BRODIE

GILLIAN SHIRREFFS

into books

Brodie by Gillian Shirreffs

First published in the United Kingdom in 2023 by
Into Books (an imprint of Into Creative)

Hardback ISBN 978-1-9163112-8-2
Paperback ISBN 978-1-9163112-6-8

Cover design and typesetting by Stephen Cameron.
Flower illustrations by Nina Kilmurry-Webley.

Typeset in Garamond.
Printed and bound by CPi Group (UK) Ltd, Croydon CR04YY

For sales and distribution, please contact:
stephen@intocreative.co.uk

Dedication

To the amazing staff and volunteers at the
Beatson Cancer Centre, with heartfelt thanks.

And to Ronnie. Always.

Acknowledgements

A grateful thanks to all the teachers who inspired and encouraged me, especially Mrs Hamilton at St Machan's and Mrs Shaw and Mr Gallagher at St Ninian's. Thank you to the wonderful staff and students of the Creative Writing department at Glasgow University and to my incredible DFA supervisors, Dr Elizabeth Reeder and Dr Kate Reid. Many thanks to the brilliant Alan McMunnigall and the talented and generous writers I've met through his classes at *thi wurd*. A heartfelt thank you to Neenah Public Library where I wrote much of Brodie and to my Fox Valley friends for your love and support. A special thanks to Dr Stephanie Long for believing in Brodie and gathering together the fabulous women of the Brodie Book Group. A resounding thank you to my amazing publisher, Stephen Cameron, for his creativity and vision, and to Jan Kilmurry for her kindness and encouragement.

Finally, I'm indebted to Brodie's early readers and cheerleaders and to my family and friends who've supported and believed in me, and in my writing. Thank you!

Part One. Violet
1988 - 1990

Chapter One

My earliest memory is of the bookshop at 66 St Vincent Street. I spent a short eternity there, mid-shelf, mashed together with identical copies of myself. We were not getting along at all well, so it was a great relief when Sandra Galbraith's long fingers shoogled me free.

She already had a copy of *Collected Poems* by Philip Larkin in her hand and as she made her way to the till, we became pressed together, quite inappropriately. At the cash desk a young man with unseemly fingernails deposited me, followed by the rather ill-tempered Larkin book, into a plastic bag that had the words John Smith & Son emblazoned on the front.

The journey that was to follow was relatively painless. After a short jaunt on the subway, we arrived at Sandra's Victorian flat in Glasgow's West End. Its tall, draughty windows and exquisitely intricate cornicing seemed to fit with my initial read of this, my first, however brief, guardian.

After placing me on a coffee table, Sandra carried the John Smith & Son bag towards a wall covered entirely with bookshelves. She selected a home for my cantankerous companion, slipping him into his allotted berth on the uppermost of the two shelves that appeared to have been dedicated to poetry, in between a copy of *The Poems of John Keats* and Larkin's *The Whitsun Weddings*. I thereby deduced that her preference was to organise books alphabetically by genre.

I brooded in my resting place for the remainder of the afternoon.

After taking time to gather myself, I set about the task of learning as much as I could about my slender-fingered saviour. By merely observing my surroundings, I felt I was able to glean something of the essence of her soul. Not only was an entire wall of her sitting room replete with books, they also covered her stripped and polished oak floorboards in irregular molehills. My initial appraisal seemed to reveal that books were her primary concern in life. However, I was to discover in the days ahead that this was not quite the full story.

My companions on the coffee table included a small decorative plate with a portion of crust from a slice of burnt toast; a china mug festooned with pink peonies; four towers of jotters – each approximately twelve high – and a pile of A4 lined paper containing, I would later learn, some very poorly written essays on *Hamlet*.

When the light from the bay window had only just begun to fade, Sandra reappeared. She marched to the corner of the room and turned on a radio. As she headed back towards me, a self-important voice proffered an opinion on the imminent withdrawal of the Soviet army from Afghanistan.

Sandra's left hand nudged me towards the stack of essays and, on the spot I had a moment earlier occupied, her right hand deposited a plate piled high with potatoes, peas and a large battered fish. She settled herself on the floral couch and then, using only a fork, made short work of her meal.

I would learn that this was her ritual: dinner and the radio partaken on a couch I have since come to imagine was bought years earlier from Laura Ashley, the reward of her first year's teaching salary.

Sandra's figure was that of a woman who appeared to enjoy, and engage lustily in, both eating and exercise: she was neither skinny nor fat, but rather an upturned rectangle, with magnificent shoulders – suggesting an upper body strength which would no doubt have been the envy of many members of the less fair sex.

When the food was gone, she closed her eyes, another nightly practice, and rested the plate, empty but for the fork, on her knees. Her face wrinkled briefly as a second disembodied male voice offered an assessment of the Afghan situation and she fell asleep.

After a time, Sandra stirred and came back to life. She removed the plate from her knee and returned it to the table. She then stacked the mug and the smaller plate, crust and all, on top of her dinner plate and slid the whole assemblage a few inches further from me, towards the jotter towers.

The phone, which I imagined to be sitting on a small table in the hall, rang mid-way through a rousing piece by Tchaikovsky. With the help of her impressive arms, Sandra removed herself from the comfortable-looking indent she had created in the cushions and strode to the other side of the sitting room. Thankfully, she did not close the hall door behind her so I was privy to one half of the conversation that followed.

Sorry, Jane. I was about to call. I've just finished dinner.

(   )

Of course.

(   )

I know.

(   )

That's not fair. I wouldn't forget her birthday.

(   )

That happened once. Years ago.

(   )

There's no need to nag. As a matter of fact, I've already got her a present.

(   )

Today. I went shopping after my lunch with Mark.

(   )

He's fine. I don't know why you insist on worrying so much. Anyone would think he was the baby of the family, not you.

(   )

These things take time. It's not even six months since she left.

(   )

A book.

(   )

The Prime of Miss Jean Brodie.

(   )

No. Actually. It was his idea. Mark said it would make the perfect gift for a spinster teacher to give to her sixteen-year-old niece.

So that was it. I would never find my way onto the four-and-a-half-shelf prose section of the wall of books. I was meant for somewhere else. Someone else.

I was quite sure that this would not be a good thing. Sandra,

I had decided, would make for a fine guardian. Instead, I was to be handed over to an unknown girl.

When Sandra reappeared, she lifted me off the table and ran her hand over my cover. She then studied me, front and back, before gently turning my first few pages, after which, she laid me back down, even closer to the jotter towers.

She picked up the stack of dishes and left me for the night.

The next day – a Sunday in the middle of May – began with a great deal of clattering in a room not too far away. A room I astutely assumed to be the kitchen. As if to confirm my hypothesis, an exquisite aroma began to waft under the door suggestive of a fried breakfast of bacon, sausage and perhaps a slice or two of black pudding.

These items were confirmed when Sandra trooped towards me bedecked in a floral dressing gown, not dissimilar to the couch on which she proceeded to sit. In addition, a fried egg and one slice of thickly buttered bread – plain not pan – fought for the remaining space on her plate.

After a few mouthfuls, breakfast in hand, Sandra rose and headed to the radio in the corner. As she returned to her spot, a play featuring a bank manager, the bank manager's cruel wife and the bank manager's much younger half-brother (who happened to have a fondness for meeting up with the cruel wife in hotel bedrooms) interrupted my thoughts and occupied them for next twelve or so minutes, by which time Sandra's plate was clean and her eyes were closed.

A little later, the radio informed us it was ten o'clock. Marking began.

Sandra ploughed through the pile of *Hamlet* essays, red pen in hand, shaking her head and muttering about undeveloped arguments and ill-chosen quotes. At some point after twelve o'clock, she reassembled the pile, I presumed by highest mark to lowest mark, and set them aside, stacking them on the cushion next to her, only to snatch them up moments later in order to retrieve the bottom two essays. These she spread out on her lap.

Raising her eyes heavenwards, she proclaimed, 'It appears, Miss Stewart, that despite the weeks we have dedicated to its study, you are not in the least familiar with this play. The *to be, or not to be* soliloquy is in Act Three, Scene One, not, as you assert, in Act One, Scene Three. And you, Paul Anderson,' she said, poking at his scribblings with the sharp end of her pen, 'If you were so intent on copying someone, you should have chosen more wisely than the lazy article, nay dullard, who is Marie Stewart.'

Sandra's mood did not improve when she moved on and began to tackle the first of the jotter towers. I discovered these belonged to her second-year class. The lively commentary that accompanied this portion of marking suggested there were more than a few slothful miscreants in this group.

Between tower one and tower two, Sandra eased herself off the couch and disappeared from the room. I hoped she had retired to shower and dress and had not in fact left the property, still in her night attire, with the intention of carrying out any of the punishments she had threatened to rain down on her lackadaisical pupils – especially the rather elaborate one she had concocted for Alan Baird, who, it seemed just to torture Sandra, committed the sin of many a misplaced apostrophe. However, minutes after the radio informed me it was three o'clock, she reappeared in her rose-covered dressing gown, peony patterned mug in hand, and set to work on the remaining towers.

I am not sure what had occurred when she left the room, perhaps she added something of a calming nature to her tea, but the remainder of the marking passed off quickly and quietly and by five o'clock, everything else having been swept up and removed, I was alone on the coffee table.

An hour or so later, Sandra was back. She was wearing an ensemble of brown plaid skirt and cream blouse and carried a plate with a meal that was a carbon copy of the previous night's dinner. It too was swiftly demolished and, as before, Sandra sighed, sank further into the couch cushions and closed her eyes.

I took this opportunity to study the face of my erstwhile guardian. Granted her eyes were closed, but I had already committed their specifics to memory – each one a swirl of hazel and amber, the left marginally favouring a lighter hue. What this new inspection revealed, in particular, were the lines buried in her brow, deep even as she rested. I wondered as to their cause, thinking that a mere Paul Anderson, a Marie Stewart or even an Alan Baird could not have etched them so profoundly into her pale skin. I also thought again about her age.

When she had rescued me from the confines of that cramped bookshelf, I had thought her young. Or not old. Perhaps in her middle thirties. Her slim fingers were smooth and her left hand soft against my cover. I had since recalculated upwards and had settled on a figure somewhere between forty and forty-five. The evidence was not conclusive, but the presence of a sixteen-year-old niece – produced by a younger sister – and this, her lined brow, pushed me towards the upper end of my estimate. Regardless, I decided she was a handsome woman who suited middle age and was perhaps even born for it.

The phone rang, interrupting my analysis. Sandra opened her eyes. She waited until it stopped before she roused herself. Ten minutes later, she had forsaken me and was, I presumed, seated at the hall table I had conjured earlier.

I heard what I later learned is the noise that is produced when a telephone is being dialled – the kind with the rotating circular disc over the numbers.

Did you phone?

(　　　　)

It must have been Jane. No doubt intending to remind me about Violet's party. Again. Are you going?

(　　　　)

I know, but it's not Violet's fault.

(　　　　)

You're being paranoid.

(　　　　)

Jane won't invite her. It's inconceivable.

(　　　　)

Because that creature stopped being any part of this family months ago.

(　　　　)

No. She's not Violet's aunt. Not anymore.

(　　　　)

Do you want me to come over?

(　　　　)

I'll just stay. It's as easy to get to work from yours.

(　　　　)

I bet you haven't even eaten.

(　　　　)

We don't need to go out. I'll pick up some shopping on the way.

(　　　　)

It's no problem. What are big sisters for?

Chapter Two

Sandra returned to the flat two nights later.

As she eased off her shoes, I noted that her olive-green suit both accentuated the amber in her eyes and complemented her sallow skin. It also flattered her figure as it, along with the silk blouse she was wearing, cinched her in at the waist. I speculated that perhaps there was someone she was trying to impress – a fellow teacher, the ticket booth attendant at the subway, perhaps even a stranger she passed each day on her way home from work.

Unhappy with the limitations of my knowledge, I supposed I would just have to wonder. Or perhaps occupy myself with the invention of a handsome suitor.

I was glad of Sandra's presence. I had felt her absence keenly, having become convinced that the Larkin book was scowling at me from its lofty perch. I had begun to feel not a little perturbed by its menacing stare and was mightily relieved when Sandra deposited two jotter towers to my left, obscuring its view.

Instead of battered fish, dinner was two square sausages and a fried egg. The radio featured a poorly mediated exchange between two politicians arguing about the future of education. This discussion resulted in Sandra becoming quite animated. She suited the flush that entered her cheeks.

She began to address the jotter towers: 'Oh yes. More testing. That sounds like a marvellous idea. And so original.' She gesticulated as she continued, 'What do you think, Martin

McDade? Would an increase in examinations enhance your educational experience – or just further interfere with football trials and your constant chatting up of the hordes of young ladies who seem so taken with those blond streaks of yours? Or you, Claire Burns? You're a sensible girl; do you think it would be judicious of me to dispense with the breadth and depth of the curriculum and merely teach to some politician-mandated test?'

She exhaled, rubbed her temples and headed towards the disembodied voices.

Pachelbel's Canon in D Major filled the room.

She gathered half a dozen jotters to herself and began to appraise the efforts within. It seemed Beth Campbell had excelled in the task Sandra had set her fourth-year pupils – a particularly difficult interpretation from the 1985 past paper. In so doing, Beth buoyed her teacher's mood, so much in fact, that Sandra was able to maintain her good humour even in the face of James Laird's less than stellar effort.

She was on her fifth jotter when the doorbell rang.

She appeared annoyed as she got to her feet.

I, however, was delighted and hoped it might be a visitor who would not only be permitted across the threshold, but who would be invited into this, Sandra's inner sanctum, for my perusal.

I could hear Sandra's voice in the distance.

'You could just have phoned.'

A woman, younger and prettier than Sandra, followed her into the sitting room. She sat on the armchair to the right of the couch.

Sandra remained standing.

The woman began to speak. Her voice carried a note of entreaty.

'I'm sorry. I need to talk about Mark and I don't want the kids listening in. You know what they're like.'

Jane was a petite version of Sandra. Her shiny hair was cut into a short bob, which suited their face shape. Sandra's shoulder-length hair did nothing to showcase the fine bone structure with which they had both been blessed.

Sandra paced as Jane embarked on a lengthy monologue.

Much to my delight, as a result of her tirade, I was able to glean the grim details of the misfortune that had befallen their brother.

It seemed that Mark's wife, Ruth, had left the marital home on Christmas day and, without even the decency of a waiting period, had moved in with one of Mark's childhood friends. This friend, Tom, had been a fixture in the lives of the Galbraith girls since they had both, in fact, been girls. In one of her many fits of pique, Jane declared she did not know whose betrayal she felt more keenly, Ruth's – her former sister-in-law and best friend since university – or Tom's – someone she had thought of as part of the family. Mid-outburst she proclaimed: had everyone, herself included, not always expected that someday Sandra and Tom would actually get their act together? If they had, she asserted, none of this would have happened.

It was at this point in the diatribe that Sandra seemed no longer able to contain her irritation.

'I have to stop you there. That's just ridiculous. There was never any act to get together. We're friends. Were friends. That's all. It's as well Tom's parents aren't alive. Can you imagine?'

Jane shook her head. 'It's all such a mess. I wish I'd never introduced them. I know Mark blames me.'

Jane began to cry.

Sandra sat down in the Sandra-shaped dent in her floral couch and stared across at the bookshelves. After some minutes had passed, she pointed out to Jane that this situation was not about her and assured her sister that it was ludicrous to think Mark held her in any way responsible. If he had not been in touch, Sandra reasoned, it was simply because he was too busy dealing with the infidelity of his wife and the highly questionable morals of his former friend.

Jane began to squeak a response. Sandra continued on in a measured tone.

By the time Jane left, it had been agreed that she would desist from any further contact with Ruth – she had tearfully confessed to two strained meetings at two different coffee houses. She would also ensure that Ruth was not mentioned by anyone at Violet's birthday party and that if Ruth had the audacity to send a card or a gift, it would be hidden and would not be remarked upon. In return, Sandra promised to convince Mark to come to the party.

I heard the front door clunk behind Jane.

Sandra stalked over to a small cabinet to the right of the bay window. I was thrilled by this development as I had spent many hours wondering as to its contents.

The polished oak door opened to reveal a surprising number of bottles. Sandra removed a twelve-year-old single malt and a stub crystal glass.

Partway through her second drink, she left the room and returned with a fountain pen. She then picked me up and, taking great care, wrote the following inscription:

20th of May 1988

To my dearest Violet on the occasion of your sixteenth
birthday: may all your teachers, now, and in the future,
be worthy of your keen mind and gentle heart.

Much love,

Aunt Sandra

She set me back down and I watched with interest as the whisky tally rose to four.

The next morning, Sandra looked decidedly crumpled.

Whilst eating burnt toast, she crammed jotters into a large embroidered satchel that was adorned with finely stitched snowdrops and daffodils. She snatched me up and eased me in. I thought I might suffocate, pressed as I was against so many quarrelsome neighbours. To ease my distress, I concentrated on events beyond the thermal prison.

Sandra exchanged pleasantries with, what sounded like, an elderly gentleman, at, what I presumed to be, a bus stop. My main clue to this was their shared annoyance at the lack of punctuality of the Glasgow city bus service. The elderly gentleman did not really have anything to rush for. 'But still,' he said, 'it's the principle of the thing.'

Sandra was sure she would miss registration entirely and might even be late for period one. 'It's my second years,' she said. 'They'll be hanging from the lights if I'm not in the room before them.'

Her companion commented that he did not know how she did it, as it was his view that the youth of today bore a striking resemblance to wild animals. Well, not all of them, he qualified. This caused them both to laugh. As we finally got on the delinquent bus, over her shoulder (or at least that is how I imagined she was doing it), Sandra said, 'They're lovable rogues, for the most part.'

When I was emptied onto the top of her desk, I was able to observe that none of the children had, in fact, suspended themselves from any of the fixtures or fittings. Such behaviour, it seemed, had been averted due to the intervention of a fine figured colleague with a free period.

In response to her expression of gratitude, Mr Callaghan assured Sandra he was always happy to help.

Sandra tugged at her rumpled skirt. I noticed her face begin to redden.

I wondered if this was as a result of embarrassment due to her awareness of the toll the previous night's excess had taken on her normally faultless appearance or if the apparent warmth that had entered her cheeks was, in fact, an unbidden reaction to Mr Callaghan's kindness and his strong, chiselled features.

Within seconds, the class grew restless. A pupil named Sean Devine roared in the face of the boy next to him. Mr Callaghan responded by frog-marching the young reprobate from the room.

As the door closed behind them, Sandra bellowed, 'Second year, I don't see pens. I don't see jotters. I do, however, see a number of bags on desks and I count at least five of you still wearing blazers.' She then lowered her voice and adopted a dangerous tone to conclude, 'You have precisely one minute to rectify this situation or I predict a large number of you will be joining Mr Devine at the lunchtime detention I have planned for him.'

Only one member of the class, Julie Melville, a seemingly inveterate giggler, ended up sharing her lunchbreak with Sean Devine. However, also paying penance that afternoon was Paul

Anderson, who had, it seemed, earned a two-week detention as a result of his plagiarised *Hamlet* essay.

Little happened during the remainder of the school day: pupils entered, sat in rows and listened to impassioned speeches on *Educating Rita*, Seamus Heaney, the evil that is a comma splice and various other points of punctuation and grammar. It was not until a little after the final bell that my interest was once more aroused.

Mr Callaghan, David – as he became when the room was childfree – dropped by to check that Sandra had survived the rigours of the day. She assured him that despite the bumpy start it had been most agreeable. She detailed her success in putting that rogue Devine's gas at a peep by having him spend his thirty-minute detention seated next to Giggles Melville whilst completing an exercise out of *The Fundamentals of English Grammar*.

Her next topic was Paul Anderson and her belief that he could be a candidate for university, if only he would apply himself. She then asked David if she could trouble him for his opinion.

She picked me up and handed me to him.

I was distracted by the warmth of his palm, but was still able to hear her enquire as to whether he thought I would make a good birthday present for a sixteen-year-old.

'Boy or girl?'

Sandra's forehead furrowed.

'Girl,' she said. 'My niece. Violet. She's at St Edmund's. I spoke to you about her last year when she had that imbecile Nelson for English. You told me not to get involved.'

David turned me over in his hands.

'I remember suggesting you were being a little harsh.'

'That's as may be, but he hardly gave them a scrap of homework all year and I was forced to supplement his pitiful efforts.'

'I'm sure your niece was delighted.'

He looked down at me and said, 'I think *The Prime of Miss Jean Brodie* is an excellent choice, but I'd suggest you also pop a crisp twenty-pound note into her card.'

After a pause, he added, 'You've not been modelling yourself on the bold Jean all these years, have you?'

'I think not. Unlike Jean Brodie, I've yet to enter my prime.'

A girl dressed as a wood nymph ran into the room and announced, 'Miss. Miss. You've to come.'

'Pardon?'

'Sorry, Miss Galbraith. Mr Bell said to get you. We were in the gym rehearsing and John Forsyth went and fell off a chair. Mr Bell said to run quick and catch you before you were away.'

Sandra overlooked the girl's use of the vernacular. On her way out of the room, she waved at a glass-fronted cabinet, instructing the pupil to bring along the first aid kit. 'And don't dilly-dally,' she said, sternly.

David followed them out. He switched off the lights as he left.

Shadows lengthened and danced until the room was dark, save for the times the waxing moon escaped from behind whichever thick cloudbank held it captive and lit up the far wall with its classroom display on *Flannan Isle*.

Early the next morning, a cleaner broke the stillness of the room.

I had been able to hear her, and her colleague, as they worked their way along the corridor. Mostly their complaints were about litter louts and the onset of arthritis, so I had been expecting a certain face and shape when the door finally opened. However, the person I had mentally assembled bore little relationship to the girl who entered.

As she worked methodically from the back of the room to the front, I heard the two voices once more and realised my mistake. The first shouted, 'Laurel? You're not still in 204? You'll need to pick up the pace.' The other added, 'It's three minutes a room. No more. Or we'll end up doing half of yours.'

There was then a loud tut and first voice said, 'I hate when we get lumbered with a new one.'

Ignoring the voices, Laurel continued to mop the floor in long even strokes. Once she seemed satisfied, she began to straighten the items on Sandra's desk. Her slight fingers picked me up and placed me on a class set of *Language Alive*, only to change her mind and sit me on top of a stack of lined A4 paper.

She turned to leave. Hesitated.

She lifted me again, smiled at my cover and leafed through my pages, stopping briefly in chapter three to read Miss Brodie proclaim, 'The Philistines are upon us.'

The first voice screeched, 'Laurel!'

She abandoned me on an obelisk made out of copies of *Wuthering Heights*, some of which were decidedly maudlin.

When Sandra arrived, she emptied jotters from her embroidered bag onto the space on her desk that had been newly created. She then removed me from my elevated position and dropped me into the now empty satchel. It was to be a long day listening to Sandra's muffled voice imploring her students alternately to learn and to behave.

Before my unceremonious imprisonment, I noted that Sandra seemed transformed. She was dressed in a tailored skirt suit with a fetching lavender blouse, tied in a loose bow at the neck. The tinge of grey her complexion had betrayed the previous day had been replaced by a vigorous glow. I wondered if we might be stopping off for a drink with David after work.

This was not to be.

Sandra's actual plan was to take me to her sister's house. Once there, I would be wrapped and made ready so that I could be presented to Violet on the morning of her sixteenth birthday.

Chapter Three

Jane's house bore little resemblance to Sandra's flat, except a similar penchant for florals. The ceilings were lower and bereft of cornicing and the sitting room had no bookshelves; instead, in pride of place, there was a television set of the smallish squat variety.

As Jane set down two cups of tea, Sandra explained that there had been no point in her attempting to wrap me as she had neither the materials nor the wherewithal. Added to which, she cajoled, Jane was the one well-known for her expertise in the art of gift-wrapping. Jane handed her sister a tag and said, 'Can you at least manage this?'

She then, rather disconcertingly, laid out scissors, Sellotape, a thick sheet of paper embossed with daisies (I would later learn that, oddly, this was Violet's favourite flower) and a small reel of purple ribbon. She got to work. Her fingers, like her elder sister's, were long and agile but they conducted their business with a nervous energy that Sandra's hands lacked.

The paper felt tight against my cover.

In order to distract myself from both the discomfort and the indignity of the situation, I concentrated on the sisters' voices.

In reply to Sandra's enquiry as to whether it would be a grand affair, Jane said, 'Grand? I doubt it. It'll mainly just be the young ones. Violet's asked all the usual girls and I've let Thomas invite a couple of boys from school. And then just a few folks from work and you and Mark. He is coming?'

'He promised,' Sandra said. 'And I plan to phone and remind him in the morning, so he won't have much choice.'

The edge in Jane's voice melted a little. Regardless, I suspected she was not fully at ease in the company of her elder sister. I filed this thought.

Talk turned to Violet's other presents. It seemed Jane had finally relented and Violet's big surprise would be a stereo system for her bedroom. 'She's been asking for ages, and you know what Drew's like when it comes to his wee girl; I didn't even stand a chance,' had been her assessment of the situation.

Over the two years that were to follow, I would overhear many an argument involving this contention: Jane's belief that her husband was too soft on their daughter; that Violet had him wrapped around her little finger. Typically, Drew's response would be to enumerate their daughter's many virtues and then provide his own view, with examples, that Jane was, in fact, too soft on their son, Thomas, who, in Drew's opinion, warranted a much firmer hand.

I would quickly conclude that Drew possessed the stronger case.

The morning of Violet's sixteenth birthday – Friday, 20th May, 1988 – began, what was to be, an intriguing day in terms of the intricacies of the Galbraith/Munro family relations. After a noisy start with Violet's discovery that she now possessed her very own stereo system, she turned her attention to the small pile of gifts on the coffee table, of which I was one.

I heard Jane say, 'Your Aunt Sandra dropped hers off because she wanted it to be here for you when you got up. And she also wanted me to wrap it for her.'

'Thanks, Mum, it looks great,' Violet said.

I felt her hands on my expertly wrapped form.

She read the gift tag aloud, turned me over in her hands and said 'Let me guess… a book.'

She was laughing as she said it.

I wondered if perhaps she was mocking her aunt, and, in turn, her aunt's choice of gift. However, as she carefully untied the ribbon and peeled back the Sellotape, I found myself reassured. I immediately became convinced that she would make a fine guardian.

She began to inspect me and came upon the inscription Sandra had written. As she enunciated each word, I scrutinised her.

Violet was tall. Her skin was fair, a milky white, with a light dusting of freckles. Her eyes were large ovals, dark hazel in colour, and her hair was a mix of auburn and red, which spiralled neatly over her shoulders.

'That's so lovely. Can I phone her? Please?' she said, after reading the inscription a second time, more quietly.

'I wouldn't, if I were you,' Jane said. 'She'll be rushing to get ready for work. You know how grumpy your Aunt Sandra can be. Why don't you phone her later?'

Without a word, Violet acquiesced, and, after placing me on the smooth plaster of the mantelpiece, turned to her brother's present.

'I think this one is a… record,' she said before carefully removing its identical daisy wrapping paper to reveal *Perfect* by Fairground Attraction.

Thomas, who, that August, would turn from a precocious twelve-year-old into a sullen thirteen-year-old said, 'I thought it would make the *perfect* present.'

He was tall and fair, like his sister. His hair, however, was an arresting shade of red.

Violet caught her brother in a vigorous hug, despite his attempts to evade her arms. Jane ordered her to release the wriggling body and both children disappeared to get ready for school.

In Violet's case, despite being on exam leave and turning sixteen that day, she was still required to don her uniform – a pleasing colour palette of green blazer, grey skirt, white shirt and a tie with alternating stripes of yellow and green – and traipse off to St Edmund the Martyr, as, that year, the twentieth of May was the date the estimable Scottish Examinations Board had chosen to timetable Standard Grade German. Despite the ill luck of the situation, Violet did not complain.

After an uneventful seven hours, my guardian skipped back into the room. I was struck by her cheerful disposition and then by the fact that this excess of chirpiness was not in fact nauseating; rather, both it, and the young girl who possessed it, were quite captivating.

Violet's response to Jane's enquiry about the German exam was, 'Better than expected.'

After this pronouncement, she danced around the room singing snippets of the pop songs of the day until her mother insisted that she go upstairs and change out of her school uniform.

The next incident of note was the doorbell ringing at a little after five o'clock.

Jane went out into the hall and from there I heard her say, 'I thought we weren't going to see you until tomorrow.'

'I just took a notion,' said a familiar voice. 'I was at the bus stop and the number 76 pulled up.'

'That's not like you. She's getting changed, but she'll be down in a minute. Please be nice about her birthday shoes. I know they'll not be to your taste.'

'Not those awful Dr Marten boots?'

Jane nodded in assent as Violet thudded down the stairs.

After she had embraced her aunt, she pointed at her feet and said, 'What do you think, Aunt Sandra?'

'I think they're the height of fashion,' her aunt replied.

I was glad of Sandra's surprise visit and found myself harbouring a vague hope that she might snatch me up and say she had made a terrible mistake, giving Violet a bottle of perfume in my place. However, she did not even glance in my direction, not until Violet rescued me from the mantelpiece.

'Thank you so much. And for the twenty pounds. It was far too generous.'

'Not for my favourite niece.'

'Your only niece,' Violet said.

'True,' her aunt replied.

'Did you know we're doing it for Higher English? Mrs Shaw already told us.'

'I thought you might be. You'll enjoy it. There's a film too. We've got a video cassette in the department. But you can't watch it until after you've read the book.'

'I wouldn't. I'm going to start reading it as soon as my exams are over. It's only eleven more days. I can't wait.'

'I'm quite sure you can't. Freedom,' Sandra said. 'For the summer, at least. Then it'll be Highers and off to Glasgow University to study English.'

'Or Edinburgh University to study accountancy,' Jane said.

A sound, like that of someone in pain, escaped from Sandra's throat.

The sisters exchanged a glance.

Violet was looking down at me. I was still clasped in her hand. As she twirled, she said, 'I love the inscription. I'm going to keep this book forever.'

'To remind you of your old auntie when she's shuffled off this mortal coil.'

Jane interrupted Violet's laughter. 'Don't be so morbid, Sandra.'

She left the two of them in the sitting room and went off to start dinner. Violet made a space for me on the glass coffee table and sat next to her aunt. She then told her how excited she was to have Mrs Shaw for Higher English. In Violet's opinion, Mrs Shaw was the best teacher at St Edmund's and she felt lucky to have gotten her in fourth year and to have her again in fifth, especially after having had Smelly Nelson in third year.

Sandra gave Violet a reproachful look but said nothing in Mr Nelson's defence.

'It's an important year. I'm glad you've got Kate Shaw,' she said. 'But you know I can always do some work with you, too.'

'I know and if I need anything, I will ask. Just maybe not for any extra homework.'

Sandra smiled and I guessed this newfound glow had as much to do with a fleeting thought of David Callaghan as it did with her niece's gentle teasing.

Sandra stood up. She leaned the top half of her body into the kitchen and, competing with the sound of some rather enthusiastic banging and clanging, said she would not be staying for dinner. She had a slew of marking she needed to dispatch.

I perceived Violet's disappointment and also noted that it was lost on Sandra who sashayed out of the house declaring she was looking forward to seeing them the following day.

'Noon, not two,' Jane shouted in her wake.

Dinner, a combination of Violet's favourite foods (mashed potatoes, square sausages, fish fingers and garden peas) was eaten in what the family referred to as the dinette – a somewhat cramped space beyond the sitting room. Whilst pushing peas around his plate, Thomas expressed his displeasure that Aunt Sandra had not left anything for him.

'It's not your birthday,' Drew said.

'I know, but she usually gets me something on Violet's birthday so I don't feel left out. And she gave her a present and money. That's not fair.'

'Maybe she'll bring you something tomorrow,' Jane said.

'He shouldn't be expecting anything,' Drew said.

At this point, perhaps sensing the tension between her parents, Violet said to Thomas, 'Maybe if you'd actually come down to see her, she might have had something for you in her big bag of tricks.'

'I didn't even know she was here,' Thomas said. 'You should have called me.'

An argument ensued.

'She was here to see me. It's my birthday. And anyway, there's no way you didn't hear her. She's not exactly got a quiet voice. I heard her the minute she came in and I had The Smiths on.'

'Thanks! Just rub it in that you've got a stereo system in your room. It's not fair,' Thomas said, turning to Jane. 'It's not, Mum. She always gets everything.'

The bickering continued until, while Jane was getting the trifle, Drew sent Thomas to his room. When Jane returned to find that her boy had been exiled, she shook her head at Drew and said, 'He's only twelve, for goodness' sake. And he hasn't even had dessert.'

Jane heaped a large helping of trifle into a bowl and disappeared upstairs, leaving Violet and Drew alone to finish the birthday tea and clear up the table.

After they had both left, Jane returned and began to straighten up the sitting room. I was moved to the sideboard in the dinette along with a copy of *Smash Hits*, the *Radio Times* and that day's *Glasgow Herald*.

Fortunately, I was at the top of the pile.

Chapter Four

My position on the sideboard in the dinette was not the ideal vantage point from which to digest the birthday party, but I made a valiant effort.

The gathering leaked into every part of the house.

Violet and her friends came downstairs after a while and settled themselves in the sitting room. Despite this, I could still hear music pounding through the ceiling. It emanated, I presumed, from the new stereo system. It seemed that at least one of the girls had stayed behind to test the rhythmic appliance to its limits. I found myself of the opinion that someone should go upstairs and insist the ill-mannered disc jockey come down and join the birthday girl.

The noise from above competed with both the merriment of the adults who had congregated in the kitchen and the din of Thomas and his young guests, a number far greater than that which he had been given permission to invite. These ran from room to room acting out a mock battle, which descended into a water fight, which, in turn, slid into actual hostilities resulting in a bloodied nose and banishment to the garden.

In the midst of what I can only describe as pandemonium, the sitting room door was pushed open by Mark Galbraith.

Violet shrieked with delight. She lurched towards her uncle. Despite her impressive height, she was forced onto tiptoes in order to throw her arms around him.

In addition to being a towering figure, Mark was handsome to boot. His deep-set eyes shared the intensity and intrigue of Sandra's, but the face that held them was altogether of a more conventional allure. Furthermore, his frame was well proportioned to his height. It seemed, at least to the casual observer, that he would make quite the desirable catch.

This was in contrast to the notion I had pieced together of him from what I had overheard. In particular, the concern Sandra had expressed over her brother's delicate state as a result of his failed marriage. I had expected Mark to be weighed down by misfortune and, if I am honest, to have more apparent flaws. Whereas the man who was now holding court, and who, it seemed, was loved by Violet – a young woman I considered to be most discerning, despite our brief acquaintance – did not have the look, nor the presence, of someone who had been thrown over for another.

Violet's shouts brought Jane and Sandra from the kitchen. Sandra greeted her younger brother with warmth. Jane also gave him a hug but I noted something akin to coolness in her manner.

Mark followed Violet to the couch, where space had been made for him, and sat next to his niece as she finished opening the present she had been in the process of unwrapping. She gave brief but enthusiastic thanks to her friend, Nicole, before turning to the neatly wrapped gift Mark held out to her.

'I hope you like it,' he said as Violet untied the ribbon that held his gift intact.

'I love it.'

'I got it in that old bookshop you like so much. Voltaire and Rousseau.'

'Even better,' Violet said, grinning at the battered boxset on her lap.

She removed one book at a time.

'I remember you waxing lyrical about the joys of Tolkien last summer after you read *The Hobbit*, so I thought you'd enjoy them. Although, if you're anything like your Aunt Sandra, your heart will always belong to that first adventure in Middle Earth.'

'Don't listen to him,' Sandra said. 'You'll love the trilogy.'

Mark winked at his niece and said, 'I think you'll find there's something in the card too, so that you can stock up on more of that terrible music.'

'You like The Smiths, Uncle Mark,' Violet said, accusingly. 'And Aztec Camera. You're the one who got me *High Land, Hard Rain*, for my Christmas.'

'Our shared taste in popular music might be why your mum and dad thought it was a good idea to have you move your collection upstairs.'

This earned Mark a second hug.

Sandra said, 'Look at that. Always the golden boy. There he is taking credit for your gift, Jane.'

'I know. But what can you do? He's always been everyone's favourite. And, for once, there is something in what he says. If she'd played *What Difference Does It Make?* up full blast, one more time in here, she might have had to find somewhere else to live.'

'She wouldn't have had any trouble finding new digs,' Mark said. 'Sandra and I would have been fighting over her.'

'You might be that size now, little brother,' Sandra said. 'But cast your mind back. I pack quite a punch.'

'Don't worry. She's going nowhere. Not for another year or two,' Jane said, before announcing that, as Mark had now arrived, she was off to find matches so that she could light the candles on Violet's birthday cake.

I noticed Drew enter the room. He stayed to the side while Mark and Sandra held centre stage. I wondered if there was a story behind this.

Fortunately, I would not have to wait too long to discover this particular family secret: of Drew's financial difficulties and Mark's part in them.

It seemed Drew had been badly advised and had invested his family's lifesavings in a venture that had been unsound from the outset. A venture that had been set up, and, in its first year, run by his brother-in-law. A venture from which Mark Galbraith made a handsome return.

After *Happy Birthday* had been sung and Violet had blown out the candles on her cake, she disappeared upstairs. Jane and her friends retired once more to the kitchen. Drew, when I turned my attention to him, was nowhere in sight so I concluded he was refereeing the activities of Thomas and his unruly comrades in the back garden, although I had no firm evidence for this supposition. This left Sandra and Mark alone in the sitting room.

Mark idled by the mantelpiece.

'Stop it. I know what you're doing,' Sandra said.

'I'm just looking at her cards. Who would have thought? Sixteen.'

'Stop.'

'I'm not looking for one from her. Don't be ridiculous.'

'You do yourself no favours. You need to move on.'

'After ten years of marriage. You think it's that easy?'

'No. But it has to be better than what you're doing to yourself.'

'What?' Mark said. 'What am I doing to myself?'

'Ruth told Jane. About you sitting outside Tom's flat in your car.'

'So, Jane is still seeing her,' Mark said. 'I knew she wouldn't be able to help herself.'

'Twice and she won't do it again. She promised. She knows where her loyalties lie. But that's not the point.'

'I only did it a few times. At the start. I just needed Ruth to talk to me. To explain. I haven't been near his flat in months,' Mark said.

'Because they moved.'

'No. Because I realised it was stupid. And beneath me.'

'I hope that's true,' Sandra said. 'You're so much better than this. You need to draw a line.'

'I know but what I keep going back to is how did I not see it coming? When did it start? Was it going on for years? He was my best man, for God's sake.'

'At least you're talking about it now,' Sandra said.

'Do I have an option, with you two interfering in my life?'

'That's not fair. I've been trying to help. Staying over when I can. Making dinners. And I haven't pried. But I was shocked when Jane told me. She said Ruth was scared about what you might do. That's why they moved.'

'Well that's stupid,' Mark said. 'As if I was going to do anything. I just wanted her to explain. Nothing else. But she wouldn't. She has a cheek telling Jane anything. Never mind that she thinks I've lost the plot.'

The conversation continued in circles until one of the women from the kitchen burst in and asked if they wanted tea or coffee. To the woman's delight, Mark offered to help and followed her into the kitchen. Sandra sat for a moment, then she smoothed the navy-blue dress she was wearing and rose to her full height. Once standing, she turned to face the large mirror hanging above the couch and, after inspecting her face, gently touched the traces of grey below her eyes. As she did, Violet and Nicole spilled through the door.

'Roddy Frame, definitely,' Violet said, before taking in the scene and asking, 'Why are you on your own?'

'Your uncle abandoned me with the promise of a cup of tea.'

'We're down for more cake,' Violet said. 'That's if Mum and her cronies haven't scoffed it all.'

'Careful. It may be your party, young lady, but that isn't an excuse to forget your manners.'

Violet apologised and explained that she and Nicole were starving after so much dancing.

'It did sound like a herd of baby elephants might fall through the ceiling at any moment.'

Violet apologised for a second time.

'Off and get your cake,' Sandra said. 'I could die of thirst waiting for your Uncle Mark. It seems he prefers the company of your mother's friends.'

Violet laughed and headed for the kitchen, leaving Nicole, looking a little nervous, in her wake.

'Miss Galbraith. I can bring your tea out, if you'd like,' she said.

'Thank you, Nicole, but I am more than capable. I was just enjoying a moment of solitude.'

The girl smiled.

'How are you getting on at your new school?' Sandra asked. 'You're missed back at Westbrae.'

'Thanks, Miss. And thanks for introducing me to Violet. She's been great. It made a big difference already knowing somebody in my registration class. My mum said to be sure to thank you, if I saw you today.'

'How is your mum?'

'A bit better since we moved. It was hard for her. Still living in the house.'

I was able to infer from what was discussed that Nicole's father had died the previous summer after a long illness.

'You're looking well,' Sandra said, I presumed to move away from such an unhappy subject. 'Not so thin. And I'm glad my niece hasn't been too bad an influence on you. I see you have the good sense not to share her taste in footwear.'

'Yes, Miss.'

Violet's head appeared around the kitchen door.

'Come and get some cake, Nic.'

'On you go,' Sandra said. 'I'll be there in a minute.'

There may be a number of reasons why this unremarkable exchange has remained so vivid, despite the passage of time. The one I would venture as, perhaps, most notable, is that this would be the last opportunity I would ever have to study Sandra Galbraith at such close quarters.

The rest of the day passed with people moving to and fro and the noise above me becoming increasingly loud. At some point in the early evening, Drew banged on the wall nearest me and, directing his voice at the ceiling, shouted, 'Keep it down, girls,' which seemed to have the desired effect.

Sandra and Mark left together in the late afternoon. Shortly afterwards Drew gathered up Thomas's friends and drove them home. The women in the kitchen left in dribs and drabs and, by nine o'clock, the only people in the house were the four members of the Munro family.

Drew settled himself in the large armchair. Thomas was on the couch. Jane refused to sit down with them, citing the amount of clearing up she still had to do. Violet seemed unaware of the others and spent an unfeasible length of time pirouetting around the room.

After a lengthy discussion, Thomas and Drew agreed to watch the film, *Ghostbusters*. It was far from Drew's first choice. He had taped it weeks before and it seemed he was now regretting having done so.

Before bed, Violet retrieved me from the sideboard and placed me on top of a pile of neatly folded wrapping paper on the coffee table. I remained there while she ate supper – roasted cheese, with, as per her request, only a little pepper.

Once she had finished, she carried me upstairs to her room.

Chapter Five

Violet's bedroom was clean and in good order.

The décor appeared to have been chosen in an era that predated her fondness for The Smiths and Dr Marten boots. The soft furnishings, other than the tightly woven brown carpet, were peach, cream, or, as in the case of the matching duvet cover, curtains and wallpaper, a combination of both. These had broad vertical stripes alternating between the two with tiny bunches of peach flowers embossed on the portions that were cream.

I noted that nothing was violet, or, indeed, any shade of purple or blue.

The room consisted of a single bed which, I would learn, had another single bed cleverly stowed underneath; two wardrobes, in what appeared to be cream-coloured Formica, one either side of Violet's bed; an oak desk with an inelegant black plastic chair on wheels; the birthday stereo system, in black; a tall, free standing oak mirror; and a second door, identical to the one through which we had entered. This enigma bothered me greatly until days later when Jane entered the bedroom carrying a stack of freshly washed towels and sheets and, opening the mystery portal, dispensed with her heavy load.

Between the two doors stood the most important item of furniture: a small oak bookcase with four shelves.

Each shelf held a row of books, which appeared to be catalogued simply by height. For instance, the books on the bottom shelf were arranged from left to right as follows: *An*

Illustrated Treasury of Celtic Fairy Tales, Aesop's Fables for Children, The Complete Tales of Beatrix Potter, Tales of Mother Goose, A Child's Garden of Verses, Fairy Tales of the Brothers Grimm, The Happy Prince, Alice's Adventures in Wonderland, Pippi Longstocking, Carrie's War, Watership Down, James and the Giant Peach, Enid Blyton's Bedtime Stories, The Wind in the Willows, Heidi, Charlotte's Web, Charlie and the Great Glass Elevator, Rapunzel, Thumbelina, The Little Red Hen, The Old Woman and Her Pig, The Gingerbread Boy, Snow-White and Rose-Red, Chicken Licken, The Princess and the Pea, The Saga of Noggin the Nog, Nogbad and the Elephants, King of the Nogs.

I was pleased to note there were no similar issues of overcrowding on the upper shelves. I was also pleased to note that those shelves were populated by books that seemed, to me, to be more suitable for a young woman of Violet's age and intellect.

Violet placed me on her pillow and filled the room with music, courtesy, according to the record sleeve, of Aztec Camera. As she lay back onto the bed, she lifted me up with both hands, stretching me above her head and in the same dizzying movement pulling me close to study my review page – excerpts of glowing appraisals from *The Sunday Telegraph*, *The Scotsman* and *The Observer*. She consumed each one then turned to Sandra's inscription and read it for a third time. Finally, I was set down on the carpet for the night, which, given its coarse texture, was considerably less comfortable than my previous lodgings.

Before the record finished, Jane knocked on the bedroom door, which she pushed open as Violet shouted for her to come in.

'Light out,' Jane said.

'Just a wee bit longer. Please?'

Jane explained that it was not a negotiation and added that it had been a long day and if she could hear the racket from Violet's room, it must also be keeping poor Thomas awake.

Violet pointed out, quite gently, that there was only one song left.

In reply, Jane said, 'Anyone would think it was your birthday weekend. That one song and no more.'

I imagined Violet's wide smile as her mother departed.

The stylus arm left the record and Violet got up and turned off the light. I feared she might tread on me, but fortunately, back then, she was still quite an expert in the art of negotiating a safe path back to bed in the dark.

The house was quiet when Violet woke up. She opened the curtains, admitting the early morning sun and then, appearing to think better of the idea, she stepped over me and went back to bed. It was not until the smell of bacon made its way under her bedroom door that she roused herself and headed downstairs in her pyjamas.

I presumed this would be the last I would see of her for a while, which was disappointing, stranded as I was on the uncomfortable carpet. However, within ten minutes she reappeared with a mug of, what I presumed to be, tea, in one hand and a small plate with a bacon roll in the other. She placed these on her desk, to the right of neatly piled books and papers, and then, in an act of charity, she retrieved me from the floor and sat me on the polished surface to the left of her breakfast.

Violet picked up her bacon roll and began to eat, clearly enjoying each and every bite in a way that reminded me of her aunt. Once the plate was empty, she stowed it under her mug and turned her attention to a geography textbook. As she began to take notes, Jane entered the room.

'There's another roll down there for you, if you want it.'

Without lifting her head to greet the intrusion, Violet replied that she was fine.

Whilst straightening her daughter's duvet cover, Jane said, 'I think you should have today off. The full day. Your next exam isn't until a week on Monday.'

'I know, but then I have two in a row,' Violet said. 'I'll be ready on time. I promise.'

'Well, you know how busy the Garden Festival gets,' Jane said. 'And your Aunt Sandra won't be happy if we're late.'

After reading another chapter, Violet pulled various items of clothing from one of the cream-coloured wardrobes, tried on different combinations, paraded in front of the mirror in each, settled on one and tidied up the clothes that were now strewn all over her bed. At nine-fifty, she left the room in a red jumper, a black miniskirt, black and red striped tights and her beloved Dr Marten boots.

On her way out, she lifted me off her desk and moved me to the bookshelf.

I was pleased with the spot she chose – on the top shelf, in the middle.

Due, it would seem, to my height, my neighbours were a copy of *Northanger Abbey*, to my left, and a copy of *The Hobbit*, to my right. The Austen book was a bit stuck up for my taste, but the copy of *The Hobbit* was friendly, if a little nervy.

I found the day long and the ticking of the clock bothersome. The family did not return until after six and it was seven-forty before Violet re-entered the room. She sat down at the desk and returned to her textbook. Her face radiated heat and light. I surmised this was a lingering indication of the excitement of the day.

Drew knocked on the door at nine o'clock. He told Violet about a feast of roasted cheese waiting for her in the kitchen. Before she followed him downstairs, in a quiet voice, Violet asked 'When can we go and see Auntie Ruth again?'

I learned five things from the conversation that followed.

Firstly, Violet was in the habit of referring to Tom as Uncle Tom, an arrangement I presumed was longstanding.

Secondly, father and daughter had visited Auntie Ruth and Uncle Tom on a number of occasions.

Thirdly, each time they had done so, it had been under the guise of Drew working late and then picking Violet up from Glasgow's Mitchell Library: a place she sometimes liked to go after school in order to study in peace and quiet, or so she told her mother.

Fourthly, the conspirators would have to tweak this arrangement somewhat as Violet was now off school on study leave.

Fifthly, Violet was eager to thank Auntie Ruth and Uncle Tom for the birthday card and money they had sent to her father's work address.

By the end of the conversation, Drew had assured Violet he would give another visit some serious thought. I was left with the impression that whilst he was prepared to engage in a clandestine relationship with the two aforementioned outcasts, he was uncomfortable that he had allowed his daughter to become embroiled in the subterfuge.

In the days that followed, Violet fell into something of a routine: she would study in her pyjamas until one or other parent returned home from work and insisted she shower, get dressed and come down for something to eat.

It was evident she took her studies very seriously, seemingly to the exclusion of all other daily tasks, barring one. Every few hours, she would disappear for a short time.

I would hear the thud, thud, thud of her feet as she descended the stairs and minutes later, I would hear the stomp that signalled her return. Violet would push open the door, still in her pyjamas and Dr Marten boots, with a mug of tea, which she would place on her desk. She would then open the top drawer and remove two, sometimes three, rich tea biscuits from her secret hoard. Studies would cease until the mug was empty and each biscuit had been savoured.

I, for my part, did my best to ignore the niggles and petty jealousies of the bookcase. To help in this endeavour I would imagine myself following Violet out into the world to experience it as she might. Unfortunately, this practice began to cause unsettling episodes of dissatisfaction, which resulted in an increasing sense of frustration. I began to resent the restrictions and limitations that marked my existence.

To add to my vexation, there were many things I wanted to know. What tormented me most was the mystery of Auntie Ruth and Uncle Tom. Had Drew and Violet found a way to see them? If so, where and in what form had this encounter taken place and why, when Mark Galbraith had been treated so badly, would Violet and Drew – in my view, fine specimens of humanity – want to continue a relationship with those who had betrayed him? It is important to remember that at this time I was not yet in possession of the truth of the affair: that

Mark Galbraith was, in fact, the villain of the piece. I would learn this in the months that were to come.

As the day of the first of her two remaining exams approached, Violet's anxiety became almost palpable. The numerous reassuring words delivered by her parents, who popped their heads around her door with increasing frequency, did little to ease her angst.

'But I'm rubbish at geography,' she would say. 'It's my worst subject, by far.'

They would tell her it would not be as bad as she thought; that it was only one subject and she was on track for top marks in the rest; that this was the last time she would ever have to have anything to do with geography, other than the odd trip to the continent – a remark Drew delivered with a half-smile – as it was not going to be one of her Highers.

This final assertion seemed to be the only one to offer Violet a modicum of relief, but even that knowledge did not stop her tears on the evening before Standard Grade Geography.

The dreaded exam came and went and Violet appeared to survive it unscathed. She said nothing about what had transpired in the exam hall in my hearing, and spent that evening at her desk munching rich tea biscuits as she studied for her final exam.

Drew and Jane each delivered a mug of tea over the course of the evening.

Both seemed happy that a weight had been lifted from their daughter. The normal call for lights out did not happen until well into the wee small hours, when Jane tiptoed in, kissed Violet on the forehead and said, 'That's enough now.'

Chapter Six

I spent most of the next two years on my shelf in Violet's bookcase. However, there were exceptions. The most notable of these was the excursion I took in the autumn of 1988.

I had become all too familiar with the humdrum rhythm of life in the bedroom, when, after months of confinement, Violet stretched out her hand and touched my spine.

She eased me free and placed me on her desk, on top of a rather irritable German text book. Next, I was packed into her school satchel along with the self-same curmudgeon. My other companions were a fluffy green pencil case, a textbook containing mathematical problems, a set of Higher English exam past papers, a shiny pleather purse in orange, a front door key on a metal keychain in the shape of the letter V and a bus pass.

I had expected to emerge somewhere in Violet's school – the cloakrooms, the dinner hall, a classroom. In fact, I was imprisoned all day and am disappointed to report that I have yet to see the inside, or the outside, for that matter, of St Edmund's as I was not released until well after the clatter of the final bell.

The majority of the journey Violet undertook after school, was, as far as I could tell, on foot, with the exception of a short spell on what seemed to be a bus.

Once it was over, Violet removed me from my leather jail and placed me on a wooden desk. She smoothed open my pages and began to read.

Despite my great affection for her, both then and now, I feel it only right to give a full account of what happened, with the disclaimer that what I am about to describe may cause some distress.

Violet lifted her pencil and, without a word of warning or apology, scratched one of my pages. Lines appeared which, although their scars have faded with age, remain to this day.

She first used the graphite point to underline the words: These girls formed the Brodie set.

She continued on in this manner.

I admit, I felt aggrieved.

However, when the shock had passed, I slowly reconciled myself to her actions. I recognise that this may be hard to believe but it even became something of a game for me: trying to anticipate which words or sentences her young mind would deem most noteworthy. I hoped that these choices might reveal clues as to the inner workings of her mind. I cannot say that they did.

The phrases she singled out in my first few pages were: they were sixteen; they remained unmistakably Brodie; they followed dangerous Miss Brodie into the secure shade of the elm; I would make of you the crème de la crème.

After reading chapter one, Violet returned me to her bag.

I was jostled around for what felt like an age before we arrived at our next destination. Her fingers examined each of my companions until they found me. I was lifted up and out and handed to a tall, slender woman with large molasses eyes.

This, I would learn, was Auntie Ruth.

I had thought I would never encounter this scarlet woman and was, at this early juncture, predisposed to dislike her. However, I was taken with Ruth immediately. The mixture of warmth and grace she radiated were just a small part of her charm.

'I remember reading it,' Ruth said. 'It made such an impression on me. I must have been your age. We had a teacher very like Miss Brodie. We all wanted to be her, or, at the very least, be like her when we grew up.'

'But you're a pharmacist.'

Ruth laughed.

She told Violet that despite her teenage infatuation with a certain Miss Richardson, her own abilities had always lain squarely in the sciences. She had, she explained, been steered towards her career by a workaday Guidance teacher, who, despite lacking in the charisma department, had assured Ruth that pharmacy was a noble calling and a field of study which would entirely suit her academic strengths.

'It's funny you and Mum got put together in Halls.'

'It didn't go on what you were studying,' Ruth said. 'I was lucky to get your mum. The other girls were all a bit bonkers. And most of them hated the person they had to share with. The fact your mum and I actually liked each other was a minor miracle on our corridor.'

'It's so sad that...' Violet began. Ruth turned away and started foraging in the fridge. Violet did not finish her sentence.

'Chicken casserole? I made it last night.'

'That would be lovely. Thanks, Auntie Ruth.'

Ruth placed two pots on the stove. One contained the casserole and the other a significant quantity of potatoes. Violet moved me to the Welsh dresser and began to set the kitchen table for four.

Ruth's casserole looked and smelled delicious.

I noted that Drew and Tom accepted second helpings,

which vanished as quickly as their first. Once all the plates were empty, Ruth excused herself from the table and returned with an attractively wrapped package. She handed it to Tom, who, in turn, handed it to Violet.

He explained that they had felt bad because, whilst money in a card had been practical, it had seemed too impersonal a gift for their favourite niece on her sixteenth birthday. This was a belated remedy.

My initial reaction was not curiosity as to what was in the parcel, rather, it was to note with interest the fact that this was the first time they had seen her since her birthday.

Violet was very polite about the fact there had been no need to give her anything else and she assured them that the money had been more than generous. I did detect, however, as I am sure they did, that she was thrilled by the surprise of this additional present.

Violet was still chattering her gratitude as she undid the wrapping paper. Inside she discovered a rather elegant fountain pen and a suede notebook with gold-edged pages. She declared each one to be beautiful and threw her arms around Tom. She then sprang to her feet and hugged Ruth.

Drew leaned over to Tom and shook his hand. He thanked him for their kindness, lowered his voice and said, 'You know you'll always be family to me and Violet.'

I found myself wondering how Violet would explain the pen and the notebook if questioned by her mother. I decided she would most likely keep it hidden to sidestep any such difficulty.

After a dessert of Arctic roll, Drew and Violet said their goodbyes.

As their voices disappeared into the hall, I realised I had been forgotten.

I have had the misfortune of being abandoned at other times, but on this occasion, it was not overly traumatic: being both short-lived and serendipitous. Within the week, I would both be back home with Violet and I would know more about her family than she did.

Ruth cleared away the remaining dishes before she noticed me on the antique dresser. She gathered me to herself and carried me into the next room.

Tom was sitting on a chesterfield sofa in the half dark.

He motioned for her to join him.

As she did, she handed me to Tom.

He turned me over in his hands and I knew why he was loved by Ruth and by Drew and by Violet. In his touch, I felt kindness and generosity of spirit.

He placed me on the chesterfield's cold green leather and said he would take me to work on Monday. He explained that he had arranged to meet Drew for coffee in the afternoon.

Ruth put her head on Tom's chest and closed her eyes.

They sat like this, in the gloom, for a long time. It was Tom who was first to stir. As he left the room, he turned on a standard lamp near the door. In its dim glow, I could see that there were books everywhere: on shelves; on the small table by the bay window; on the mantelpiece.

There were newspapers, too. They leaked from a wicker magazine rack onto the oriental-looking rug that covered much of the wooden floor. They formed clumps on the chesterfield opposite and on the low coffee table. The presence of so much reading material had a calming effect on me.

Tom returned to the sitting room with two glasses of red wine. Halfway through hers, Ruth broke the silence that had settled in the room.

'I still think he should tell Jane. Keeping secrets is never good. I should know.'

'He doesn't want to worry her,' Tom said.

'I know, but she must know there's something wrong. Maybe that's worrying her more. Don't you think?'

'I'm not saying you're wrong, but if he can get back on his feet without her ever finding out, then maybe that's for the best. She would never forgive Mark.'

Over the course of that night, I would piece together the unhappy tale of Drew's financial downfall and the part Violet's Uncle Mark had played in it.

Mark Galbraith had made a good deal of money from a seemingly lucrative enterprise. He then recruited Drew and a small number of equally naïve investors, exited the scheme and severed his financial ties with it. Unfortunately, Mark had failed to inform Drew that it might be a good idea for him to do likewise. As a result, Drew had lost significant sums and had been threatened with foreclosure. Tom had therefore loaned him a substantial amount of money to save the Munro family home. A loan Tom insisted should only be repaid when Drew was financially secure. It seemed Tom had been suspicious of the scheme from the start and had not only refused Mark's suggestion to invest, but had tried to stop Drew from doing so.

As I mulled over this revelation, it came to me that Mark's behaviour with regard to this scheme was most likely a fairly accurate indicator of his behaviour in other aspects of his life. For instance, in his marriage. It was, therefore, not too great a leap for me to imagine the way in which a relationship between Ruth and Tom may have developed. Why, when her husband was not the man everyone believed him to be and when she had nowhere else to turn, should Ruth not confide her troubles in this kind-hearted man? Why, under these circumstances, should his feelings for her not blossom from the platonic? Why should they not fall in love?

The next day, I accompanied Tom to a coffee shop in Glasgow's city centre. He chose a table at the window and placed me on it. I had an excellent view of life on the busy street outside and of the hubbub of activity within the café. The smell of strong Italian coffee and spiced cake was most appealing.

It had been clear from the moment of Drew's arrival that he was tightly wound. Thankfully, Tom's easy manner allowed him to relax and once he calmed down, he began to talk.

He talked as if there was no one else in the room. He described his anger, his guilt, the night terrors from which he had begun to suffer. He said lying awake in the dark next to Jane, one thought would get stuck in his head: he would see himself; he would watch as he got out of bed; he would watch as he went into the garage; he would watch as he got into his car; he would watch as he turned on the engine and let the exhaust fumes do their job.

When Tom finally spoke, his voice was gentle.

He was glad Drew had confided in him. They had known each other for such a long time. Tom understood that things were difficult: the money, the house, the sense of betrayal. But it would get better. And there were the kids. And Jane. And there was no need to pay the money back. Tom was secure; he had no need for it. He had simply saved it for some notional rainy day. He was glad it had been of help.

Back on Violet's desk that night, I tried to fully comprehend the gravity of what I had heard. I admit, I could not. But I was troubled by it for a long time.

Over the weeks that followed, I came to fear that Violet had finished reading the story of Jean Brodie at school, courtesy of a class copy. This was a great disappointment to me. I was, however, opened and used as a hunting ground for quotes each time she had a homework essay. I was also removed from the shelf during her prelims and was well-thumbed in the spring of 1989 when she was studying for her Higher English exam.

Once her examination was over, Violet placed me in her bookcase.

She would never again remove me from it.

Part Two. Heather
1990 - 1991

Chapter One

In the autumn of 1990, when Violet had been away at university for less than two weeks, Thomas, now a spindly fifteen-year-old, pushed open the bedroom door.

He walked over to the bookcase and pawed at the spines on the top shelf. His hand stopped when it reached the copy of *Romeo and Juliet*, which he removed. His grubby fingers then turned their attentions to me.

Thomas passed me to a girl in his English class called Heather. I got the distinct impression that he thought there might be something of a romantic nature between them. She, however, did not appear to think anything of the sort.

Heather declined the copy of the play but seemed pleased to accept me.

I was pressed into her schoolbag. It was crowded and there was a musty smell of cigarettes. I found myself next to Heather's diary, which proved to be a rather miserable acquaintance.

We were on a school bus when Heather removed me from her bag. She was sitting in a seat towards the back. Near the front, a clump of girls pressed themselves together, talking. Not in a particularly loud way, but in a manner that suggested you had to be invited to join the conversation. Unlike Heather, they each had long, shiny hair, tied back, for the most part, in high pony tails. These formed waves of gold, copper and caramel as they laughed.

The few boys on the bus, were at the back. Except one. He was diagonally in front of us. I would learn his name was Jamie. He, too, was sitting alone.

Heather smoothed open my first chapter and began to read. I saw her face crinkle into a smile as she learned that "hatlessness" was an offence if you happened to be a pupil at the Marcia Blaine School for Girls.

I tried to imagine Heather's hair tamed by a Marcia Blaine panama hat. Perhaps then the casual observer would look beyond its jagged black spikes. They might notice flecks of sapphire in her eyes or the slight jut to her elfin chin. They might become mesmerised by the pale luminescence of her skin.

As Heather continued to read, I sensed she was pleased to discover that the girls of the Brodie set "had no team spirit" and that Miss Brodie herself "was held in great suspicion".

Jamie turned around. He said something in our direction. I could not quite make him out. It seemed neither could Heather.

'Huh?' she said.

'Get off at the Bellway stop.'

'Why?'

He did not answer. Heather closed me and dropped me into her bag. I slid down coarse canvas and came to rest beside a metal pencil case and an odorous ham and pickle sandwich wrapped in cling film.

Heather stood up.

She passed the pack of girls without a word, but shouted, 'Thanks, Driver,' as she descended the steps of the bus. I felt her jump, land and begin to run. Jamie shouted for her to slow down. She ran more quickly.

The contents of her bag grumbled. It seemed that they were

well used to this sort of treatment. I longed to be back in Violet's room and cursed myself for every time I had wished to escape the confines of the bookcase. We had not always seen eye to eye, but now, being jostled around in this cold jail with dreary textbooks and a disconsolate diary, I missed my old bookshelf companions. Mostly, I missed Violet.

To distract myself from this unsettling sense of longing, I imagined what Violet might be doing at this moment.

I decided she would likely be in the library. I thought of her as I had seen her in the Mitchell two years earlier. Her hair was shorter now, of course. She had had a university cut. At least, that is what I chose to call it. Unfortunately, if the desired effect had been to make her look older, it had failed. However, if it had been to give her a more interesting air, it was a roaring success; her corkscrew curls looked decidedly mischievous in this modish chin-length style.

I imagined her coming home for a weekend and discovering I was missing.

I heard her shout her brother's name. I watched her drag him by his skinny arm into her bedroom and growl, 'Where is it?' Or, perhaps, 'What have you done?' Even better, 'I want that book back. Now. Do you hear me? Today, Thomas. I want it back today. Or you'll be very sorry.'

I imagined a crack as she applied just a little too much pressure to his wrist.

Jamie caught up with us.

I heard Heather accept his offer of a cigarette.

I felt the dizzying sensation of being dropped from a height as she let her schoolbag fall to the ground. The smell of grass intensified. Light flooded in as Heather's hand brushed against me. It pushed me aside. Her fingers searched out a small orange lighter that was trapped beneath her uneaten lunch. She removed it, leaving the flap of the bag open. This carelessness provided me with a view of the outside world.

It was a bright autumn day, but there was a distinct chill in the air. Despite this, Jamie removed his blazer and spread it on the ground. Heather sat down. Her legs extended out into the short grass and were crossed at the ankle. Jamie remained standing while she attempted to light the cigarette she held in her hand.

We were at the top of a hill. Looking down, I could see rows of houses and small children playing in the distance. The breeze blew their voices away from us. It also added an element of challenge to Heather's task. On the fourth attempt, the tip of the cigarette began to glow. She flipped the lighter up into the air and despite the vagaries of the wind, Jamie caught it. He removed a cigarette from the pocket of his white school shirt and sat down next to her.

I thought it was very bold of him to keep contraband where it might be so easily seen by a teacher. However, my early impression of Jamie was that he did not care much for rules, nor I presumed, for figures of authority.

It seemed Jamie had seen Heather's exchange with Thomas in class. He now questioned her about it in a way that suggested he thought very little of Thomas. I admit, I derived a certain pleasure from this. At that moment, as in many others, my ire for the boy who removed me from my life burned warm and deep.

Heather did not respond. Jamie asked for a second time what Thomas had given her. Without a word, she leaned over, stubbed out her cigarette, lifted me out of the bag, and handed me to him.

His hands were rough, but his grip was not. After reading my back cover, Jamie placed me on the soft material of the blazer.

'You could just have told me,' he said.

Heather shrugged.

'I didn't mean to give you a hard time,' he said. 'It just seemed a bit weird.'

Heather lay back on the blazer.

Jamie stopped pacing and sat down next to her.

Much to my disappointment, Heather said Thomas was not as bad as he seemed. It was all a bit of an act, she said. He was okay when you got to know him. They had been at nursery together; their mothers had known each other for years. She had no idea why he had given her the book, other than he knew she liked to read. His sister used to lend her books. When they were all young, she said.

Clouds ran across the sky.

Heather confessed she still had the Jemima Puddle-Duck book the Munro children had given her for her sixth birthday. She did not, however, admit something I would come to learn: that the accompanying Jemima Puddle-Duck stuffed toy still sat on her bed.

I admit, saddened as I was to hear Heather's positive appraisal of Thomas, I was intrigued by the link between the two families. It would, however, be months before I would discover the seemingly improbable fact that Heather's mum had earned extra pocket money as a teenager by babysitting the Galbraith children. In quiet moments, I would entertain myself by picturing the scene – Heather's mum attempting to keep miniature versions of Sandra, Mark and Jane occupied while their parents, dressed in 1940s finery, attended dances at the church hall. Long before this revelation, I would piece together an attendant detail: Heather had been a "late baby". Her parents, Dorothy and John Wilson, having raised a son and sent him off into the world, were well into their forties when a second bundle of joy appeared. An accident of sorts, I came to suppose.

I was pushed from the comfort of the blazer onto the grass.

An indecent amount of time passed as they cavorted on my former resting place. As they did, I thought again of my recent misfortune.

I dearly wanted to return to my former existence and found myself distressed by the fact that I could not, myself, affect this change. My only hope was that Heather would somehow learn that I had been stolen and, appalled to have played any part in such a crime, would contact Violet and return me to her.

Heather indulged in yet another cigarette.

Afterwards, she liberated a packet of polo mints from her blazer pocket. She took one then threw them to Jamie. He eased three into his hand and returned the near empty packet to her. When they were ready to go, I was returned to the bag. It was still as uncomfortable, but at least it was warmer than I remembered.

I spent the next half hour crushed between two textbooks. Jamie said his goodbyes early in the journey. I did not hear any response so presumed Heather must simply have smiled and lifted her hand to wave, or perhaps she offered nothing more than a perfunctory nod as he veered off to whatever destination awaited him.

Once inside the Wilson family home, Heather threw her bag onto the sofa. She picked through the items inside and lifted me out.

The room I found myself in was larger than the Munros' sitting room. A thick cream carpet covered the floor. There were occasional tables in dark mahogany and a number of standard lamps constructed from the same material. Across from me was a marble fireplace and to my right stood a display case filled with porcelain figurines. The sofa on which I now lay was upholstered in gold-coloured velour. It had a matching gold fringe. The two armchairs in the room were of a similar style.

The room had a distinctive smell.

In time, I would be able to identify it as furniture polish.

Dorothy Wilson appeared. She was small and lithe with brown bouffant hair. Her dark brown trousers and light brown crewneck looked expensive. As did her jewellery – large pearl earrings set in gold with a matching pendant.

She began to remonstrate with her daughter.

The fact Heather had not removed her outdoor shoes was the first point of contention. The second was Heather's eye makeup. According to Dorothy, it had not been there when her daughter left the house that morning and should not be there now. The third was the time of day. Dorothy had expected Heather to be home at four-thirty and was deeply disappointed that her daughter had appeared two hours late, behaving as if nothing was wrong. I could go on. Dorothy certainly did.

Heather did not utter a word. She intermittently shrugged her shoulders and offered the occasional roll of her eyes, but provided nothing in the form of a defence.

When Dorothy had exhausted her list of complaints, she returned to the sin of outdoor shoes in the sitting room. Heather began to untie the laces of the offending articles. When she had, she removed them and lifted them up. Leaving me behind, she walked out of room in her stocking soles. Only when she had stepped into the hall did I hear her speak.

'Happy?' she said, as the door swung shut.

Dorothy dissolved into one of the armchairs. Her face was

in her hands, so I could not see if she was crying.

The noise from above suggested that Heather was once again wearing her outdoor shoes.

Chapter Two

I was still on the sofa when John Wilson opened the sitting room door. His steel rimmed glasses and the matching silver-grey of his thick, wavy hair made him look like he might be Heather's grandfather rather than her father.

Dorothy lifted her head out of her hands. Despite the absence of any sound suggestive of sobbing, she looked like she had, indeed, been crying.

John asked what the fight had been about.

'I think a better question might be, what has she done now? Don't you?'

'Sorry. What did she do?'

Dorothy did not begin by explaining that Heather had arrived home from school two hours after she had been expected. Instead, she complained at length about the "sheer cheek" that had come out of their daughter's mouth. This seemed somewhat disingenuous as I had only heard Heather say one word to her mother, and that had been muttered from the other side of a door.

John tried unsuccessfully to appease his wife. When she finally told him about Heather being late, he agreed that such behaviour was not acceptable and said he would go upstairs and speak to her. Dorothy told him to take Heather's ruined dinner up, while he was at it. She then left the room.

John sat down on the armchair nearest to the window.

I could hear drawers and kitchen appliances opening and closing in the next room. I presumed this was as a result of the force with which these actions were being undertaken. Each time there was a particularly loud thud, John would glance over at the wall that separated the two rooms. It was on one such occasion he spotted me. He was leaning down to pick me up when Dorothy appeared with a tray.

'Here,' she said. 'And you can take that book up, too. It would be nice if your daughter refrained from treating the lounge as her own personal dumping ground.'

John pressed me between the inside of his left arm and side. The cotton of his shirt was smooth and cool. I could feel the outline of his ribs; the rise and fall of his breath.

Dorothy placed the tray into his hands and said, 'Don't be long up there, or your dinner will be ruined as well.'

When he reached the top of the stairs, he called out to Heather. She opened her bedroom door. It looked like she, too, might have been crying.

'Here you go, sweetheart,' he said, handing her the tray. 'Do you mind if I come in?'

She stepped back and let her father enter the room. As she did, she smiled at him and at precisely that moment, I caught a glimpse of the girl who lived deep inside of her. I felt safe for the first time since Thomas had snatched me from the top shelf of Violet's bookcase.

Like the sitting room, Heather's bedroom was commodious.

An ornate oak desk sat under the bay window. Heather placed the tray on top of it. Her father moved a French dictionary aside to create a space for me to the right of the tray. This placed me directly in the path of a cold draught that pushed its way through a tiny fissure in the wooden frame of the window.

To divert my attention from the Arctic blast, I examined the contents of the tray. Heather's meal did not look in the least bit ruined. It was presented on a brown stoneware plate patterned with orange flowers and consisted of fillet of salmon, poached, I think, four potato croquettes and a generous helping of garden peas. The tray also held a glass of water and a large yellow pear, sitting on a miniature version of the brown dinner plate. Silver-plated cutlery – a knife, a fork and a fruit knife – peeked out of a cream cotton napkin.

Heather moved to the corner of the room. An armchair was heaped high with clothes. She pushed them aside and lowered herself into it. John eased the leather chair out from under her desk. He turned it around to face his daughter and sat down.

'Do you want to tell me what happened?' he said.

Heather's hands were in her lap. She started to pick at the already peeling turquoise paint on her fingernails.

During the silence, whilst her dinner continued to cool, I undertook an inspection of the room. The walls were beige and the carpet was a pale mauve. Heather's furniture looked to be antiques, in dark lacquered wood. An imposing wrought iron bed had been pushed up against one of the walls. It was thick with bedding in white and various shades of blue. Four oversized pillows were arranged against the wall to create a seating area where I imagined Heather might like to read. In between the middle two pillows there was a trio of cuddly toys: the stuffed Jemima Puddle Duck, an ancient looking Scottie dog wearing a green and yellow tartan coat and a tiny koala bear whose nose and ears appeared to be fashioned out of leather. In front of them was a fluffy pyjama case in purple with black stripes. It was the size and shape of a well-fed, sleeping cat.

'I'm not annoyed,' John said. 'I'm worried about you.'

Heather looked up. Her eyes appeared even darker in the dim light from the window.

'Talk to me.'

Heather's attention returned to her fingernails.

In a voice that was barely audible, she said she had stayed behind at school to do her homework. She said she was sorry. She had lost track of the time.

'I'll speak to your mother,' John said. 'Explain what happened.'

He asked Heather if she wanted him to put her dinner back in the oven.

She shook her head.

Once he was safely downstairs, Heather walked towards the desk. She unwrapped her cutlery and selected the fruit knife. She lifted the pear to her face and inhaled. After doing so, she held the fruit just above the smaller of the two plates and turned it in her hand as she carved off thick slices. These she devoured, skin and all. Within a moment only the core remained.

She dropped it onto the empty plate and set the knife next to it.

I thought it was odd that she ate the pear first, letting the salmon, potato croquettes and peas grow even colder. I have thought it over a number of times since, but I have no explanation to offer.

Still standing, Heather lifted up the fork and pierced a potato croquette with it. She ate it in three bites. She did likewise with the others on her plate. She then ate the peas. The salmon remained untouched.

Heather picked up the dinner plate. She held it in one hand and the larger of the two knives in the other and left the room. I heard a nearby toilet flush. When she reappeared, the plate had been scraped clean. She put it back onto the tray and picked up the glass.

In one continuous motion, she drank almost half of the water. She placed the glass back on the tray and walked over to the bed.

I was mesmerised as she lifted up the fat cat pyjama case, unzipped it and slipped a small ornate bottle out from between white and blue checked fabric, that I presumed belonged to her pyjamas.

The word Ouzo was written in exotic lettering on the label of the bottle.

Back at her desk, Heather topped up the water glass with a generous splash of the clear liquid. It smelled strongly of aniseed. After returning the bottle to its hiding place, she sat down on the armchair and drank her doctored water one sip at a time.

The room was in near darkness when the glass was empty. She returned it to the desk and lifted me up.

In the corner near the bed there was a lamp with a dark blue lampshade. Heather used her free hand to turn a small bronze knob. With each click one of the three bulbs flared. With this same hand, she plumped up the already plump pillow nearest to it and made herself comfortable.

She flicked through my pages, from back to front, stopping at the inscription. Her sharp knuckles kneaded my spine. She mouthed the words Sandra had written. She paused. She mouthed them again. This time she slowed over the words "keen mind" and "gentle heart" as if tasting each one.

I sensed sadness. Or at least I imagined I did.

I was closed and banished to the chilly desktop. Once there, I performed an inventory: the tray topped with its crockery and cutlery; the aforementioned dictionary; a small brass clock; a black plastic rectangular repository holding pens, a pencil, a ruler and a compass; an unopened packet of polo mints; a glass paperweight with bubbles and swirls depicting an ocean scene; a Bank of Scotland desk calendar turned to October and a jam jar half-filled with twenty pence pieces.

Heather turned her attention to her schoolbag, which leant against the armchair. She spilled its contents onto the carpet and, picking through them, selected her diary and the pencil case. From this, she chose a pencil with a sharp point at one end and an eraser at the other.

She re-plumped the pillow and began to write with a fluid hand. When she had filled four pages, she set the diary and the pencil on the carpet next to her bed.

Long after the light had been turned off, I was still engaged in the task of imagining what those pages might reveal.

When Heather opened the curtains the following morning, I was once again assaulted by an unwelcome gust of air.

I watched her dress.

Her translucent skin was pulled taut over her slight frame. She was thin, but not, in my opinion, skinny. Her stomach was flat and there was dip from her ribs to her hips, but her legs and upper arms appeared muscular and gave the impression of physical strength.

When she was ready, hair freshly spiked, she returned the diary to her schoolbag and left for the day. This action was both sensible and prescient as a few hours later her mother entered the room in order to perform an extensive search.

She began with the tallboy. She opened one drawer at a time, removed the contents and, finding nothing of an incriminating nature, returned each item to its correct location. Despite being ill-attired for the task – dressed as she was in a white blouse tucked into a rather smart coffee-coloured skirt – she lay flat on her stomach and checked beneath each piece of furniture in a manner that suggested she was practised in the art of yoga.

I am quite sure she would also have inspected the insides of the wardrobe, but for the fact its ornate key had been removed from the lock. This, too, I presumed, was safely stowed in Heather's schoolbag.

Before resigning herself to defeat, Dorothy sat down on Heather's bed, inches from the pyjama case, and scoured the room with her eyes. Thwarted, she retreated with nothing more than the tray.

The search may not have revealed what Dorothy was looking for, but I found it illuminating. Heather's room, whilst it showed little of her personality in its furniture and fabrics, revealed more of her identity when pried apart. For instance, the items of school uniform that lay strewn on the armchair and on the carpet, bore no similarity to the neatly folded black apparel that filled two of the mahogany drawers. Similarly, the drawer that contained makeup and personal grooming accoutrements was well-organised and scrupulously clean.

I began to think that somewhere, beneath the surface, Heather was more like her mother than she may have liked to admit, even to herself.

I also believed I had learned something more of the relationship between mother and daughter. I made assumptions about Dorothy's overbearing nature and need for control. I had yet to learn that these traits, were, in the main, borne out of concern.

When Heather came home from school, she appeared to have a sense of what had gone on earlier in the day. Like her mother, she thoroughly inspected the room. I wondered if a trace of Dorothy's honeysuckle-sweet perfume still hung in the air, no longer perceptible to me.

Heather removed the bottle of Ouzo, tilted it from side to side as if to check its level was unchanged, put it to her lips and tipped back her head.

When she was done, she loosened her school tie and exchanged tights for thick-knit socks. As with the previous evening, she did not remove her uniform – in contrast, Violet had, without fail, changed out of hers every day after school.

Chapter Three

Heather pulled books and jotters from her bag and sat down at the desk.

I was pushed aside as she set to work on what appeared to be chemistry homework. Next, she opened a maths textbook. There were three insistent bangs on a wall below us. I detected what I thought might be anxiety when, moments later, Heather's mother called up the stairs, asking her to come down as dinner was on the table.

After opening the packet of polo mints and crunching two of them, Heather complied with the request. She returned minutes later carrying a tray. This time, her meal consisted of slices of cooked ham, boiled potatoes and broccoli. The fruit for the evening was an orange.

She began by methodically peeling it over her dessert plate. This was a disconcerting sight as the fingernails that took such care were pockmarked with the final remains of the turquoise nail polish.

When she had finished removing the skin, she ate the orange segment by segment. She then ate three of the four boiled potatoes and all of the broccoli.

She left the room with her plate and fork. I heard the nearby flush of a toilet and when she returned, both the remaining potato and the ham were gone.

Heather supplemented her water with a liberal measure of

Ouzo. The half-empty bottle was then slipped beneath the layer of clothes on the armchair on which she proceeded to sit. She drank from the glass in the same manner she had the previous evening.

After an hour or so, I heard noises suggestive of the fact John Wilson was home from work. Heather's response to this was to consume two more polo mints.

She seemed to allow time for a parental debrief before she went downstairs with the tray. Within minutes, I heard her footsteps on the stairs once more. I tried to make sense of sounds I was not, at that moment, able to identify but now know to be the scrape and rumble of a hatch in the ceiling of the upper hall being opened with a retractable stick and a ladder being pulled down.

Before climbing up into the attic, Heather returned to the bedroom. She re-stashed the bottle of Ouzo then retrieved me from the desk.

With her schoolbag slung diagonally over her body she scaled the ladder using only her right hand for assistance; I was in her left. Near the top, she stretched the hand that held me up into the black square above us and used the bottom edge of my spine to press a switch. My horror at being used in such a way vanished in the instant this action, and my part in it, transformed the darkness into a yellow glare.

The attic was an elongated triangle with floor to ceiling rough-cut wooden beams. The flooring was a jigsaw of plywood covered, in part, by offcuts of Persian-looking carpet. On top of this haphazard arrangement lay a kaleidoscope of bric-a-brac. The exposed lightbulb that hung from the rafters illuminated a sea of household items the Wilsons had retired from service.

Heather made her way through decades of miscellany to,

what appeared to be, the back wall of the attic. I marvelled at the multitude of coats and formal wear, which I suspected had not been worn in decades, suspended from a steel pole that stretched from one wall to the other.

Heather parted the rack of extravagant attire midway: between a blue taffeta ball gown and a long silk dress in emerald green. The material of the dress felt soft against my cover as Heather pushed her way through the clothes. Once on the other side, I beheld the makeshift room that would be my home for the next two decades.

Nothing here betrayed even a hint of Dorothy Wilson. I might have believed she had never set eyes on this hidden portion of her home. However, having witnessed her conduct earlier that day, it felt almost impossible that this place could actually have avoided falling prey to her shadowy techniques of surveillance.

I estimated this portion of the attic accounted for one fifth of the overall floor space. It seemed odd, therefore, that a section this size might have been spared the Wilsons' appetite for storage, bearing in mind the surfeit of tired-looking furniture, obsolete electrical goods, once-loved model cars and trains, boxes of crystal glasses and stack upon stack of forsaken books that spilled from one groaning mound to the next on the other side of the fabric divide.

By comparison, our side was desolate. In the middle of the plywood floor was a large off-cut of red-swirled carpet. On it, brown couch cushions were arranged on three sides of a wooden coffee table. The actual back wall of the attic was sandstone, blackened by age. Against it stood a long, low bookcase, which housed an interesting collection of books. Many from, what I presumed to be, Heather's childhood. Others appeared to have been cherry-picked from the book mounds beyond. These tended to the literary, with titles by Sir Walter Scott, Charles Dickens and George Eliot. Others still had stickers on their spines that led me to believe they may have been pilfered from the school library or, to be more generous, acquired from a second-hand bookshop with an unscrupulous approach to the provenance of its merchandise – *To Kill a Mockingbird, Sunset Song, Of Mice and Men, To Sir with Love, The Outsiders, Rumble Fish, The Tempest, Twelfth Night, Much Ado About Nothing, Macbeth, Hamlet, King Lear.*

Heather placed me on the coffee table. The only other tenant was an oversized confectionery tin that declared itself to be a receptacle for Cadbury Roses. I would learn, however, that what it did in fact contain was a vast collection of cigarette ends.

This knowledge came early in my time in the attic for, after setting me down, Heather dug into her schoolbag for the orange lighter. To my horror, she placed it on top of me. She then lifted out the metal pencil case and put it by my side. When it was open, I could see that it contained a pen, a pencil and four cigarettes. She sat one of the cigarettes on my cover next to the lighter and turned her attention to a small window in the slope of the rafters. She stood on her tiptoes and began to wrestle with it. She pushed it open to the full extent of its rusted arm then removed the lid of the ashtray masquerading as a sweetie tin, retrieved the cigarette and lighter from my cover and sat cross-legged on a cushion. After smoking the cigarette in similar fashion to the way she had drunk the Ouzo, slowly, she sprayed the air in front of her with a can of Mr Sheen she kept in the reference section of the bookcase.

I never saw Heather drink alcohol in the attic. I presumed that either the pungent smelling liqueur had disabused her of the notion or that the Ouzo had been an anomaly, acquired by

82

means she found herself unable to repeat.

I remained in my original position for an age, neither shelved nor read. During those weeks, on schooldays, my only entertainment before Heather arrived home would be a miniscule brown mouse who would on occasion appear, check for food and leave disappointed. Most nights, thankfully, Heather would materialise at some point.

The weekends were a different matter. On those days Heather, dressed entirely in black, would appear late in the morning and would stay for a few hours. On one such occasion, she brought a battery-operated cassette player with her. After that, every week a new cassette would be added to the growing collection neatly arranged on top of the bookcase. Her taste in music did not overlap with Violet's at all. Heather's preference seemed to be for solo female artists or songs from musicals. She played the tape marked Les Misérables with annoying regularity. The volume was always turned to low.

The first time Heather brought a visitor into the attic was a school day. I knew by the length of the light from the window that it was around noon. She appeared in her uniform and stocking soles. At her back, pushing his way through the wall of garments, was Thomas.

'Are you sure she'll not be back?' he said.

'Are you scared?' Heather asked.

'Your mum is a bit of a dragon.'

'We're not all as lucky as you,' Heather said and made a face as she added, 'And there's no need to rub it in.'

Thomas apologised, conceding that he was, indeed, fortunate.

It was then, as the conversation turned to the fact that Dorothy Wilson was ancient (a hundred years old by

Heather's reckoning), that I learned she had, in fact, babysat for Thomas's mother, and, perhaps more astonishingly, for his Uncle Mark and Aunt Sandra. A fact they both seemed to find hilarious, although I suspected there was a bitter edge to Heather's apparent amusement.

'I don't care how nice my mum is,' Thomas said, 'she'd kill me if she knew I was dogging school.'

'It's the last day before the Christmas holidays. No one cares,' Heather said. 'Did you want to sit around all day and play Monopoly?'

I could not help but wonder, why, when this was the first instance I was aware of that Heather had played truant, she had chosen Thomas Munro as her accomplice. It seemed to me that Jamie would surely have made a much more interesting partner in crime.

Heather motioned for Thomas to sit on the cushion next to hers.

As I watched him, I began to suspect that he was also curious as to why he was there. I also noted that he had stretched in the two months since I had last seen him. His arms and legs now looked too long for his body and he had changed his hair. It was no longer short and neat. His red locks now tended to a floppier look. I imagined he might have mistakenly thought that it gave his appearance more appeal, perhaps even made him look a little edgy. If this indeed was his logic, it was defective.

When he had made himself comfortable, he said, 'I thought you were going out with Jamie.'

'So?'

'So, won't he mind?'

'Mind what?'

'Me,' Thomas said. 'Me being here.'

'Why would he care? He's away up north to his granny's. And he knows we're just pals.'

'Sure. No worries,' Thomas said.

His face told me a different story; I got the distinct impression he was less than happy at his designation as a friend.

Heather produced two cigarettes.

'Want one?'

'No. You're alright.'

'Worried it'll affect your footballing prowess?'

She smirked as she reached over to prod him with her free hand.

Thomas took the cigarette. Heather reached into the waistband of her skirt and handed him the orange lighter.

'Your secret's safe with me,' she said.

It was quite clear that Thomas did not enjoy what I suspected was his first experience of smoking. This, however, seemed to be lost on Heather. She pushed at her cushion and lay back. Thomas let the cigarette burn in his hand and then stubbed it out in the open tin.

Heather was now on her second cigarette. Thomas watched as she formed her mouth into a circle and let the smoke escape in rings. He moved his cushion closer to hers and lay back.

'Are you and Jamie pretty serious?'

'Not really,' she said.

Neither I nor, I suspected, Thomas, was convinced by this.

'I don't mean to be rude,' he said, 'but he seems a bit weird.'

'I'm sure your pals say the same about me.'

'Nah. You're interesting.'

'That's why the other girls stopped inviting me to things years ago, is it?'

'I wouldn't worry about them. Stuck up bitches.'

Heather set her mouth into a circle. A series of perfectly spherical grey rings escaped from it.

Thomas declared he was hungry. Heather lit a third cigarette. He asked if they could raid the kitchen. She looked at him askance and asked if he was feeling brave. She said the kitchen was strictly Dorothy's domain and that her mother's dark powers would alert her if anyone dared to trespass. Thomas laughed, but looked nervous.

Heather discarded the crushed end of the final cigarette I would see her smoke that day. She relaxed back into the cushion and closed her eyes. Thomas was still on the one next to her. He raised himself onto his elbows. I felt my concern grow. After he had spent an indecent length of time staring at her, he stood up and began to examine the contents of the bookcase.

I was relieved as this kept him away from Heather and from me. He ran one freckled hand along the books until he came to the copy of *To Kill a Mockingbird*. He plucked it from its place.

He began to read, in a ridiculous accent.

Heather opened her eyes.

'Really?' she said. 'You do remember Scout's a girl?'

Thomas adapted his voice accordingly.

'And she's from Alabama, not Wales.'

Thomas threw the book in her direction.

Heather smoothed its cover as she picked it up from the rug.

'Didn't you like it? I loved when Mrs Shaw did it with us,' she said.

'It was alright. A bit long.'

'You're such a cretin.'

Thomas responded by suggesting that Heather was a lot more like Dorothy Wilson than she might like to admit, at which point, his visit was over.

The following day when Heather visited the attic in regulation black, she had two cassettes in her hand. One was a medley of Christmas songs. The other an album by Suzanne Vega. I would hear the Christmas tape only once, but she played the Suzanne Vega tape over and over and over. The constant repetition did not thrill me at the time, but later, when the attic was silent for so long, I would miss that soulful voice.

Three things I would not easily forget happened over those Christmas holidays. The first occurred the day after Heather had skipped school. It was the most troubling. Even though she had already been in the attic twice that day, she returned in the evening, later than she would normally appear.

Heather sat down on her usual cushion. The Roses tin was on the floor next to her. She lit a cigarette but did not smoke it. Instead she stared at it as it burned, her eyes lined red. When just the stub at the end was left, she knocked the ash into the tin, pushed up her sleeve and held what remained of it next to the whitish blue skin of her forearm. I felt my distress turn to relief as, a second later, she stubbed the cigarette end out on the inner rim of the tin. But then, as if in a trance, she started to run one fingernail back and forwards across the same small spot of skin until it started to bleed. Only when her nail was entirely covered in blood, did she stop.

I was at a loss to understand what had happened or why. All I knew was that I could do nothing to help, which was a matter of profound sadness to me.

Chapter Four

Days later, I heard the voice of Dorothy Wilson boom through the fabric wall. In addition, there were two other smaller voices I could not identify. In their girlish tones, they referred to Dorothy as 'grandma'.

I gathered from the bits of the conversation that I could hear more clearly that this was an expedition in search of toys that had once been Heather's but had long ago been forsaken. I also gathered that one little voice belonged to a girl called Kirsty and that the other belonged to one called Elspeth.

The search seemed quite particular. The rummaging noises would often be met with remarks like, 'Not that one, Elspeth. That's too old for you,' or 'I think that's broken, Kirsty,' or 'That would be a bit too messy, don't you think?' The girls sounded very obedient as their replies were mainly limited to, 'Yes, Grandma.'

Despite spending so much time on my own and being inquisitive by nature, I found myself pleased that the foraging did not breach the rack of clothing. This led me to realise that I had grown to care for Heather; I was willing to forfeit my own curiosity if it meant her secret lair remained undiscovered.

The search ended when Dorothy declared, 'That's a good find, Kirsty,' and 'KerPlunk! Well done, Elspeth.' She promised the girls Heather would play with them when she got back from her piano lesson and then instructed them to put the other toys back into some semblance of order. Her final words on the matter were that they should look lively about it as lunch would be ready in fifteen minutes. Dorothy then retreated, noisily, down the ladder.

The first I saw of Kirsty was her hand.

It pushed its way through between two bead-encrusted evening gowns and, bit by bit, was followed by the rest of her tiny body.

She squealed in delight.

'Ells! A den!'

An even smaller version of Kirsty appeared between two of the long capes in Dorothy's collection – the velvet one and its cashmere neighbour. This diminutive intruder began to jump up and down, clapping.

Despite matching floral dresses and the fact that each girl's hair was held tightly in place by thick pleats tied with yellow ribbons, it was obvious that these petite strangers were related to Heather – beneath their blonde fringes were bright little eyes flecked with sapphire.

'Sweeties!' Elspeth shouted, as she pointed at the tin.

Thankfully, Kirsty was her grandmother's granddaughter. 'No,' she said, firmly. 'You'll ruin your lunch.'

I sensed the younger sibling was on the brink of sedition when, from somewhere beneath us, I heard Dorothy bellow, 'Lunchtime!'

The attic was silent until days later when Heather appeared with a new cassette. I got the impression it might have been an unwanted Christmas gift. Instead of adding it to her neatly arranged collection of music, she placed it on top of the foreign language dictionaries in the reference section of her bookcase and slid it back until it could no longer be seen.

From somewhere beneath the folds of her black clothing, her

lighter appeared, followed by a solitary cigarette. She had only just begun to look relaxed when the metal steps of the ladder rattled. Within seconds there was no trace of the cigarette, or, for that matter, of Heather.

It was not like her to forget to pull the ladder up behind her. I decided this oversight was evidence of the detrimental impact the Wilson family Christmas guests were having on her.

From the other side of the attic, I heard her say, 'I don't think so.'

'But Grandma lets us,' a voice, I identified as Elspeth's, countered.

'No. Back down now. You could fall and break your necks coming up here without an adult present. You too, Kirsty. Down.'

It was Kirsty's turn to protest.

'But you're here. And you're an adult. Sort of.'

'Don't be cheeky. Down. Now.'

It would be a year before I would hear, or see, those little girls again.

I was to learn more about them when, in an exciting turn of events during the last days of the school holidays, Heather invited Jamie up to the attic.

When he first arrived, she assured him they had the house to themselves for hours as her dad was at work and her mum was visiting some boring old friend in Edinburgh. Jamie stacked one cushion on top of another and made himself comfortable. He removed a packet of cigarettes and a lighter from the pocket of his jeans. He held the packet out to Heather. She took one then headed to the window to open it. This she did with difficulty. I noted Jamie did not offer help.

'I can't believe you had someone else up here,' he said.

'It was just Thomas.'

This answer did not seem to appease him.

'Anyway,' Heather said, 'I'm sure you snogged some wee Teuchter when you were up in Inverness.'

'What if I did?'

'Exactly. Whereas, I didn't get off with Thomas. So, can you leave it?'

Heather perched her narrow frame on the edge of one of Jamie's cushions. He reached out with his free hand and pulled her into his chest. She lay back and began to smoke.

'What was her name?'

'Who?'

'The Teuchter.'

'Are you jealous?'

'No. Just asking.'

'I'll tell you what, at least she was a bit friendlier than you.'

Jamie was laughing. Heather dug her fist into his ribs. He raised himself onto one elbow and they began to kiss.

I was very concerned by this as both cigarettes were still burning. Thankfully, however, they took a break from one another long enough for Heather to snuff out the glowing remains and discard them in the tin, that was, at this point, on the verge of overflowing.

While she was on her feet, Jamie said he was cold and asked her to close the window. Her response was to mock him for being a delicate flower. He, in turn, patted the cushion next to him and suggested she sit back down and warm him up.

When they had finally finished frolicking on the floor, Jamie asked if Heather had missed him when he was up north. She said she had been too busy with her big brother's brats to even notice that he was gone and went on to complain that it was the same every Christmas – Jonathan and his hoity-toity wife, Natalie, would arrive from London, their annoying children in tow, and would then proceed to spend the week gallivanting around Glasgow seeing all Jonathan's old university friends, while Heather was stuck looking after their spoiled brats.

Worse, it seemed, was that these girls were the apple of Dorothy Wilson's eye. According to Heather, their grandmother could not see past them and she let them away with murder, and, worse still, sided with them every time they were cheeky or broke something or went poking about in Heather's room. They could do no wrong, apparently, unlike their unpaid slave.

Jamie did not appear overly perturbed that Heather's holidays had been ruined by a couple of pocket-sized hellions. He announced he had things to do and people to see and said he was going to head into town. Heather convinced him to have one more cigarette. He did and then left.

Heather put on the Suzanne Vega tape, made herself comfortable on the cushions and closed her eyes. I watched her as she slept. Her chest rose and fell. I could see the outline of her ribs through her black, cotton top. I scanned the rest of her body: the black of her leggings hugged her athletic legs; her wrists and ankles created angles in the blue-white of her skin. She had kicked off her black sandshoes and I could see that her feet were smooth and white, like porcelain.

I was, however, distracted by the lime green polish that covered the nails of her long toes in faultless strokes. By contrast, the mess of colour on her bitten fingernails was a vibrant red. Not for the first time, I wondered at the jumble of precision and chaos that seemed to co-exist within Heather.

When school recommenced, life in the attic reverted to its pre-Christmas routine. Despite the lack of success with which his expeditions had always been met, even the small brown mouse reappeared. I presumed he had been well and truly spooked by the increase in human traffic, because he was absent until some point at the end of January.

I decided to name him.

It seemed to me that Mr Lowther would make a fitting sobriquet.

Mr Lowther adopted a new habit, which involved inching his way around the perimeter of my portion of the attic in the early morning. On one such occasion his painstaking search for crumbs was rewarded. He discovered half a polo mint, dropped by Heather the previous evening.

After her third cigarette of the evening, she had peeled back the silver paper from the wrapper and attempted to remove the first sweet in the packet. This proved to be tricky and resulted in the fragile circle of mint breaking in two. Heather was left with one half and the other half bounced across the floor and came to rest under the bookcase.

I suspected that Mr Lowther was able to detect its presence when his whiskers began to twitch more than normal. With only a little crouching, his tiny body vanished into the impossibly small space. The mint must not have rolled too far as I was still able to see the tip of his tail as he retrieved it. He re-emerged with it snug in his mouth and scampered back below the fabric curtain. I presumed to feast on it in the comfort of the burrow I imagined he had constructed for himself in the far eaves.

The evening following Mr Lowther's mint discovery,

Heather brought her diary and a pen into the attic. Before even lighting a cigarette, she began to write in the notebook. When she had finished, she put down her pen and, taking pains to do it cleanly, tore out the page containing the entry she had only just composed. She produced the orange lighter from her waistband, lifted the piece of paper by one corner, held it above the Roses tin and set it on fire.

I admit I found this bewildering, but it proved less unexpected than her next action, which was to pick me up.

Her fingers were sharp and bony.

She sat, cross legged on the floor and began to turn my pages.

Despite having already started chapter one, she began again on my first page. I could feel the effort it took for her to banish her thoughts and concentrate on reading, word by word and sentence by sentence. After an hour of such close communion, she shut me over and placed me back on the table.

I found myself in a different position to the one to which I had grown accustomed; a little closer to the pungent tin than was comfortable.

Each of the following evenings, when Heather came up to the attic she sat, cross-legged and started to read. On the third night, she reached my final page.

I like to believe that the story contained in my pages gave Heather succour. I had detected a change in her as she read – a release of tension, perhaps. Over those three evenings I felt, or so I imagined at the time, that Heather was caught up in my pages: striding out behind Miss Brodie on Edinburgh's Middle Meadow Walk, more Sandy than Mary McGregor; taking tea on a Sunday afternoon in Miss Brodie's flat, surrounded by the girls of the Brodie set and, on that final night, I sensed her fingers clasp at the grille of Sandy's cloistered cell as Heather peered at the woman who had once been the girl who betrayed Jean Brodie.

She lay me down on the table. This time, in a spot I found quite satisfactory. After smoking a cigarette, slowly, as was her habit, she stubbed it out and wrote at length in her diary.

I was very curious about this entry as I suspected I was at its heart.

Chapter Five

The weeks that followed were uneventful.

Thankfully, the Easter holidays provided welcome relief from the tedium to which I had been forced to become accustomed.

Once again, the last day of term was signalled when, late one morning, Heather and Thomas appeared in their school uniforms. Thomas seemed more relaxed. He caught the cigarette Heather threw in his direction and held his hand out for her lighter before she had even had time to produce it from her waistband.

'Alright,' she said, 'hold your horses.'

She lit her own cigarette then, leaning towards Thomas, she passed him not the lighter, but the cigarette she had just lit. He exchanged it for his unlit one and Heather took it as her own. I felt this practice was most unsanitary, although I had seen worse examples of poor hygiene during Jamie's visit. It also led me to wonder if Heather's assertion that she and Thomas were no more than friends should be called into question.

Despite the still glowing grudge I held against him, I was forced to acknowledge that Thomas was not wholly abhorrent, when, after Heather asked him how Violet was doing, he provided us both with a full account.

I was happy to learn that she had settled well both into the halls of residence and into university life itself. She had apparently become bosom buddies – Thomas's description

– with someone called Emily, who was her roommate. He seemed unsure of this new friend, due mainly to the fact, it seemed, that her hair was a different colour each time Violet brought her home. It had been green in February, he reported, making a face of disgust.

Heather commented that she liked the sound of Emily, and her hair.

Thomas ignored this and went on to explain that Violet would spend the Easter holidays at home. Despite what he said, reading between the lines, I got the impression he was not delighted that he would have to share the attention, or the family bathroom, once more. He was careful not to betray his sibling jealousy being, it seemed to me, smart enough to realise that Heather's fondness for Violet worked in his favour.

I, however, was not fooled by him.

The conversation turned to events at school. They both seemed very happy with the effort their English teacher was expending to prepare them for their Standard Grade exam. They were less enamoured with some other members of staff, who, they claimed, were disinterested and lazy. A particular chemistry teacher, Greasy Gifford, came in for more criticism than most. According to Heather, he was more interested in telling bad jokes than teaching. According to Thomas, he needed to have a shower more than once a week. Whilst talking about Greasy Gifford, an incident that had taken place outside of his classroom was mentioned.

The story went that Jamie, on his way to music, walked past as they were queued along the corridor wall, in anticipation of being granted entry into their chemistry classroom, and there was an altercation.

Heather asked what that bully Damian Dickson thought he

was doing, punching Jamie in the ribs, for no reason. Thomas suggested she ask her boyfriend. She said she had and that he had no idea, except that Dickson was a nutcase. Thomas's face failed to hide the fact that he was not convinced of the veracity of what she had been told.

'He's a friend of yours,' Heather said, 'What was he playing at?'

'It's not for me to say.'

'What's that supposed to mean?'

Thomas shrugged and said, for a second time, 'Ask your boyfriend.'

It was clear Heather was unhappy. It was equally clear that this was making Thomas very uncomfortable.

He tried, unsuccessfully, to change the subject.

Heather lit a cigarette and passed it to him.

'Just tell me,' she said.

Thomas puffed on the cigarette and then handed it back to her. They continued sharing it in this manner until, when there was almost nothing but the filter left, Heather stubbed it out in the tin.

Thomas broke the silence.

'Damian says Jamie snogged Leanne at a disco in town.'

'Leanne Bryant? That's rubbish. Even if he wasn't going out with me, he can't stand her. He hates that whole gang of nasty bitches.'

'I didn't say he snogged her. Julie McIvor told Damian. She said she saw them eating the faces off each other.'

'She's another one. Why would he even believe her? She's always been a stirrer. I bet she said it because she wants to break him and Leanne up. And as if Jamie would be seen dead at some disco in town with any of them. Not exactly his style.'

Thomas made a valiant attempt to mask the fact he was unconvinced, but I could tell he was sceptical, even if Heather chose not to notice.

'How long's he going to be up north?' Thomas asked.

'Almost the full two weeks. He's really close to his gran. He lived with her for a bit when he was wee.'

This time successfully steering the conversation away from Jamie, Thomas said he was thinking of going to the Mitchell Library one day during the holidays to study. He asked if Heather wanted to come along. She looked a bit unsure until he told her Violet had studied there for all of her school exams.

Heather said she would try to make it, but added her mother had made it very clear that the outside world was out of bounds until the exams were over. Thomas ventured that even Dorothy the Dragon would surely make an exception for a visit to the Mitchell.

It was now Heather's turn to appear unconvinced.

Thomas began to rummage in his backpack. He produced a large silver rectangle. As he unwrapped it, he said, 'Want one? They're cheese and ham.'

Heather declined, preferring to light a cigarette instead.

'I don't eat meat,' she said, 'Not that my mum pays any attention.'

'I forgot. Sorry. I've got a bar of chocolate in here somewhere?' he said, reaching back into his bag.

Heather shook her head and said, 'I'm good. Thanks.'

Thomas demolished the stack of sandwiches. He then dug two bars of chocolate out of his backpack and devoured both.

'What amazes me,' he said, apropos of nothing, 'is that your mum lets you hang about up here all the time.'

'She's too busy drinking her gin and tonic to care. That's when she's not off out doing charity work for the church. As long as I'm locked up in the house, she's not bothered. It doesn't matter that I'm up here in their dumping ground of an attic.'

'Really?'

'Honestly, I don't think she cares as long as I'm under lock and key.'

Heather went on to hypothesise that things might have been different if she had not been her parents' "little accident" – a term she said she had once overheard her father use when he had consumed a little too much whisky.

'You know she's sixty in July? She can't stand having a teenager in her precious house. And she blames me for the fact my dad's still working.'

Heather then went on to speculate that, in fact, Dorothy was the reason her father kept pushing his retirement out by another year and another year.

Before Thomas left, he attempted to solidify the Mitchell Library arrangement, suggesting they meet up the following Wednesday.

Heather said she would let him know.

At first light the next day I heard unexpected noises from the hidden part of the attic. Moments earlier I had detected Heather's footsteps on the metal steps and had expected her to appear, but instead, I was treated to a cacophony of scraping and scratching, grating and scuffing.

The first piece of furniture to appear through the fabric wall was a small collapsible breakfasting table in light oak. Heather heaved it to a spot under the window and pushed it tight against the rafters. She disappeared. When she appeared again, she was dragging a rather attractive looking upright chair – its wooden trim was painted white; its back and its seat were upholstered in a cheerful fabric bedecked with song birds. She positioned the chair to face the table; its back to me. She vanished a second time and returned carrying a wicker wastepaper basket. She placed this under the table. She left a third time. When she re-materialised, her arms were piled high with books and jotters. She stacked these on the table and sat down, facing the rafter wall. She emptied the pockets of her long black cardigan and placed their contents – an assortment of pens and pencils – in a neat pile to the right of her study materials.

She spent the rest of the morning at the table with her back to me, reading and writing. It was around noon when she finally stood up and stretched. After massaging her lower back with her hands, she sat on one of the cushions and lit a cigarette.

Before she returned to her books, clearly dissatisfied with her earlier interior design efforts, she rearranged the furniture. She shoved the coffee table, with me on it, from our central spot. Once we had been pushed up against the far wall, she hauled her study table into our former position. The only advantage of this new arrangement was that she moved the chair to the other side of the table, I presumed to take advantage of the light from the window in which I had previously bathed. Fortunately, this meant she would now face me as she worked.

She pressed play on the cassette player and sat back at the table.

Taking advantage of the fact I could now actually see the table top more clearly, as Heather was no longer blocking my view, I was able to take note of which subjects she was studying. In addition, thanks to her body language and facial expressions, over the days that followed I was also able to learn which she found most arduous – chemistry and Latin.

Heather was reading from a history textbook when Dorothy roared, 'Lunch!' from somewhere below us.

Heather worked hard for her exams. Watching her do so was not the most fascinating activity to observe, so I found other ways to amuse myself: keeping a close eye on her nicotine addiction; counting the number of times I heard Suzanne Vega in a day; monitoring the imbalance of time spent on certain subjects – perhaps unsurprisingly, chemistry and Latin proved to be the poor relations.

Her last exam fell on a Friday, according to the timetable she had affixed to a portion of wall above the bookcase. When she arrived home that afternoon, Jamie followed her through the fabric curtain, which led me to conclude there was no one else in the house.

They got straight to the business of kissing. As they were lying on the floor, Jamie began to remove his clothing. Heather asked him what he was doing. Her voice sounded quite playful at first.

Jamie laughed and suggested she do likewise. He told her it was time. He put his hands on her legs and started to move them up under her school skirt.

Heather pulled back. She said that they had talked about this. She said that she still was not ready.

At first Jamie seemed understanding, but his tone soon changed. He started to say things that were obviously designed to hurt – about her looks, her figure, the fact that, not surprisingly, none of the girls at school wanted to be friends with her. It was at this point that he informed Heather he was sick of waiting for her to grow up. He said there were other girls in their year, prettier girls, who were more than happy to oblige – Leanne Bryant for one.

Heather's voice was quiet but firm. She asked him to leave.

After he was gone, Heather curled herself into a tight ball. As she rocked back and forth, I longed for John Wilson to push his way through the fabric curtain and take her in his arms. Despite her protestations about elderly parents who lacked the energy and inclination to care for a teenage daughter, this was not what I had witnessed the evening he had sat with her in her bedroom. I saw a man who loved her.

Even Dorothy Wilson's antics could be interpreted as love, granted of quite an unhelpful variety. I would have been happy even to see her, at that moment, break into Heather's place of refuge.

I imagined the capable arms of Dorothy Wilson wrapping themselves around her daughter: Dorothy's body swaddling Heather's narrow back, as they rocked back and forth together.

Not for the first time, I felt helpless.

It was worse than when Sandra had first pushed me into that canvas bag. Worse even than when Thomas had removed me from Violet's bookcase. I was powerless. My imagination was all I had. It was the only means by which I was able to navigate my own difficulties and it could provide Heather no assistance.

Chapter Six

The anguish I had experienced diminished only slightly in the days that were to follow. Days that saw Heather's visits become infrequent. I was forced to comfort myself with the thought that she might be spending time with friends, friends of whom I was unaware.

I would even have settled for her spending time with Thomas. Having witnessed Jamie's behaviour, I found myself able to view Thomas in something of a more generous light. I was therefore not unhappy when he appeared through the curtain mid-way through the summer holidays.

It seemed to me that he had grown, perhaps by two inches or more, since I had last seen him. His hair, unfortunately, had grown by the same degree. It did not have Violet's curls, but at this length it had a decided wave and covered his left eye on an almost permanent basis. His clothing had also changed. He was dressed entirely in black. I was suspicious that everything except his increase in height was for Heather's benefit. It seemed to be working.

Within moments, they were both cross-legged on cushions, smoking. The conversation revolved around Heather's latest fight with Dorothy. It seemed Heather had been invited to spend the last two weeks of July in London with Jonathan and his family. Dorothy had refused.

'Do you care?' Thomas asked. 'I thought you said they were just angling for some free babysitting.'

'I know, but what right has she to stop me from going. I'm sixteen. I could get married for God's sake.'

'Too right,' Thomas said. 'She's a total dragon.'

The end of his cigarette glowed as he inhaled deeply.

Lying back, Heather rounded her mouth and produced smoke circles. I always enjoyed this and had not seen her do it in months.

'Jonathan phoned on Sunday,' she said.

More grey rings escaped from her lips.

'I was the only one in.'

Thomas stubbed out his cigarette on the inside rim of the tin.

'I know I moan about him but he does care. He said he feels bad that I've had to grow up here on my own. He remembers being a teenager in this house. He said it's why he got out. And then moved to London.'

Heather offered Thomas another cigarette. She lit it for him and then lay back.

She looked up into his face as they shared the cigarette.

'I'd miss you,' he said.

Heather laughed, but not unkindly.

'You're an idiot,' she said. 'Anyway, Dorothy the Dragon says no, so it's not happening.'

'What about your dad?'

'He's worse. He pretends to care, but he's never going to rock the boat. It's taken me long enough, but I've learned that now.'

The cigarette was finished. Thomas leaned down, a little awkwardly. Heather reached up and, to my surprise, they began to kiss.

I saw little of Heather for the remainder of the school

holidays and had to presume that the young couple were finding the Munro house an easier place in which to conduct their burgeoning relationship. I also, during those long days in which I had little else to think about, imagined that Dorothy Wilson might be somewhat content in her daughter's choice of companion, knowing his family as she did. I, however, was less content. Thomas would not have been my choice.

I had not forgiven him. I would not forgive him. It was his underhand and unconscionable behaviour that had taken me from Violet.

Once school began, Heather returned. I would not, however, see Thomas again. This led me to hope that whatever romance had existed had been short-lived.

The attic appeared to be Heather's preferred work space and it seemed that fifth year brought with it a lot of work.

Late in the autumn, I began to detect a difference in her.

In the evenings, when she would climb up into the attic to do her homework (and smoke and listen to music), I noticed that whilst she still secreted objects in the waistband of her school skirt, they were held in place more snugly than before.

As the weeks wore on, she began to limit herself to one cigarette per visit. Her waistband went from neat to uncomfortably tight and, as the draft from the window in the rafters turned bitter, indicating winter had commenced, Heather began, after having sat down on her favourite cushion, to undo not just the button of her skirt, but the zip also.

I admit, in those moments, I did not understand the significance of the thickening that had occurred around her middle, or of the dark circles that had become a permanent feature of her ashen face. I did not even begin to comprehend, not until after she was gone.

My final evening in the attic with Heather was in the December of 1991.

That night, as had become more common, her eyes were a spider's web of red. She sat down at the study table and wrote in her diary. It seemed as though she was writing the same thing, over and over, page after page.

Once she was happy with the substance of the opus she was composing, she carefully tore out the final page of the notebook and diligently copied this dissertation onto it. When she had finished, she folded over the piece of paper and wrote the words 'Mum and Dad' on the other side.

The attic fell silent.

Thankfully that first silence only lasted a week. It was broken by the voice of Dorothy followed in close succession by the sing-song sentences of Kirsty and Elspeth.

It seemed the two imps had convinced their grandmother to allow them to look for toys in the substantial toy pile that lay beyond the fabric partition. Once more she left them unattended and once more, they broke through to my part of the attic.

Immediately, they began to paw at Heather's belongings: the books on the low bookshelf; the pens and pencils she had left on her study table; the tin that had once contained Cadbury's Roses.

It was the younger of the two girls, Elspeth, who headed directly for the metal container. Her disappointment at the lack of confectionary stored within was quickly replaced by the glee she derived from the fact she had discovered a secret transgression.

'Look!' she exclaimed, as she held the open tin out to her sister.

'Put that down, Ells.' Kirsty said, 'It's disgusting.'

'Should we tell Grandma?'

'No. And put the lid back on it. It stinks.'

Kirsty then explained to her sister, not for the first time I imagined, that it was not nice to tell tales. However, I thought perhaps Kirsty might be more concerned by the fact that Grandma Dorothy would be so upset about Elspeth's discovery that she might mistakenly take out her wrath on the small child delivering the news, rather than on the absent daughter who had committed the crime.

Before Dorothy summoned the girls for lunch, I would learn that instead of playing truant from school on the last day of term in order to spend the day in the attic with me, Heather had, in fact, played truant from school in order to catch a train to London.

Elspeth provided these details whilst marvelling at the boldness of her big cousin and wondering aloud what else she might find out about Heather if, when she had finished this reconnaissance mission, she also searched her bedroom.

Kirsty was not in the least enamoured with this notion and told Elspeth that she was not to go creeping about in Heather's room.

Elspeth continued to pout as Kirsty said, 'That's not a nice thing to do.'

From the look in the younger sibling's eye, I was quite sure that, at the first opportunity, she would scour her cousin's bedroom in a manner reminiscent of the investigation I had observed her grandmother undertake.

This memory led me to wonder, not for the first time, why, in the many months I had been here, Dorothy had never broken through the fabric curtain and performed a fingertip search of the space.

I speculated that she may have carried out a thorough inspection prior to my arrival and decided that there were too few places to hide contraband. It was also possible that Heather had been correct and it was just too much effort to come all the way up here to snoop on her truculent teenager. Perhaps most likely, I thought that Dorothy may have decided that it was in her best interests to leave well enough alone because as long as Heather was happy to hole herself up in the heavens of the house, her daughter would be safe from the dangers and the temptations of the outside world.

My musings were interrupted by Elspeth complaining that if it was okay for Kirsty to touch Heather's things, why shouldn't she. In fact, Kirsty had done nothing worse than settle herself on a cushion, in order to read *Jemima Puddle-Duck*. She closed over the book and said she did not think Heather would mind as long as she put it back where it belonged when she was finished. Elspeth then asked if Kirsty thought that they should take some of the books back to London for Heather. Kirsty replied that she would ask their father and then, very firmly, advised Elspeth to remember that they had been instructed not to mention anything about Heather in front of Grandma or Grandpa. Elspeth's face fell into its now familiar frown.

As they disappeared back through the divide, I heard Elspeth say that she hoped when the baby came it would be a boy because she did not want to have to share her toys with it. Kirsty responded in a growled whisper that they had been warned not to say a word about the baby while they were at their grandparents' house.

It was at this moment that I truly understood the significance of the missive Heather had written to her parents and knowing what I thought I knew of them, and of Heather, I believed that I would never again see my runaway guardian. This was a difficult reality for me to process.

Heather, through Thomas, had been my only connection to Violet and the life for which I still longed. With her gone, I might be forced to face what seemed like the inevitable: that things would never again be as they once were.

Yet despite moments of desperation, in the years that would follow, I kept a flicker of hope alive that one day, somehow, I would return to Violet and to 'life before'.

The first Christmas after the baby was born, the girls wormed their way through the divide. Elspeth appeared to be delighted with the new addition, despite the fact that it was a girl. Rather than being a toy thief, it seemed the baby had turned out to be a far superior plaything than any Tiny Tears doll. Elspeth's only unhappiness seemed to stem from the fact that she was not able to spend Christmas in London with it. Kirsty appeased her with the assurance that Heather and the baby would not be lonely because they would spend Christmas Day at Grandma and Grandpa Tate's house with Auntie Eleanor, Uncle George and the boys.

'I know,' Elspeth whined, 'but it's not fair. I wanted to go there, too.'

I confess the notion that Jonathan and Natalie Wilson had agreed to make a home for Jonathan's wayward teenage sister, and her baby, in their London abode was something of a revelation. It was, however, a comforting one.

A good number of Christmases later, I would overhear the news that Heather had moved back to Scotland as she, having worked in a large bookshop since leaving school, had been transferred to the chain's Edinburgh store as the newly appointed manager. At this juncture, Kirsty and Elspeth were in their middle teens and had returned the Cadbury's Roses tin to active service. As Elspeth stubbed out her second cigarette of the afternoon, she struggled to contain her excitement about their mother's clever ruse that would see them spending Boxing Day at Heather's flat in the Canonmills district of the city. Apparently, the clandestine plan involved a visit to fictional friends who had recently moved north from London. I waited anxiously for a report on how the visit had gone. Days dragged. I was finally forced to accept that the London Wilsons must have departed.

By the time Kirsty reached her late teens, she would be the only grandchild to visit the Wilson family home over Christmas. The first time I watched her push her way through the fabric curtain alone, I remembered Elspeth's long treatise the previous year about the fact she was almost sixteen and her parents could no longer force her to spend Christmas in miserable Glasgow with Dorothy the Dragon. Kirsty only climbed the stairs to the attic a couple of times that year and once the following. That visit would be the last one she would make.

Thankfully, during that final time we were together, she was in no rush to go back downstairs. Her first task was to examine the cassettes on top of the bookshelf. I had not heard music for such a long time. I dearly hoped she would choose the Suzanne Vega tape, for old times' sake.

Instead, she chose a tape I had rarely heard Heather play. As Kirsty moved her head in time, captivating female voices sang about, amongst other things, a cruel summer and the fact that Robert De Niro was both waiting and talking Italian.

Whilst listening to the music, Kirsty performed an appraisal of Heather's book collection. The books she chose to remove from the bookcase suggested that her literary inclinations were rather catholic. After what appeared to be considerable deliberation, she chose Sunset Song over the others and sat down on a cushion to read. However, as she made herself comfortable her eyes seemed to alight on me. Within moments the Grassic Gibbon book was on the coffee table and I was in her hands.

At the precise moment her fingers touched my cover, I experienced something akin to the sensation a jolt of electricity might provoke. Years earlier, I had made a deliberate choice not to allow thoughts of loneliness or abandonment to enter my consciousness, but the tenderness of Kirsty's touch brought with it an irresistible thirst for the society of humans. I could not have known then that it would be many more years before this drought would end.

As she held me, I willed her to take me with her.

I imagined being on a train to London – the sights, the smells, the sounds. I imagined life in a bookcase in the front lounge of a busy household in the city, a bay window opposite and the bustling street outside. I imagined Heather coming for a visit and seeing me there. I imagined her taking me back to Edinburgh. I thought that perhaps from there, I might find my way back to Violet.

Instead, Kirsty did little more than flick through my pages and read the inscription Sandra had written so many years earlier. She then placed me back on the table and left the attic, taking the Grassic Gibbon book with her.

Over the years that followed, I had no way of knowing if the Christmas visits by Jonathan Wilson and his family had ceased. What was perfectly evident was that if they had not, no one was interested in climbing up into the attic and making their way through the fabric curtain.

As time crawled along, I would occasionally hear noises. For the most part, it would be the sound of John Wilson climbing up the metal stairs in order to add to the various groaning storage piles that were situated close to the entrance of the attic. This would invariably be accompanied by the sound of Dorothy supervising his efforts.

Despite her bluster, the snippets of conversation I was able to overhear were suggestive of a tender relationship. On one occasion, John uncovered a teddy bear that had once belonged to Heather and called out to Dorothy to let her know what he had found. She climbed up to join him.

His discovery of Little Ted caused them to reminisce about their daughter as a young child. I heard the sound of Dorothy sobbing and John's attempts to comfort her. He assured his wife that things would get better between them; he said that one day soon Heather would agree to see them again. Dorothy cried even more loudly. I tried to imagine the scene that was blocked from my view – Heather's parents surrounded by the chattels of a lifetime, some twenty years older than when I had first observed them, clinging to that soft toy and to one another. The sound of grief subsided when John finally coaxed Dorothy downstairs.

My liberation from the attic came shortly after, in a way I would not have wished for nor imagined, with the death of John Wilson.

The first I knew of a change in circumstances was when Dorothy employed three men to pack up the attic. It took them at least an hour to learn not to question her judgement. Before they did, they insisted on continually checking if she was sure she wanted some item or other packed in a box as opposed to them disposing of it. An example of this was a damaged lamp that, in one man's opinion, looked like it had come out of the ark. Dorothy pointed out to him that it was a Tiffany lamp. In response, a gentler male voice said, 'But are you sure you want it packed? It's got a crack and I'm sure that flat you're moving to is lovely but it's not a big place like this. We could just pop it in the skip.'

Each time, Dorothy would thank the man for his concern and mention, again, that her son had recently moved to a large home in Kingston upon Thames and may want the item. She would then issue the instruction to wrap it carefully and put it in a box marked sitting room or in one marked kitchen or in one of the ever-growing number of boxes marked Jonathan.

Late in the afternoon, a third man, having been issued with a stack of tissue paper and various instructions delivered in a very Dorothy-manner, grumbled as he dismantled the fabric curtain. My first glimpse of him was when he lifted a particularly full ball gown off the rack and I was able to see the room beyond. He called the other two men over to look at what he had found. They gaped as they peered through the breach in the fabric partition. The oldest of the three said, 'You've got to be kidding me. There's more?'

As if on cue, Dorothy rattled up the metal stairs. The chief complainer took her to task about the fact there was a hidden part of the attic almost as big as the bit they had just packed up. Dorothy gave him no quarter, pointing out that it was not nearly as big and had hardly anything in it. The kind-hearted man intervened again. He said they would be done in no time; it was just a few wee bits of furniture and a bookcase, after all.

As the men finished off in the main attic space, Dorothy sat down on Heather's study chair. Despite being, by my calculation, eighty-one years of age, she was remarkably unchanged. The main difference in her appearance was her hair. It was now silver-grey and cut into a short bob. Her carefully applied makeup hid most of the other effects of age, but it could not hide her sadness.

It seemed I was not the only one to notice this. Hours into the day, the man who was in charge, and happened to be the only one who appeared in possession of a healthy dose of compassion, silenced yet another complaint when he said, in a low voice, 'Can't you see the woman's grieving?'

This was the man I would come to know as Alan Mackintosh.

It was he who packed up the bookshelf. After stacking all the books into boxes, he came over to the table and, motioning to me, said, 'This one, too?'

Dorothy returned from wherever it was in her head that she had retreated.

She looked unsure as to what he meant.

He picked me up and used me to point at an almost full box.

He repeated, 'This one, too?'

She reached out and took me from him.

'It was my daughter's,' she said.

He smiled and nodded.

'Should I pop it into that box?'

Dorothy's grip on me tightened.

She looked up into his face and said, 'Have you got a daughter?'

'We weren't that lucky.'

'A son?'

'It's just me and my wife. And the two cats.'

Dorothy pressed me into his hands and said, 'Maybe for your wife, then. If she likes to read.'

Part Three. Iris
2012 - 2013

Chapter One

I sensed that Alan Mackintosh was not sure how to react to Dorothy's suggestion that he take her daughter's copy of *The Prime of Miss Jean Brodie* home to his wife. To his credit, his response was gracious.

Holding me in his warm fist, he said, 'That's very kind of you. My wife loves to read.'

After the people and boxes had gone, I lay alone at the mouth of the attic.

I thought about Mr Lowther.

I had long ago imagined that his bones must be somewhere in the eaves of the roof, turning to dust. Despite his lengthy absence, I was sad to leave the memory of him behind. In the short time we had been together the antics of the tiny brown mouse had made attic-life more bearable.

My sense of loss was amplified by the knowledge that I would soon be taken even further from the life to which I longed to return.

Fingers reached up through the opening and plucked me from the only home I had known for over twenty years. Strangely, in that instant, I found myself grateful. Although, perhaps this was simply a reaction to the fact I had been perched, rather precariously, on the edge of a groaning chasm.

Alan Mackintosh was holding a toolbox in one hand and me in the other when he told Dorothy they would be back at ten the next morning. He said he and the boys would pack up her

BRODIE GILLIAN SHIRREFFS

bedroom and the final bits and bobs from the kitchen and then she would be on her way. Dorothy reverted to the Dorothy of old. She informed him the house keys were being handed over at noon and said she would prefer if he arrived by nine o'clock at the very latest. She was emphatic: under no circumstances did she want to be there when the new owners arrived to take possession of her house.

Alan nodded and agreed to demands I was sure he felt were unnecessary.

When we got to his car, he put the toolbox on the passenger seat. He then placed me on top of it; I was less than happy to note that I would have to balance on the lid of an uncomfortable metal container for the entirety of the trip.

We made slow progress as we journeyed through Glasgow. It was clear that unlike many of his fellow drivers, Alan was both courteous and careful. Even so, he was forced to apply his brakes unexpectedly a number of times. On the most extreme of these occasions, I skidded across the uneven lid and was launched into the air. After striking the sharp edge of the car's glove compartment, I came to rest in the passenger footwell. Alan was kind enough to scoop me up when he stopped at the next red light. He did, unfortunately, sit me back on the lid so I was relieved when, not long after, our journey ended in the neatly paved driveway of a pleasant looking semi-detached property.

Alan had just stepped into the front porch when he collapsed. I had been in his left hand and fell to the floor as he dropped to his knees. The crash of the toolbox and the noise of its contents spilling onto coarse brown carpet tiles alerted his wife.

She cried out when she saw Alan. She grabbed at him and then pushed through the front door into the world beyond. She shouted for help. Still shouting, she burst back in and, without stopping in the porch, careened into the house.

When she returned, she was speaking into the phone in her hand. A male voice boomed out of it. He told her to speak more slowly and then asked her to repeat the address. He asked what her name was and calmly began to deliver instructions.

As directed, she put the phone face up on the floor.

Iris pulled at Alan until he was no longer in a heap. Despite the tight quarters, she managed to rearrange him so that he was lying flat on his back. She performed every task the voice on the phone commanded her to do.

A young woman appeared. She crowded into the porch next to Iris and Alan. She knelt down. She took over the work of resuscitation in a manner that seemed more confident, more robust. She continued in her efforts until the paramedics arrived.

Throughout all of this, I lay next to a sturdy geranium. In the tumult it had toppled over and some dark earth from its clay pot had, most inconveniently, spilled onto me. The next day, when the same young woman came to see how Iris was doing, she set the geranium upright and brushed the soil from my cover.

She held me out as Iris opened the door to her.

I confess that up until this point I could not have described Iris. My memory of her was shrouded in a clutter of anguish. As she stood before me, I could see that her distress had settled into her face. It had carved itself onto her soft skin in shadows and lines. Her eyes were swollen and red so it was difficult to identify their exact colour; I thought perhaps some shade of brown. Within a day, I would decide they were light hazel in hue. Her dark hair, whilst appearing that it had not been brushed, fell in compliance around her shoulders.

Iris did not look at the woman I would come to know as Helen. Instead, she stared at me.

'It was lying over there,' Helen said, by way of explanation.

Iris had the same absent expression that I had seen on Dorothy Wilson's face the day before. Despite her obvious confusion, she accepted me and stepped aside to let Helen enter the house. As she did, I noticed how much smaller Iris was than the young woman who had cleaned me and rescued me from my predicament.

It was apparent that they did not know each other.

I would come to learn that Helen had only recently moved next door. Her new home shared a thick wall with the house in which Iris and Alan had lived for most of their married life. The fact that these two women were strangers, made Helen's earlier actions all the more interesting to me.

From a combination of the statements Iris made whilst expressing her gratitude and from the actions I myself had witnessed as I lay coated in a film of soil, I pieced together what had transpired once Alan had been taken away.

This, then, is the record of events I was able to assemble: Helen drove Iris to the hospital; Helen sat with Iris until a doctor appeared and delivered the news that Alan was dead; Helen brought Iris home and waited with her until her sister arrived hours later.

Iris carried me into the sitting room and put me down on the coffee table. Despite the heat of the room, the glass on which I lay felt cold. I was hopeful that at some point soon I might be moved to the mantelpiece. It looked like an ideal spot and I was concerned that in my current position I was in danger of being cleared up and swept away. The mantelpiece, in contrast, looked like a safe place: somewhere I might be left alone to observe the movements of my new home.

Iris insisted she make Helen a coffee.

As she walked through the door that led to the kitchen, two cats ran between her feet. Iris demanded to know what they had been up to and threatened them with exile if she found as much as a trace that they had been on the work surface. The creatures disappeared under the couch and I saw not another sign of them until after Helen left, leading me to believe that they were indeed guilty.

Iris returned from the kitchen with an oddly shaped terracotta mug. She handed it to Helen who sipped at the hot drink as she tried to console a woman who was beyond consolation.

'You couldn't have done anything,' she said. 'The doctor told you that.'

Iris was in an armchair. She sobbed as she tried to speak. Her nose was running. It was impossible to hear what she was saying.

Helen stood up. She placed the glazed mug near to me on the table. She handed Iris a tissue from the pocket of her jeans then rubbed her back until the older woman's body stopped shaking.

'Will your sister stay again tonight?' she asked.

Iris shook her head.

'Is there someone else?'

Iris said a friend was coming over after work. As she spoke, she looked up into Helen's face. It seemed as though she wanted to ask something but did not have the words available in order to form the question.

Fortunately, Helen seemed to intuit the information Iris sought. 'I work shifts,' she said. 'At the hospital. I'm on early shift this week.'

The ghost of a smile flitted over Iris's face. She said that Alan had guessed Helen was a nurse because of the hours she kept. Iris started to cry again. The young woman held her hand. She did not contradict the man she had met only in death.

Helen offered to make Iris something to eat but Iris said

she was not hungry.

'Have you eaten anything today?'

Iris shook her head.

'A slice of toast then. I'm sure I can figure out where everything is.'

Despite the noise from the next room, Iris did not raise her head until Helen returned carrying a plate in her hand. On it, next to the two slices of toast, with jam, there was a chocolate biscuit whose wrapper declared it to be a Jacob's Orange Club. Helen said she thought a little sugar might help.

Even though Iris appeared to be perhaps twenty years Helen's elder, she complied with the order to eat as much as she could, which, in this instance, turned out to be little more than a half slice of toast.

As Iris ate, Helen asked for the name of her family doctor. She nodded when Iris said it was Dr Garvey. Helen asked if she had the number to hand.

'I don't. We never have any need of a doctor.'

'I'll look it up,' Helen said. 'It's best they know. Someone should really come out to see you.'

In the end, Helen had to take the phone from Iris and talk to the person on the other end. When she did so, she introduced herself as Dr Helen Lang, Mrs Mackintosh's neighbour.

It seemed Iris was too grief-stricken to attend to what was being said because, days later, when her sister declared that it was very lucky she had that nice young doctor living next door, Iris was incredulous.

Her sister, Morag, would utter many insensitive things over the weeks that followed, on one occasion commenting, 'At least you and Alan couldn't have a family. Can you imagine? The poor kids.

Having their dad drop dead on them like that, at the front door.'

One of Iris's friends would eventually take Morag to task. This, however, was not the reason Morag's visits grew less frequent. Mercifully she lived in Dundee and had a very important job and two teenage boys. This meant, according to Morag, that she could not possibly keep running backwards and forwards to Glasgow, especially when she felt it was time for Iris to start getting on with her life again, which, by Morag's reckoning, was less than two months after Alan's sudden death.

Although, to be fair to Morag, she was the one who, during that first week, in order to make room for the plate of fondant fancies, lifted me up and, using my spine to carefully nudge at a candlestick, made room for me on the mantelpiece. This was fortunate for the reasons I had already supposed and because of the sanctuary it provided. Neither of Iris's frighteningly agile cats were able to jump up onto the mantelpiece thanks to the fact it was sprinkled with candles and picture frames, making it a poor landing zone. The same could not be said of the coffee table.

Holly and Ivy were not much more than kittens when I first arrived. Taking their names as a clue, I presumed they had been a Christmas present from Alan to Iris. He could not have known how prescient the gift would be; in those first weeks, Holly and Ivy provided more solace than any of the humans who tried to comfort his widow. The few times I saw Iris smile that year, were each preceded by the ridiculous acrobatics of one, other, or both cats.

Holly and Ivy looked like photographic negatives of one another: the patches of white on Holly were patches of black on Ivy and vice versa. Within days I had developed a preference for the smaller cat, Ivy. Unlike her sister, she had never stepped on me or attempted to swat me across the table top.

It was Ivy who seemed drawn by a magnetic force to her

mistress's ankle, to the extent that I sometimes worried she might create a hazard. However, each time I thought that either she might be stepped upon or cause Iris to trip, she moved at just the right moment and angle to prevent disaster.

Holly was less affectionate. She was the performer of the duo and relished being the centre of attention. A case in point was the day of the funeral.

Morag had stayed over the night before and was up early to fuss over every detail of the ceremony. She made numerous calls on her phone regarding items with which she was unhappy. She arranged for the hearse to come earlier. She added coronation chicken vol-au-vents to the purvey menu. She castigated Iris's friend Geraldine for a spelling error in the order of service – the name of Morag's elder son, who was to be a reader, was Marc with a c, not Mark with a k, apparently.

Her final call was to Alan's friend Douglas to relinquish him of his duties as a pall bearer. Iris had been sitting silently throughout on the armchair that had, I had now gleaned thanks to a comment by Morag, previously been Alan's not hers. It was only when her sister said, 'Iris doesn't know what she was thinking. It wouldn't be right. Uncle Ian and our male cousins will be the pall bearers,' that Iris spoke.

'That's enough. Douglas should have a cord. He and Alan have been friends since primary school.'

It was at this moment that Holly chose to leap from somewhere on the far side of the couch on which Morag was sitting. She landed, claws extended, on the unsuspecting lap. Morag squealed and threw her mobile phone into the air. The phone was closely followed by Holly.

By the time Morag retrieved the device, its screen was a mosaic of broken glass.

Chapter Two

Iris paid no attention to me for almost two months and may have ignored my existence for even longer had it not been for her friend Diane.

Diane was one of a gang of three – Iris's best friends from school.

I thought of this trio as an indissoluble group as they were in the habit of arriving and departing together. I was not sure if this was a longstanding foible or if it had been instituted only as a means of safety for occasions when it was necessary to cross the threshold of someone who had been recently widowed, perhaps in the vain hope that this arrangement might insulate individual members from the lurking dangers of awkward conversation and tsunami-like grief.

The women had only just sat down, each with a glass of red wine, when Diane stood up and made her way to the mantelpiece.

In an act I thought of as ill-judged given the circumstances, she picked up the framed wedding photograph to my right and said, 'You really were a beautiful bride.'

The friend I had learned to identify as Geraldine said, 'Although, we may never forgive you for those peach dresses.' She was laughing as she added, 'Those puffed sleeves. Remember?'

'They were the height of fashion in 1987,' said the third

friend, Emma.

'They were terrible,' Iris said. 'Looking back.'

Despite her efforts to keep the conversation light, Iris's eyes betrayed the fact that she was only just managing to get through the visit. This was something I was used to observing. In a short matter of weeks, Iris had learned how to keep her despair under control, for the most part, until her guests would leave. Once they were gone, her body would become an awkward ball of bone and sinew and she would sob into the upholstery of Alan's armchair.

Diane put the picture back down. As she did, her hand brushed my cover.

Her touch was unexpected.

'*The Prime of Miss Jean Brodie?*' she said, picking me up. 'We did that with Miss Galbraith back in the day, did we not?'

I felt the revelation wash over me.

There was a connection.

Perhaps all was not lost.

Diane's hands were dry and a little cracked, despite the overpowering smell of what I presumed to be lavender hand lotion.

Looking at Iris, she said, 'What's it doing up here?'

Iris's face revealed a familiar mix of fatigue and bewilderment. She said, 'The girl next door gave it to me.'

'The doctor? Why?' Diane asked.

'I don't know.'

Diane put me back on the mantelpiece in precisely the spot from which I had been removed. I spent the next few moments worrying that as I was once more in Iris's consciousness, I may no longer be able to hide in plain sight.

When I was able to concentrate on what was happening around me, the four women were talking about Sandra. I was dismayed that I had missed part of the conversation.

'Do you think she was having it off with Mr Callaghan?' Geraldine said.

'Definitely,' Diane said.

'Definitely not,' Emma countered.

'You've lost me,' Iris said.

'Keep up,' Emma said, in a manner that suggested gentle teasing rather than irritation. Smiling, she continued, 'Those bold girls are suggesting that Miss Galbraith and Mr Callaghan were having an affair.'

'Absolutely not,' Iris said. 'Miss Galbraith would never have been interested in him. He was too young, for a start. And I think she might have been more partial to someone else.'

Diane rounded on Iris and said, 'You never mentioned that at the time.'

'I wouldn't have thought it at the time. I didn't spend a lot of time thinking about our teachers and their love lives. That was more your department.'

'So?' Geraldine said. 'Spill.'

'Not long after we were married, Alan and I were at Kelvingrove Art Gallery on a Sunday afternoon. We went to see that big Egyptian exhibition.'

'Uh huh,' Diane said, impatiently.

'We were walking through the gallery bit and we saw Miss Galbraith and Miss Airlie,' Iris said. 'They didn't see us. They were looking at a painting. It was a landscape.'

'Miss Airlie? The Art Teacher? I don't see it,' Diane said.

'They looked like two halves of a whole. That's what Alan said.'

'Your Alan was always such a romantic,' Emma said.

Iris lowered her head. She did not cry. Instead, she made fists with her hands. I knew that her fingernails would be digging into the soft skin of her palms, leaving them, not for the first time, with deep, purple scores.

Geraldine poked Emma in the arm and said, 'That was your fault.'

'Diane started it,' Emma growled back.

Ignoring them both, Diane lifted up the wine bottle and said, 'A wee top up? Anyone?'

When the three friends left, Iris cried for a while and then went out into the kitchen. She returned with a fresh bottle of Merlot. By the morning, it was empty. As the sun rose, she made a telephone call and left a message. She said she was sorry. She would not be in that day. Some sort of bug, she said.

Late in the afternoon Helen stopped in. Iris asked her about me.

'It was in your porch,' Helen said.

Iris shook her head in a way that suggested she was puzzled. She contorted her face and said, 'That doesn't make sense.'

'I found it. The next day,' Helen said. 'On the floor. One of the plants had been knocked over. The book was sort of under it. Could Alan have had it with him? Maybe it was a present for you.'

Iris walked over to the mantelpiece. She drew me to herself.

'I don't know,' she said.

Helen, as I had seen her do many times in the preceding months, smiled a smile that appeared almost to be the physical manifestation of an apology.

Iris took me back to Alan's armchair. She touched my cover as she spoke.

'He was packing up a big house. He might have got it there, I suppose. He wouldn't just have taken it though. He would never have done that.'

Helen changed the subject.

'I remember reading it at school,' she said.

'Me too,' Iris said. 'The teacher who did it with us was a bit like Miss Brodie. The girls and me sometimes called her that. Not in her earshot. You wouldn't have dared.'

'It was a man who did it with us,' Helen said. 'Mr Callaghan. He would throw his hands in the air and say in his best Morningside accent, *if only you would listen to me, I would make of you the crème de la crème.*'

'Did you go to Westbrae Academy?' Iris asked.

Looking a little unsure, Helen answered in the affirmative.

'That was my school,' Iris said, 'Although, I left in 1982.'

Helen's voice sounded kind as she said, 'I was born in 1987.'

Iris grimaced.

'Alan went there as well. He was two years above me. The first time he asked me out was at a school disco at the start of second year.'

'The first time?'

'Uh huh. My mum would have killed me if I'd said yes,' Iris said. 'But he was persistent. We started going out when I was fifteen.'

Looking a little confused, Helen said, 'So Mr Callaghan was a teacher when you were there?'

'He was. And we thought he was old. He was probably only in his thirties.'

'He was pretty ancient when I had him,' Helen said. 'I think he retired at the end of my sixth year.'

'Was Miss Galbraith still there?' Iris asked.

'I don't remember the name.'

'You wouldn't have forgotten her. Not if she'd been there,' Iris said. 'She was a force of nature.'

Iris stared down at me. She began to flick through my pages. She stopped at the inscription Sandra had written almost a quarter of a century earlier and read it aloud.

She said, 'I wonder if Violet lived in that house. The one Alan was packing up. I might call Peter. Ask if he knows anything. He was working with Alan that day. He said to keep in touch.'

'Maybe that's what to do,' Helen said. 'When you feel up to it.'

Ivy jumped from the carpet onto the space between Iris's right thigh and the arm of the chair. She put her head down and nudged me with her pink nose. She was purring as she did it a second time. Helen said she had never seen the like – a cat jealous of a book. Iris disagreed. She countered that it was more a case that Ivy liked her creature comforts and was merely angling to get the whole thing to herself.

With that, Iris eased herself up from the chair, taking care not to cause the cat to topple onto the floor.

As she put me back on the mantelpiece, I saw Ivy roll across the length of the seat cushion and stretch all four legs into the air.

I was beginning to begrudge the cat her comfort when Holly flew across the room. With incredible sureness of paw, she touched down on Ivy's exposed stomach. In the melee that followed, two cats became one.

Iris had the good sense not to intervene.

Within minutes, Holly and Ivy were cleaning themselves on the rug in front of the fire as if nothing had happened.

Chapter Three

Helen's visits, unlike those of other friends, for instance the gang of three, did not diminish.

She popped in every week, often more than once. The only exception to this was the time she drove down to the Lake District to visit a friend. It seemed her job did not afford many opportunities for travel.

I have found myself wondering, when I have occasion to think about their lives, if they are still as close as I watched them become over the fifteen months I spent in Iris's home. I like to imagine that they are.

In the January after Alan's death, Helen asked Iris if she would consider going to a bereavement group. She said that there was a good one locally and that she knew the man who organised it. She explained that a GP friend, James Buchanan, had lost his wife years earlier. He must only have been in his forties at the time, she said. Helen explained that she had mentioned Iris to him and he had said he would be happy to talk to her about the group.

'Sometime. Maybe,' was all Iris said.

Six months passed. Neither the group nor James Buchanan were mentioned. Then, a few days after Alan's first anniversary, Iris said that she would quite like to meet the man Helen had told her about. She asked if Helen might bring him for coffee one Sunday afternoon.

The following day, I watched Iris scribble something on her 2013 National Trust calendar. I had to wait until the following week when she turned July over to reveal August to read what she had written. It was not particularly easy to make out but, in the box assigned to August 11th, after much scrutiny, I settled upon "H and J coffee".

I decided that this arrangement had been made as the two neighbours chatted over the wrought iron fence which I had recently begun to imagine separated Iris's beautifully tended back garden from the equally well-maintained but lower maintenance one I had invented for Helen.

That summer Iris had become quite dedicated to the care of her garden, or so it seemed. In the evenings, and on weekends, she would often don what appeared to be the sort of clothing a person might wear if they were intending to remove weeds, trim hedges or plant flowers. She would then head into, and then through, the kitchen.

I would hear a noise I believed to be the back door closing with a thunk and would picture Iris stepping out onto a neat path that led to a manicured square lawn surrounded by an herbaceous border whose tenants were in constant need of dead heading – this was a term I had learned years earlier whilst listening to Gardeners Question Time during my brief sojourn with Sandra. Beyond this, I envisaged a green wooden shed hemmed in by clumps of bushes and flowers that had been given permission to live a less ordered life.

It helped that Iris was a disciple of The Beechgrove Garden, so I was able to conjure all manner of colourful blooms: peony, phlox, daylily, petunia, marigold, fuchsia, dahlia and, hugging the south west corner of the garden shed, a particularly ancient and determined clematis in a shade of purple so dark that the outer edges of its petals appeared to be black.

The beginning of that summer also seemed to signal a change in Iris's eating habits. For almost a year I had watched her bring her evening meal into the sitting room in order to eat it in front of the television in a manner that suggested she was not able to derive any pleasure from the food on her plate. In the first weeks and months after Alan's death, when she was in my presence, this food consisted of little more than bread, usually in the form of a sandwich. The few hot meals I saw her eat had been hand delivered by concerned individuals who I took to be well-meaning co-workers and friends. These she would start, but never finish. This source dried up reasonably quickly, at which point I rarely saw her consume anything other than cheese sandwiches and the occasional slice of toast.

In the early days, to supplement these meals, Iris would drink a bottle of red wine before bedtime. She may have convinced herself that this was a form of sleep aid, but if the number of times I watched her return to the sitting room in the middle of the night and curl up in Alan's armchair to watch television proved anything, it was surely that red wine was an ineffectual weapon in the battle against insomnia.

In stark contrast, Iris had now begun to appear from the kitchen with a procession of colourful salads. She would still eat them from a plate balanced on her knee, but she had begun to do so without the need for the constant din of the television. This new routine did have one downside: Holly.

The naughtier of the two cats appeared to have become obsessed with a desire to taste the slices of ham that typically accompanied the array of assorted leafy greens, pink skinned potatoes and miniature yellow tomatoes. Iris would inform Holly that she was being rude and, in addition, that human food was not good for non-humans – the high salt content of honey roast ham could easily damage a cat's delicate kidneys, she would say. Holly seemed unconvinced and, when her mid-air gymnastics were thwarted, she would yowl and mewl until she was banished to the garden. Unpleasant noises aside, I was pleased that Iris had begun to take better care of herself and of her dietary requirements – in part because it made my daily observations more interesting.

Iris was also drinking fewer glasses of wine and was up in the night less. Unfortunately, this meant I now had limited access to Cary Grant films and snooker.

I counted down the days and eventually the morning of the eleventh of August arrived. I was disappointed to note that Iris was in her weekend uniform of shapeless jeans paired with an oversized cotton shirt, so I was pleased when, after lunch, she reappeared wearing a skirt – something Iris rarely did, even on work days – and shoes with a kitten heel. In addition, she was wearing an attractive blouse I had never seen before. Its floral pattern in shades of blue complemented her sallow skin.

Before her guests arrived, Iris plumped cushions and fussed over her appearance in a small round mirror normally reserved for checking her face just prior to leaving the house. In the past, it had seemed that this practice was to ensure she had erased any evidence that might indicate to those on the outside that she had been crying.

The doorbell bonged. Iris disappeared and returned with her guests.

James Buchanan introduced himself in a way that suggested he was self-possessed. He was a man of somewhat indeterminate age, but my guess was that he was most likely somewhere in his middle sixties. His face was worn, yet attractive. His hair was grey with only a slight suggestion of the black it must once have been. Despite his years, he appeared athletic. His clothes, whilst they could be thought of as those of a younger man, did not seem out of place on his tall body – well-fitting jeans, a white shirt under a navy sports coat with an expensive looking cut. On his feet he wore beautifully constructed leather shoes that were, I suspected, Italian in origin.

Helen was at James's side. Her long hair was loose and she had applied lipstick in coral pink. I was more used to seeing her waves tamed by a tight bun and her face sans makeup. Whilst this alternative look did not necessarily enhance the natural beauty with which she had been bestowed, it did suggest that she had chosen to make something of an effort with her appearance.

James brought a light into the room that I had not known was missing.

Despite this, Iris appeared ill at ease as he and Helen settled themselves on the couch. In contrast, as I observed the scene, unnoticed, I was sure I could sense that James had immediately warmed to Iris.

As Iris hovered, I found my focus alight on the kitchen door. It was ajar. This led me to become distracted, for just a moment, by the absence of Holly and Ivy.

My curiosity was aroused and I wondered where they might be as they normally appeared, as though summoned by an unseen force, whenever anyone would visit. Indeed, in those summer months, if they happened to be outside, their lithe bodies would invariably slide into the room through a small, rectangular top window that Iris left ajar for the purpose. That day, however, the window was closed.

It seemed I was not the only one to have this thought;

seconds later Helen asked their whereabouts. Iris explained that she had put them outside. She said the last she had seen of them, Ivy was stretched out in a patch of sun and Holly was stalking what she hoped was a vole, rather than the young robin that had recently, and rather foolishly, taken up residence somewhere in the midst of the buckthorn.

Iris explained that whenever she was unsure if a guest might have allergies, she thought it best to err on the side of caution and remove the cats altogether. James assured Iris that he was an allergy-free animal lover. This information appeared to cause her to relax, a little. She then confessed she hated the notion that anyone might think of her as a crazy cat person. I was suspicious her admission revealed the truth behind the expulsion.

James folded his navy-blue wool jacket into a square and set it down on the couch next to him.

'Some of my best friends are crazy cat people,' he said. 'In fact,' he added, 'I have a cat called Gordon. Or, more accurately, an enormous ginger moggy I call Gordon condescends to live with me.'

There followed a brief discussion about Gordon, who, according to James, was prone to behave more like a footloose lodger than a devoted family pet, despite the love James and his daughter Laurel had for years lavished upon the capricious creature. This tale of the ungrateful tomcat seemed to amuse Helen and Iris. The two of them laughed, something I had never seen them do in concert. Iris then retired to the kitchen.

In their host's absence, James said, 'I'm amazed at how well she's doing. It's only been a year?'

'That's right. It was last July. The 17th.' Helen said, 'I think she found the first anniversary really hard. She didn't open the door to me for a week.'

'Milestones are difficult. You know that,' he said. 'Even years on.'

'To be honest, I'm not sure how well she's doing, really,' Helen said, 'but she does seem better than she was.'

Being in James's presence appeared to have a noticeable effect on Helen. I found this odd, given the obvious age difference. Her slight reserve, with which I was so familiar, was gone. I wondered about her relationship with this much older man and was curious to know how they had met and come to form what appeared to be, at the very least, a close friendship.

I was not forced to concoct a story to mollify my inquisitive nature as the conversation that would follow provided a satisfactory explanation, at least in answer to the first of my questions: how their lives had come to intersect.

Iris brought a tray in from the kitchen and placed it on the coffee table. She pointed out which mug belonged to whom and insisted they help themselves to her homemade carrot cake. This was a surprise to me. I could not fathom how it might be possible that I had not been aware of her baking in the kitchen. I found myself once more frustrated by the fact that so many things were beyond my ken.

It was at this point in the afternoon that something odd happened.

Iris took her mug and sat down on the armchair on the far side of the coffee table. This was the first time I had ever seen her walk past Alan's armchair in favour of the one opposite.

James put down the rather generous slice of cake he was in the middle of eating and began to describe aspects of the bereavement group. He told Iris how many people met, how often and where they held their meetings: eight or ten of them depending on the week; seven o'clock on the first and third Wednesdays of the month; in the parochial hall. He mentioned details about a few of his fellow members: Frank's wife died three years ago after a long battle with illness; Patricia's husband was killed in a skiing accident over a decade ago; Aileen lost her husband to septicaemia last year, leaving her with two small children.

Iris stared at her mug as he spoke, turning it slowly in her hands.

James said his own wife had died when she was just forty. Iris lifted her head and looked at him. He said his daughter had been a teenager at the time.

'I was a disaster,' James said, 'and that wasn't fair on my daughter. She was only sixteen.'

Helen touched his arm. She spoke gently as she said, 'I'm sure she doesn't think that. You had just lost your wife.'

'Yes. But it was my job to take care of her,' James said.

As I observed this scene, I began to sense that I was not the only one who had detected the intimacy between them. Iris's eyes were fixed on Helen's hand, which still rested on James's arm.

Chapter Four

My thoughts had turned, as they were wont to do, to my own predicament – trapped in one place whilst longing to be somewhere else.

'How did she die?'

Iris's question brought me back into the room. It seemed out of place, escaping as it did from the mouth of the woman I had observed for over a year.

'She was hit by a car,' James said. 'A drunk driver.'

Iris shook her head. She said she was sorry for having asked.

He told her not to apologise.

James said it was good to be interested in the lives, and even in the deaths, of others. He said it was something he had learned after years of watching the people in the group. In his opinion, it represented a step forward when a bereaved person was able to focus, even briefly, on someone other than the loved one they themselves had lost.

Once he was finished delivering what seemed like a heartfelt but well-worn speech, Iris brought a coffee pot in from the kitchen in order to refresh her guests' drinks. Then, as an apparent nod to his earlier point, she said 'How do you know each other?'

Helen was the one to answer.

'I ran into James at the hospital one day. He was putting up a poster,' she said. 'We just got talking.'

Whilst this answer did seem somewhat plausible, the body language I had observed between Helen and James suggested there was far more to their story than this innocuous beginning.

By the time each of them had finished their second cup of coffee and James had eaten a second slice of cake, Iris had promised to go to the next meeting of Living with Loss at the parochial hall. This, however, did not signal the end of the visit. At the very moment I was expecting James to rise to his feet and offer his thanks for a pleasant afternoon, he sat further back in the couch and asked Iris about Alan.

This came as a surprise.

A few months into Iris's widowhood, I had noted that those who visited began to studiously avoid any mention of Alan's name. I was grateful for James's breach in protocol.

In the weeks after Alan's death, I had taken great pleasure in listening to Iris talk about him – repeating something he would always say or remarking upon things at which he had been particularly good.

I remembered his touch fondly and wanted to learn more about him. Unfortunately, Iris was rarely able to finish any such anecdote without dissolving into tears. I had, therefore, never before heard her speak at any length about him or about their life together. I had also never heard her express anger towards him. In the course of the next hour, she did both.

As she spoke, James nodded. When she got upset, he leaned towards her but did not intervene. When she fell silent, he told her that everything she had said, everything she was feeling, was completely normal.

It was almost dinner time when James eased himself off the couch. Helen, who had said very little throughout the course of the afternoon, also stood up but she did not leave the room.

I listened to James and Iris's goodbyes in the distance. He said he was looking forward to seeing her the following Wednesday and then shouted a last farewell to Helen.

Iris did not come back into the room. Instead, I heard her footsteps on the stairs and a door close on the floor above. Helen removed one of the books from underneath the coffee table and began to flick through its pages. I found myself captivated by the graceful way that she held herself and wondered if she had perhaps studied dance in her younger years. Iris's entrance interrupted my reverie.

'Are you okay?' Helen asked.

Iris said that she was, but her face betrayed the truth.

'Do you want me to stay for a while?'

'Maybe. If you've got time.'

The women took the dishes into the kitchen. I heard a key turn in a lock, the sound of a door handle and Iris's voice as she called out to Holly and Ivy.

Holly careened into the room. She vaulted onto the couch and performed a version of feline ballet, with claws, on the spot James had recently vacated. Having reclaimed this particular item of furniture, she executed a move akin to a grand jeté and landed on the floor. Her next exploit involved a stealth manoeuvre under the coffee table, on the hunt, I presumed, for hapless cake morsels that had fallen to the floor from the china tea plates.

Ivy was at her mistress's heel when she returned to the sitting room. As soon as Iris had taken a seat, in Alan's armchair, the smaller of the two cats was on her knee.

'I'm sorry if that was too much,' Helen said.

Iris assured her that she was fine. She said she thought

145

speaking about things would likely help, in the long run.

'Are you sure I can't get you a glass of wine?' Iris said. 'Or prosecco?'

'I'm sorry. I better not. I've hardly eaten today,' Helen said.

'I've got crisps.'

'Okay,' Helen said. 'Just a small one.'

Her acquiescence seemed to cause the heaviness to lift from Iris's voice.

Once a bowl of crisps and two tall glasses filled to the brim were on the table, Iris said, 'So tell me again how you know him.'

Helen did not elaborate on the story of their first meeting, but she did tell Iris that she had gone to the group for a short time.

'As part of your job?' Iris asked.

'No.'

Helen put down her glass and began to speak. She said that her sister had died of a brain aneurism. Helen was fifteen. Her sister had just started university.

Helen's parents shut down. They rarely mentioned what had happened and talked less and less about Emily as the years went on, at least in Helen's presence. It was a quiet house after that, she said. Except for the noise of one or other of her parents crying in the middle of the night.

Helen said that when she had gone to the group, it had been the first time she had spoken to anyone about losing Emily, whilst sober.

'You didn't say,' Iris said. 'Why didn't you say?'

Helen said she did not find it easy to mention Emily. She

said the group had helped, but she still found it difficult to talk about her sister's death.

'You should have said.'

'I know. I'm sorry.'

Helen offered nothing further about her sister and Iris did not to press her on the subject.

After a short silence, the conversation turned to the banal. Helen mentioned that a new Italian restaurant had opened near the hospital. A few of them had tried it after her shift on Friday. The food could be better, apparently. According to Iris, the weather was disappointing for August, although, she added, Heather the Weather on the BBC did claim it would get better from Tuesday.

After Helen was gone, Iris's phone rang. She held it in her hand, staring at it. Just as I expected the phone to fall silent, she answered the call.

Hi.

(   )

Bugsy? Really? Good for him. You must be proud.

(   )

If you think Marc would want me there.

(   )

Of course, I want to come. I just didn't know if he'd be happy with his old auntie sitting in the front row, cheering him on.

(   )

Six thirty. December fifth. I'm writing it on the calendar as I speak.

Iris did not write anything on the calendar. She did, however, finish the bottle of prosecco.

On her way to bed, she walked over to the mantelpiece and, to my surprise, picked me up.

The carpeted staircase was steep and I was a little concerned for the wellbeing of us both. In addition to the remainder of the prosecco, Iris had drunk most of a freshly opened bottle of merlot. I liked to think that I was in almost pristine condition and I had hoped to stay that way. Despite the years I had spent in various spaces that could be deemed unsafe for an object such as a book, I had barely a crease on my cover and, other than Violet's pencil lines that had faded with the years, my pages were spotless.

It occurred to me on my journey in Iris's right hand that I had not been afforded the sanctuary of a bookcase since the moment Thomas had chosen to steal me from Violet's bedroom. Whilst being confined to one might have been something I would have eschewed previously, at this point in my existence I was convinced I would relish the opportunity to return to the security of that life, no matter the tightness of the quarters.

I am happy to report that we did, in fact, reach Iris's bedroom unscathed.

Once inside she dropped me onto the large bed in the centre of the room and withdrew, I presumed to the bathroom. The navy-blue striped duvet on which I landed was thick and soft. As I lay on it, I traced the map of the house I had constructed in my consciousness long ago. I decided I was most likely in a room that was directly above the one in which I had spent more than a year.

Despite the dark of the night sky and the illuminating glow

from the wrought iron light fixture above the bed, the curtains were open. I assumed they would be drawn as a matter of priority when Iris returned. I was mistaken. Instead, she removed all of her clothes in full view of the window. Having done so, she retrieved a pair of brown satin pyjamas with cream polka dots from under her pillow. She climbed first into these and then into bed.

Sitting upright, Iris stretched her hand out to me. Her fingers were slick as they lifted me up. It felt as though they might be coated in a thin layer of something of a slippery nature. Iris seemed suddenly aware of this also. She wiped each hand in turn on the duvet cover, switching me between them as she did. Her grip felt secure. She held me for only a moment before setting me down on the nightstand on her side of the bed.

Its narrow top was already home to a square lamp and a black rectangular box with green lights that I would come to learn was a radio alarm clock. Their existence was unfortunate as it left little room for me. I got the distinct impression from both of them that my presence was equally unwanted.

As I lay on the wooden surface, I could feel the edge of the nightstand, sharp under my spine. I felt as though I might topple onto the floor, which, I was relieved to note was covered in comfortable-looking carpet. Carpet that had only a slight suspicion of cat-damage, unlike the chest of drawers on the wall opposite.

Iris got back out of bed and exited the room once more.

I heard her descend to the lower floor of the house.

Alone, I inspected the mirrored wardrobe doors whose plastic surround also bore traces of feline mischief and wondered what Iris had left downstairs. She returned with a glass of water.

She set the water glass down next to me, which was an unwelcome development. She then switched on the lamp and walked to the door to turn off the overhead light. Returning, she lifted the glass and took a long drink. When she had finished, she got into bed.

Iris reached out and picked me up with her right hand, which felt damp.

After reading Sandra's inscription once more, she turned to the first page of chapter one. As she read, she kept place with her right thumb. When she turned to a page on my left side, the thumb on her left hand would take over the task, inching down one line at a time.

She read the excerpt from Tennyson on my third page to herself. She then read it aloud, slowly, adopting a noticeably refined accent. I thought perhaps Iris imagined this was the way in which Sandy had enunciated each vowel sound in order to garner Miss Brodie's favour.

Each time Iris came across a sentence that had been underlined by Violet, she would note it with her thumb and then run an index finger the length of the portion that had been deemed worthy of such special attention.

Before closing me over for the evening, Iris mouthed the last words of chapter three, once more elongating each vowel.

They walked back to Crail over the very springy turf full of fresh plans and fondest joy.

It seemed to me that the water glass was just as unhappy as the rest of us at having to share the nightstand. Thankfully, a sliver of a gap existed between us. The lamp and the radio alarm were less fortunate. Had any of us had the wherewithal to rearrange ourselves in such a way that we were each bounded by a moat of space, I am quite sure the night would have passed off in more comfort. As none of us was capable of such a feat, we were condemned to hours of misery on our miniscule island of oak.

Chapter Five

The sun had just begun its leisurely climb in the sky, throwing light into and across the room, when the black rectangular box at my back shrieked in order to declare that it was six twenty.

Iris's hand emerged from under the duvet and slapped the top of the noisy box. This happened three times over the next half hour until she finally roused herself and pushed the duvet back to reveal her pyjamas.

The weekend being over, Iris dressed for work. I had wondered if she would invent an ailment that morning but it seemed the alcohol of the previous night had little lasting effect.

I watched as she sat down on a stool that was positioned in front of a long mirror to the side of the window. The mirror was angled to take full advantage of the morning sun. Iris carefully applied colour to her face: she started with her eyes, moved on to her cheeks and finished with her lips.

As with Helen, I did not believe the addition of colour was necessary. Her face, in its natural state was most pleasant. The lashes that surrounded her pretty eyes were dark and long, her lips were full and there was a symmetry to her face that was most satisfying. If pressed, I would admit, however, that makeup had had a useful role to play in the many months she had spent crying and not sleeping. This, however, was no longer the case.

After brushing her hair, Iris opened one of the mirrored doors. She got onto her knees and hauled a pair of high heeled shoes from somewhere underneath the clothes that were, rather disconcertingly, in heaps on the floor of the wardrobe.

She pushed the stool to one side and inspected her appearance in the freestanding mirror. She leant in to check the makeup she had applied then ran one finger around the outline of her lips, erasing any pink that had strayed beyond the outer edge. As I studied this previously unknown portion of her morning routine, I noticed that not only was the mirror angled to take advantage of the natural light, it was also able to catch Iris's reflection in one of the mirrored doors of the wardrobe, thus providing her with a view that would otherwise be hidden. As she scrutinised her reflection in the wardrobe door, she was alerted to the fact that there a small clump of white cat hair on her black knee length skirt. This she removed with a barely audible tut.

I was led to wonder, not for the first time, where exactly Iris went when she left for work and what exactly she did once she arrived. The only concrete fact about her employment that I had been able to glean related to her boss, Darren. It seemed, from what I had heard, that he was a well-meaning imbecile whom her friend Geraldine thought to be rather attractive. Iris disagreed. I had heard this particular point debated on more than one occasion. In Iris's opinion, which seemed by far the more sensible, only someone who was partial to men who were too pretty for their own good could possibly hold this view and such an individual – Geraldine – should be very wary of entering into a relationship with a man who ranked so high on this scale, as it was bound to end in tears.

If the number of times Geraldine suggested Iris introduce her to Darren was any indication, it seemed she remained unconvinced by her friend's argument.

In terms of the substance of Iris's employment, from the snippets of information I had managed to gather I had settled upon a career in sales. Possibly, in real estate sales. I also imagined that this career was somewhat lucrative. My reasoning for this assumption was that, since Alan's death, Iris had not conducted any conversations in my presence that suggested she had any financial worries. I had seen her cry over letters that appeared to be of a formal nature, but I had also seen her cry over almost every piece of mail she received during that first year, so I did not take this to indicate anything other than the fact that any mailed communication had the power to remind her of Alan, or of his absence.

Before Iris left the room that morning, she picked me up. I had imagined that I would be confined to her bedroom for longer and whilst I was glad to be liberated from the confines of the nightstand, I was unhappy that I had not observed her room with a more critical eye; I was sure I had missed clues that could have provided me with an even fuller picture of Iris and of the extent to which she was, or was not, coping with widowhood.

Downstairs again, I found myself on the glass of the coffee table. I was immediately aware of the fact that Holly was observing me from the very corner of her eye.

Iris gave both cats instructions to be good while she was out at work. In my experience to date, Iris's definition of acceptable feline behaviour consisted merely of exercising the requisite amount of self-control to refrain from shredding items of furniture. Next, she pointed out the fact that the top window was ajar and exhorted them to come and go as they pleased. I felt it might have been safer, for me at least, if the window had stayed shut and the cats had remained beyond it for the duration.

When Iris left, Holly and Ivy each chose an armchair and appeared to fall asleep. I remained on high alert, convinced that Holly might pounce at any moment. It turned out that it was Ivy who should have been vigilant as it was she who fell victim to her sister every time she lowered her guard, which was often. Despite this activity and my aptitude for passing the time, the day seemed to drag more than normal.

The cats, who could at any moment have experienced the freedom that was to be found beyond the top window, chose not to avail themselves of it until the afternoon.

Ivy left first followed closely by Holly, who I was sure was up to no good. I feared for any inattentive garden visitor who may find itself on the wrong end of Holly's claws and in need of her mercy, a commodity she appeared to lack.

With the threat gone, my thoughts turned to Iris's connection to *life before* (this was the term I had settled on to use for my existence prior to being abducted by Thomas).

I had by this point developed a number of scenarios that might result in the return to *life before*. Unfortunately, they were all rather outlandish. The one which was least so involved a school reunion at which both Iris and Sandra were present. They would meet and speak. The conversation would turn to books. Iris would describe the strange tale of the copy of *The Prime of Miss Jean Brodie* that had appeared in her front porch on very day her much loved husband, also a former pupil, had died. Iris would talk about the solace she had found in it and would mention that within its covers it held a handwritten inscription to a girl named Violet.

My thoughts were interrupted by Iris's return.

She had only just sunk into Alan's armchair when the doorbell rang.

The expression on her face and her lack of movement suggested she was considering whether or not she could ignore it.

It rang a second time.

She roused herself.

From the hall, I could hear her say, 'Is something wrong?'

As an even more smartly dressed James Buchanan walked into the room behind her he said, 'I'm sorry to barge in on you. I would have phoned, but I don't have your number. I sent Helen a text and tried to phone her but she didn't get back to me.'

James explained that the reason for this drama, that I was pleased to be able to observe, was that he thought he must have left his wallet. He said he had only realised it was missing that morning when he had attempted to buy petrol and had discovered he was without the means to do so.

James had, apparently, promised to return with payment later that day when he had retrieved the missing wallet. Upon returning home he had checked his blue sports coat and discovered the inside pocket was empty.

Iris said that she was impressed he had been allowed to leave the petrol station under such circumstances. At which point he explained that he had known the young lad behind the cash desk for years.

'He's been one of my patients since he was a baby,' he said.

I was surprised at James's use of the present tense. I had imagined he had retired some years earlier. The look that flitted across Iris's face led me to believe that she had made the same assumption.

'I thought it might have been down to your honest face,' she said, lifting up the couch cushions.

I admit that I was sceptical about the wallet story. However, Iris's search of the couch did indeed reveal an expensive-looking leather rectangle, which she prised out of its hiding place and handed to James.

'Thank goodness,' he said. 'I tore my car apart and did the

same to the house when I got home.'

After James had declared his gratitude for a second time, Iris offered to make him a coffee. He said he better not dally in case there was already a warrant out for his arrest but added that he would be happy to take her up on the offer another time. He then offered to pick her up and take her to the Living with Loss meeting the following week. He suggested that perhaps he could have a quick coffee afterwards, if she was amenable. With that, he left.

I was unsure as to what had just transpired. It could be that James's wallet had indeed leapt from his jacket pocket and lodged itself in Iris's couch or that Holly had somehow helped with this process when she had attacked the couch the previous day. However, I found myself wondering if it had been nothing more than an elaborate ruse to see Iris again, without the presence of Helen. I weighed up both scenarios and decided that the former was less outlandish than the latter.

It appeared that Iris had also been left somewhat perplexed by James's visit. Once she was alone, she sat down on the couch where James had sat the previous day and used her right hand to feel between the cushions. I came to believe that this action allowed her to satisfy herself that a gap, large enough to swallow a wallet sized item, did indeed exist.

Holly, seeming to think there was a game afoot, joined Iris on the couch. She then tried to alternately pounce on the hand undertaking the investigation and swat at it. In contrast, Ivy chose to curl her head and tail around Iris's ankles, holding them captive. Iris gave up on the apparent detective work and instead turned her attention to first Holly and then Ivy. When both cats had received an equal number of head and chin scratches, they encouraged their mistress to follow them into the kitchen, I presumed in order that she would provide them with their evening meal.

Once the mewling had died down, the sound of Iris singing floated into the sitting room. She had an appealing voice and I was glad that she appeared to have found it in the preceding weeks. Her repartee seemed however to be limited to three songs. The one she sang most often had a pleasing tune which she held well. I was unsure of the lyrics despite the fact that I tried to unravel them each time I heard her voice begin to lilt. I was never able to do more than identify a word or two. This had less to do with the fact that Iris failed to enunciate the words clearly and more to do with the fact that she only ever seemed to sing whilst preparing a meal. My efforts were therefore invariably thwarted by the distance that lay between us.

Helen rang the doorbell two nights later and stayed long enough to drink a mug of herbal tea. Iris did not mention the fact that James had visited. Helen was on the point of leaving when she herself broached the subject.

'Thank goodness James found his wallet,' she said.

Inexplicably, Iris said, 'I'd completely forgotten about that.'

'He texted me for your number, but I didn't see the messages until late on,' Helen explained. 'We were really busy at work. You'd have thought it was a Saturday night.'

I wondered if James might be the cause of future difficulties as I was sure I could detect a slight strain in each woman's voice. As it turned out, this was not to be the case. However, during that first week I thought there might be cause for concern. Later, I would chastise myself for my seemingly unremitting need for drama. Later still, I would excuse myself as this propensity had never caused anyone any harm and, after all, I did have to find diverting ways to fill my days, and my nights.

I lay on the coffee table for the remainder of that week.

Being in this location resulted in long and anxious days as I felt myself to be at the constant mercy of Holly. In truth, however, she only joined me on the glass once and was more interested in the small plate that Iris had abandoned next to me and the leftover piece of toast it contained.

After flicking the remainder of Iris's breakfast into the air, she batted it onto the floor and amused herself until Ivy sidled up behind her. Holly hissed in her sister's direction and with Ivy suitably cowed, she consumed the erstwhile toy.

Despite the jeopardy my position on the table presented, it was otherwise a rather pleasant place to have been left, especially in the hours of daylight when the sun's rays warmed my cover. I was therefore somewhat conflicted when Iris picked me up one Saturday afternoon.

She had just finished a sandwich. As usual, Holly had been banished and Ivy, who appeared able to exercise self-control in the face of honey roast ham, had been resting between Iris's thigh and the arm of the armchair. With me in one hand and her plate in the other, Iris headed towards the kitchen, taking care not to step on Ivy who accompanied her mistress, weaving from one ankle to the next.

Chapter Six

On a bright September day, Iris carried me outside and placed me on a lacquered patio table.

I feel it is important to mention that, as I lay there, I was wholly unaware my time with Iris was nearing its end. It seems no matter how often I am reminded of the ever-present possibility of unwelcome change, each metamorphic moment catches me by surprise. I am led to conclude that I am incorrigibly naive.

The garden was not as I had imagined.

It was, for instance, devoid of grass. Instead, where I might have thought to find it, there was a slabbed patio on which stood the table with its four matching wooden chairs, each with a thick green cushion. In the centre of the table there was a green umbrella. I was glad of its presence as the glare from the afternoon sun was fierce.

The gaps between the beige slabs on which the table sat were remarkably weed free. I therefore decided that this in fact was the task that had been occupying much of Iris's time and was also likely the reason for her habit of cutting her fingernails so short.

The flowers I had imagined were, in the main, missing. However, there were clay pots containing plants I took to be fuchsias. In addition, at the rear of the garden in the shade of a tall wooden fence, there was what might best be described as a rockery. In amongst the large greyish-blue stones were pretty alpine blooms in white and various shades of purple and pink.

I spent my first moments outside alone as Iris had returned to the house to make herself a coffee in one of the oddly shaped terracotta mugs. This she also sat on the table and then lifted me to herself. She opened my pages at chapter two and began to read about the unfortunate demise of Mary McGregor.

Once more she kept place with alternate thumbs, holding me between one or other and two of the fingers on the same hand each time she stopped to take a drink of her coffee. This she did with some regularity. However, it seemed she was able to do this without losing focus on the story within my pages. Indeed, later in the chapter, Iris appeared to shiver along with Sandy in the tram-car as it travelled through the 1930s Edinburgh of Jean Brodie.

While she read, I was perfectly placed to observe my wider surrounds.

To my immediate left was Helen's garden. It was indeed separated from Iris's by a fence, but not the wrought iron one of my imagination. Instead, it was constructed of wooden panels that had been varnished, at least on Iris's side, in a colour that was a little too orange for my liking. An identical fence delineated Iris's garden from the one on my right. Hanging over it was a tree I identified as a fruit tree, possibly plum, that had given up its crop for the season.

Iris did not lay me back onto the table until she reached chapter five. She had long since finished her coffee and when she left me alone for a second time, I thought that perhaps she had gone to replenish her mug as it was now also missing from the garden tableau; I would have my hypothesis confirmed a short time later.

In the meantime, Holly jumped onto the table. She gave me an imperious look before performing a stretch that began at her chin and ended at the furthest reach of her tail. When she was done, she settled herself on the table and began to slowly lick the tips of her paws.

I was sure she was considering reaching out with the now pristine foot nearest to me and knocking me onto the slabs below when her attention turned to a moth that fluttered in the upper reaches of the umbrella. She stood up onto her back legs and tried to swat at it with one paw whilst attempting to thwart its bid for freedom with the other. Surprisingly, it was the moth who was triumphant.

Holly dropped from sight as Iris stepped back out into the garden.

It was now Ivy's turn to jump up and join me.

I thought Iris might object due to the fact that the picnic table might sometimes actually function as a place where food was consumed. She did not, however, seem to have any such hygiene concerns as instead of shooing Ivy, she stretched out her fingers to scratch behind the cat's left ear.

Iris did not pick me back up until she had finished her coffee. When she did, it was not to read chapter five. Instead, she carried me inside the house and placed me on the coffee table.

That evening when she was straightening up the sitting room before bed, Iris moved me from the glass top to the wooden shelf underneath. In common with the nightstand, this new location suffered from overcrowding.

I found myself on a stack of newspapers in the middle of the shelf. My front cover was a mere hair's breadth from the underside of the glass and my back cover rested on an overly inked copy of *The Herald*.

It was then that I discovered my propensity towards mild claustrophobia – seemingly triggered almost exclusively by tight horizontal spaces. This may seem to be an odd distinction, but I have found that narrow vertical spaces do not induce such a state.

I deployed distraction as a coping strategy.

I saw that to my left there was a box of tissues. Next to it was a stack of magazines. The bold writing on the uppermost of these declared that it was a compendium of conundrums. I remembered the man who gave it to Iris and his awkwardness as he suggested it might help to pass the time. Harry from number 34 was how he had identified himself at the door.

I had a more recent memory of Iris struggling with one of the puzzles contained in its pages, which at the time I decided was likely to be a particularly fiendish crossword. It seemed that, even though it had taken almost a year for it to happen, its well-meaning donor had been correct.

To my right, there were four books, all in some way related to grief, stacked one on top of the other. It may surprise you to learn that each one was, in actuality, more cheerful than the next.

Further to the right, there was a small collection of greeting cards that had arrived around the time of Alan's first anniversary. The uppermost was moss green in colour with the outline of a tree that had lost its leaves, the last of which had been captured in eternal descent. Unlike the original condolence cards that Morag had insisted be displayed on the shelving unit, each of these had gone directly from envelope to coffee table pile.

I remained in this less than comfortable location for an age, with only the bereavement books to amuse me. It was therefore a welcome diversion when, days later, Iris showed James into the sitting room.

She asked him to take a seat while she got her coat from the hall cupboard.

The garment in question was red. It reached to just above her knees and had five large buttons a shade darker than the wool of the coat. The cut was flattering. Beneath it, Iris wore black trousers paired with a black boatneck jumper. Her shoes were black patent. The coat was therefore a good choice as, otherwise, she might have looked just a little too funereal.

James was dressed in what I could almost have imagined were the same clothes I had observed him wear that first Sunday. The shirt, however, may simply have been an identical copy.

They left for what seemed like hours.

On their return, Iris left James in the sitting room while she prepared hot drinks. As he waited, he paced the length of the room whilst pushing his hair through his hand. He picked up the wedding photograph on the mantelpiece and appeared to study it. It was still in his hand when Iris stepped back into the room holding two mugs.

'It's lovely,' he said.

Iris nodded, in a manner that was almost dismissive.

'We were just kids,' she said. 'But you don't think it at the time.'

'No,' James said. 'Maggie and I got married the Saturday after we graduated.'

'You studied together?'

'We met over a cadaver,' he said. 'Well not really. But that's what Maggie used to say.'

James explained that they had, in fact, met in the bar during freshers' week. He could not believe his luck when she knocked into him and spilled his beer. Not the beer bit, he clarified.

'You didn't mention her. Tonight,' Iris said.

'I try not to talk that much anymore. It gives other people a chance. New folks. Like you.'

'Maybe next time,' Iris said.

James assured her that it was okay for her to take her time.

The small top window rattled as Ivy jumped up onto it from the outside window ledge. Once she had dropped down onto the carpet, she ran to Iris's feet. Holly was close behind. Stepping over them, Iris put both mugs on the coffee table and sat down on the couch. James stayed where he was, the photograph still in his hand.

'You don't look any older,' he said.

Iris snorted.

I had become aware that whenever she received a compliment, she behaved as though the person offering it was delivering a malicious untruth.

'You don't,' James said, looking directly at her.

Softening just a little, she said, 'I wish.'

Holly swatted at James's right calf as though some sort of winged creature visible only to her had landed there. It seemed, to me, that she was still bitter about her banishment during his original visit and, being a stubborn beast, was determined to wreak her revenge.

After admonishing the cat, Iris commented that Aileen was very sweet and said she could not imagine how she was able to cope with her children's grief along with her own. James said he thought that, whilst it was undoubtedly difficult, it could also be helpful to be a parent as you were forced to focus on the needs of your child, whether you wanted to or not. He cited himself as an example. If it had not been for having to keep going for Laurel, he said, he did not think he would have survived losing Maggie. He once more expressed remorse at not having done a good enough job as the father of a child who had lost her mother. He told Iris, by way of explanation, that Laurel had dropped out of school despite only having been sixteen. The accident happened a month before her Highers and she refused to sit them, he said. She had been on track for five As.

James sat down on the couch next to Iris and picked up the mug she had left for him.

Iris said it must have been awful for Laurel, losing her mum at that age.

'It was terrible,' James said. 'I don't think she'll ever really get over it. She still won't speak about Maggie.'

It seemed that to deter his daughter from leaving school James had told Laurel she could only do so if she got a job. Within a week she had done exactly that. She found work as a dish washer, then a cleaner, then she had worked in various coffee shops and after she turned eighteen, in various bars. Despite his obvious distress that he had allowed this situation to happen, he sounded proud as he told Iris that despite the fact his teenage daughter had flitted from one temporary job to the next, she had never had more than a day or two without employment.

In her early twenties, Laurel had got a job in a care home for the elderly and had worked there ever since. He said she was running the place now. He also said he thought the staff and the residents had become the family he was never really able to provide.

Iris told him not to be so hard on himself. She reached towards James's arm as she said this, but she did not touch him. I thought perhaps her face had coloured a little as she turned it away from him and picked up her mug.

'I know Maggie would never forgive me for letting Laurel leave school. She was sure she would follow in her footsteps. Become a doctor.'

At this stage in the conversation, Ivy uncurled herself from her spot on the floor next to Iris's feet and landed on the couch between them. She pressed her back against Iris's leg and she reached her paws, and claws, out towards James.

'I don't think your cats like me very much.'

'She's only playing. Ivy couldn't dislike anyone.'

'And what about her sister?'

'She's a different kettle of fish,' Iris said. 'Most of the time I'm not even sure she likes me.'

As if on cue, and much to Ivy's disgust, Holly leapt onto Iris's lap and began to roughly knead the legs of her trousers.

'Ouch,' Iris said, expelling the cat. 'See what I mean?'

Iris asked if Laurel had ever gone to the group.

James shook his head.

'She's never been interested. She did just start night school though,' he said. 'She's sitting three Highers. So, you never know. Miracles do happen.'

Iris seemed interested in James's daughter's foray back into education.

She asked where Laurel was going and what she was taking. When she heard that one of her subjects was English, she reached down and eased me out from between the Herald and the glass top.

'She wouldn't be studying this, would she?'

'You know, I think she might.'

'Well, if she needs to borrow a copy.' Iris's voice trailed. I felt her grip on me tighten. 'I would need it back though.'

To my dismay, James seemed pleased by her offer.

Part Four. Laurel
2013 - 2014

Chapter One

I am happy to report that Iris did in fact finish reading me.

It happened the following evening when, after eating a meal consisting of a sizeable slice of mushroom quiche and a salad of spinach leaves, cucumber slices and mange tout, Iris picked me up and took me to Alan's armchair.

As soon as she was settled, Ivy joined her. The small cat melted her bones into Iris's lap and was thus able to serve as a most comfortable cushion. So much so, I found it hard to concentrate on Iris as I was delightfully distracted by the sensation that is produced when the base of your spine rests on a purring pillow of fur.

Iris reached the end of my story, sat with me in her hand for a moment and then, gently moving Ivy, got up and placed me on the mantelpiece.

This action was as appreciated as it was unexpected.

From my position of safety, I mulled over Iris's offer to lend me to James's daughter. On balance, I decided it would not happen. I had felt Iris's regret as strongly as I had ever felt Heather's anguish or Violet's joy. I was therefore quite sure that it would never be mentioned again, keeping alive my hope that a return to life before might still be a possibility.

I took a moment to inspect my surroundings. I noted that I was on the opposite side of the mantelpiece to the one with which I had become so familiar when I first arrived. An advantage of this was that I had a better view of the kitchen. In fact, when the door was open, or even generously ajar, I could see the gas hob and the section of countertop on which Iris would assemble both sandwiches and salads. There was however one downside. The candlestick to my left was rather inhospitable, unlike its twin on the other end, who, whilst a little reclusive, had not been in the least bit disagreeable.

The ornament to my right, a plump little wren fashioned out of clay, was, in contrast, most diverting. Its cheerful demeanour assured me it would make for a most pleasant companion. Sadly, our fledgling friendship was to be short lived.

The following Wednesday, James arrived to take Iris to the Living with Loss group. She looked surprisingly alluring as she showed him into the sitting room. The black woollen dress she had changed into after work fell nicely over the curves that had recently begun to return to her body. The pearls she wore in her ears and around her neck complemented her skin tone and seemed to give an air of confidence, as did the slightly darker eye makeup she had chosen to apply.

Iris disappeared briefly, leaving James alone in the sitting room.

Holly lurked near his feet.

He bent his long body and stooped down to stroke her back. She was in the process of rejecting his advances when Iris reappeared in the red coat. She had changed her shoes and added a large handbag to her outfit, into which I was unceremoniously dropped.

I toppled onto an assortment of items: a small round tin containing mandarin flavoured lip gloss; two black and yellow BIC pens; a lipstick in winter plum and one in precious peach; a packet of tissues with added balm; a notebook wire-bound at the top and a miniature hand sanitiser. A moment later, Iris's purse and mobile phone bumped me as they fell inside.

I heard the front door shut and was struck with the thought that I might never return. I began to think about Alan. Despite the discomfort of my confinement, I remembered the warmth I had felt when he first clasped me in his hands.

This memory, however, served only to heighten the anxiety I had begun to feel journeying as I was, once more, into the unknown. Fortunately, the smell of soft leather helped me to resist despondency.

The noise of chairs scraping next to me suggested Iris had placed her handbag onto a wooden floor. This seemed unwise due to the financial investment I was quite sure my leather prison represented and I was reminded of a phrase I had once heard Sandra use: toffs are careless. This was a discordant thought because Iris was most certainly not a toff, although she had just shown herself to be careless.

This sound of metal dragging over wood punctuated the din of voices I could hear. When first the one noise and then the second died down, I heard James thank everyone for coming. He welcomed them to the meeting and introduced a man called Simon. It was Simon's first time, apparently.

'Thanks, James,' said a quiet voice that I presumed belonged to the newcomer. That was all Simon did say for the entire evening, which was more than I heard from Iris. When it was time for coffee, she left her handbag where it was on the floor. I presume she must have spoken then, even if just to explain that she took only a little milk and no sugar.

After the proceedings had drawn to a close, I heard James's voice, much closer than before.

'Mine, then?' he said.

In the car, James asked Iris how she had found the meeting.

She said it might still take her more time to feel comfortable enough to speak about Alan.

'I'm not even sure how I would start,' she said.

James suggested Iris start with something else. Perhaps her assertion that people were forever telling her how good she looked and how well she was doing as a strategy, in her view, to sidestep the subject that her spouse had died.

'I do hate that.'

'So, just start there. I think you'll find we all hate it.'

The radio was set to a station that played what the announcer described as popular classics. From the groans of my entrapped companions, it seemed I might be the only one of Iris's possessions to appreciate Sergei Rachmaninoff and Vaughan Williams.

Midway through The Lark Ascending, we came to a halt.

Iris was in the kitchen of James's house when her hand searched the bag for me. Plucking me from my surrounds, she set me down on cold marble.

'I remembered,' she said.

'Marvellous. Laurel will be delighted. She has a thing for old books. She's forever rummaging about in second hand bookshops.'

Until this point I had been fond of James but I now found myself unimpressed by both his words and tone. These thoughts were soon banished when he took me in his hands and declared I was a favourite of his. A classic.

'I'll put it in the lounge,' he said. 'I don't want anything to get spilled on it.'

At that I found myself in a stately room even larger than the kitchen. I was placed on a low table of thick mahogany. I had only just begun my examination of the room when James re-entered with Iris. They each held an ornate china mug.

'I hope you like white tea,' James said. 'There's only a hint of caffeine in it. Or so the marketing people say.'

I thought Iris might have preferred a glass of red wine.

James placed two coasters equidistant from me on the table and motioned for Iris to take a seat. I noticed she had taken off her shoes, something I had not been aware of whilst in the confines of her bag. The carpet under her feet was not thick but looked comfortable nonetheless. I imagined it was old and expensive, which also appeared to be true of the art on the walls. This might suggest that the room was dark but, in fact, the opposite was true. The walls were white and the alabaster of the fireplace was a smooth cream. The silken carpet appeared to have been spun from the palest palette of blue, which might have been the reason that Iris had chosen to step on it only in stockinged feet. James, Laurel, or, perhaps, a well-remunerated interior designer, had ensured that all the soft furnishings and anything upholstered favoured the shades of the carpet. In contrast, the wooden furniture in the room was drawn from the darkest of wood.

I was pleased that Iris had chosen to dress in a way that made her seem as though she belonged on the sofa on which she sat. I was also gratified to note that she had adjusted her posture to mirror the elegance of her surroundings.

'It's beautiful,' she said.

James looked unsure.

'Your house. It's beautiful.' Then, looking across the room, 'Do you play?'

I followed her eyes to the cello in the far corner.

'It was Maggie's,' James said. Before Iris could do so, he added, 'And don't apologise.'

The conversation turned to the Living with Loss meeting. Iris mentioned that she had spoken to Simon over coffee.

'Do you think it's a bit soon for him?' she asked.

James said that people come to the group at a time that feels right for them. He did not like to judge, or to discourage.

'But it's less than a month. Surely that's not right.' Iris said, judging.

James was kind in his response but did not agree with her. Instead, he reiterated his earlier point.

Iris did not seem appeased. She did, however, allow him to change the subject to Laurel.

'If I'm honest, I'm not really sure about this night school business. She's so busy with work,' James said, 'and I don't want her to be disappointed if she doesn't do well.'

'I'm sure she'll be fine. From what you've said about her.'

'I know. But at her age and she has a lot of stress at work. I'm not sure it's a good recipe for doing your Highers.'

In a state of mock indignation, Iris said, 'She's what 40? 41? That sounds pretty young to me.'

James said that Laurel had just turned forty-two, quickly adding that he and Maggie had been no more than babies themselves when she was born. Then, a little flustered, he said, 'That's not why we got married.'

Iris laughed. Even though I had seen her do this on a handful of occasions, there was a lightness to it that seemed different. I thought I might even detect something akin to happiness.

James carried the empty mugs into the kitchen.

Iris followed at his back.

This would be the last glimpse I would ever have of her.

I saw James again when he returned from driving Iris home. He was carrying a small glass of something I took to be whisky – a very fine single malt, I was sure – and had a newspaper under his arm.

He turned on a radio I had not yet noticed, set back as it was on the sideboard, and, sitting in the chair I took to be his favourite, began to read.

I remembered talk of Gordon and marvelled at the fact he had not left his mark anywhere on the décor. It was then that I saw a fat ginger paw stretch slowly into the air from somewhere underneath the sideboard – the rest of his body being obscured from view. The languor with which he performed this action led me to believe that his intense sloth had been the room's salvation.

My attention returned to James. He read two more broadsheet pages before he folded up the newspaper and drained the remnants of his drink.

I spent many hours alternately wondering about Laurel and worrying about the future. On the fifth day, she appeared.

I had stitched her together using a mixture of the features of my previous guardians. What I should have done, rather, was imagine a younger female version of James, for Laurel was indeed her father's daughter.

She had his height, his build, his long face, the hair colour he must once have had. The only aspect of James she did not possess were his eyes. I presumed she must have inherited these from Maggie. Hers were not blue; they were dark brown like the mahogany of the furniture.

Given Laurel's name, and what I now know to be the infrequency with which it is bestowed, I should also have realised that I had met her before, but it was only when she touched me that I realised she was the girl, the cleaner, I had met in Sandra's classroom all those years earlier.

As soon as I felt her skin on my cover, I knew.

It may sound sentimental to say that it was like meeting an old friend, but that is the closest comparison I have to offer. Laurel had shown me kindness once and I have found, as I sift through my past, it is such instances of grace that glisten in the grey.

Chapter Two

With hope rekindled, I listened intently to Laurel's voice.

'I love it,' she declared, holding me to herself. 'So, when am I going to meet its owner,' she added, with something I might venture to describe as a mischievous glint.

Her father said he was sure that there would be plenty of time for that. He then changed the subject, something at which he was adept.

'How's it all going?' he asked, waving his hand vaguely in the space between them.

'Fine.'

I found myself unsure as to the veracity of this statement due to the edge that seemed to have crept into her voice.

'Really?'

I presumed he had noted the same shift in tone.

Laurel dropped down onto the sofa. Without undoing her shoelaces, she eased off her trainers. She first removed the left one with her right foot and then the right one with her left foot. James almost shivered with displeasure.

Laurel opened my pages and began to read from the place her eyes fell. As she did, I found myself admiring the moss green of her cable knit jumper, a jumper that brought necessary colour to an outfit of grey combat trousers and matching socks. When I shifted my focus to what she was reading, I found her underneath the big elm in the garden of the Marcia

Blaine School: Jean Brodie caught up in a discourse about her lost love, Hugh; the young girls in her charge propping their books up in front of them, to affect an attitude of learning.

Laurel stopped reading.

'Remember Granny would talk about her great sorrow? And in front of Grandpa, too.'

'Her Bert,' James said.

'He died in the war, didn't he?'

'That's right. He was killed in The Clydebank Blitz. He'd been home on leave. They were only engaged a few days.'

'And Grandpa didn't mind? The fact she talked about Her Bert.'

'It never seemed to bother him,' James said.

'Odd though. Don't you think?'

'Maybe. But that was your granny. She paddled her own canoe. She never meant any harm by it. For her it was just a statement of fact. She suffered a great sorrow. And then after the war she married my father.'

'And they had Uncle Robert. Named for her first love. I have to say, Grandpa was very tolerant.'

'He loved her.'

Laurel bent forward and put me back on the wooden coffee table. She stretched her long arms then used them to ease herself off the sofa.

'I'd better be off.'

'No dinner?'

'No time,' she said.

She picked me up in one hand and her trainers in the other.

Once in the hall, I fully expected to be dropped in a handbag.

To my surprise, however, Laurel's version of this was a black nylon backpack. Before I was placed carefully inside, she set me down on the carpet, which was a continuation of the one I had admired in the lounge. It was as smooth and comfortable as I had imagined.

Laurel removed metal clips from the backpack. These she attached to the lower reaches of her trousers. She forced each foot into a trainer and picked up the yellow helmet that rested against the lower edge of the ornately wallpapered wall in the hallway. She twisted a purple elastic band around her dark hair to create a stub ponytail and fitted the luminous headgear into place.

I felt the backpack being hoisted up onto her back.

Slotted as I was into a rear-zipped pocket, I could feel the rise and fall of the ribs of her back as we left her childhood home. Or, to be more accurate, as we left the residence that I presumed was the home of her youth.

The journey that followed was filled, initially, with terror. It was, after all, my first experience of being transported by bicycle. However, once I had figured out that this was the way in which we were travelling, I found myself more able to relax into the situation and by the time Laurel dismounted, I had almost begun to enjoy the sensation of scudding through a city.

The following may not strictly be true, but what I think then happened was that, having negotiated the heavy door of her close, Laurel pushed the bike over the concrete floor, attached it by means of the black plastic and metal bike lock with which I had shared the journey and then ascended a gently spiralling staircase to what I can only imagine was the uppermost floor of the building.

I was released from the backpack whilst we were still in her hallway, a hallway that was markedly different from the one we left thirty minutes or so earlier. The avocado-coloured walls stretched up to the high ceiling, which was an expanse of off-white. The floor boards were bare and their polish somewhat patchy. Four doors led enticingly into rooms with interiors at which I could only guess. There was a tall, twisting wooden coat stand with various garments in differing fabrics suspended from it. Laurel removed her green cagoule and slung it over the top of a thick grey cardigan, whose resting place, it seemed to me, should instead have been a wardrobe. I was quite sure it would fair badly where it was, with a spike of wood creating an unsightly stretch mark at its neck.

Laurel used her free hand to push at one of the doors. As she did so, her sitting room opened up to me. Due to the way in which I was being held, my first observation was that the floor boards were in the same condition as those in the hall. Once I was on the coffee table, I was more able to carry out a survey of the space. My second observation was that it was rather sparse. For this reason, and several others, it was also a stark contrast to the room in which I had observed her father spend his evenings.

There was only one chair in the room. It had been placed near the bay window. I thought it must once have belonged to a set.

The chair was the only wooden item in the room that did not appear to have been constructed out of light-coloured oak. It was also the most ornate feature of the room, thanks to the delicate embroidery on its seat.

There were two bottle-green chesterfield sofas in the centre of the room. They looked as though they had seen better times.

Their front feet rested on a large rug that reached out from underneath the table. It was light green with pink flowers. It also looked as though its best days were behind it.

One wall was entirely covered by a bookcase. In the gaps between the busy shelves, I could see that it, like the other three walls, had been painted a light shade of yellow. Despite my earlier desire to be reinstalled in one, I was concerned that this particular bookcase was not for me due to its tight quarters. In addition, the books on display did not look like a cheery lot. I felt quite sure they would be less than pleased to have another join their uncomfortable ranks. In fact, on the middle shelf of five Laurel had begun to stack books horizontally in small piles on top of those shelved vertically.

Laurel padded over to the window in her socks. She closed the curtains, allowing me to see more fully both their expanse and their pattern – long stripes in yellow and white overlaid with what looked like tendrils of ivy. There were no lamps in the room, just an overhead light whose shade was distinctly off-white.

I found myself wondering where in the house it was that Laurel undertook her studies because, in this room, there were none of the accoutrements with which I had grown so familiar – jotters, notebooks in various sizes, pens, pencils, a pot for the pens and pencils, sharpeners, rubbers, and so forth. I imagined they must all be elsewhere and that at some point I would leave this room to join them, so, for the moment, I decided I would enjoy this new space and the things I might find out in my privileged position as the sole resident of the coffee table.

The first of these I discovered thanks to the small free-standing television that was positioned between one of the chesterfields and the bay window: Laurel, it seemed, was an avid watcher of quiz shows and the knowledge she possessed on a vast array of topics was impressive. I learned that she was also quite impatient with the contestants who had no business being on, for example University Challenge, in the first place.

Monday nights, I would learn, were University Challenge and it so happened, I arrived on a Monday night. Laurel's first order of business was to turn on the television and settle herself on the left chesterfield, her preferred seating option. Bangor triumphed over Aberystwyth. She appeared content with the outcome.

When it was over, she left the room and reappeared with a bowl in which there was a rather dubious meal of insipid-looking macaroni and cheese. In her other hand she held what I took to be a mug of tea – without caffeine I presumed, given the hour. She continued to watch television – news and current affairs seemed to be her second love – until she left the room to, I presumed, go to bed.

After Laurel turned off the overhead light, the room was in near darkness. The only source of light were the rays that seeped under the door from the hallway. This light stayed on all night. Whilst it was welcome, it was not the greatest source of illumination. For instance, I was unable to make out the title of any of the many books that lined the shelves of the bookcase.

The noise of the traffic outside eased. However, it did not cease altogether. Rather it decreased to a trickle. This led me to believe that I was now in the heart of the city, or, at the very least, that I had been brought to a section of it that required a cadre of its residents to stay active regardless of the hour.

In the relative quiet, I replayed the second time I met Laurel. I found that revisiting this moment, revelling in it, allowed me to imagine other equally unlikely scenarios. For instance, one in which Laurel was in fact Violet's second cousin three times removed with whom Violet would at some point in the near future make a connection thanks to a shared love of ancestral history and a website dedicated to discovering distant relatives.

Laurel opened the door at some point early the next morning. She entered the room with the sole intent of opening the curtains. On her way out, she left the door ajar. This allowed me to hear part of her morning routine – the making of breakfast. The noise of a kettle and toaster were accompanied by a voice I felt sure was a radio announcer. I was hopeful his proclamations might be interspersed with music. This did not happen. Instead, every so often his dull drone was briefly interrupted by other, equally dismal, voices.

Laurel did not reappear that morning. Moments after the opinionated man was silenced, I heard the front door shut with a thud that petered out into the rattle of what I imagined was brass hardware in the form of a letterbox and an ornamental knocker in the shape of a hook-beaked bird of prey.

During that first full day, I undertook an inventory of Laurel's books and magazines. Many of the books were duplicates of titles I had already seen, but there were some that were new to me. For instance, she seemed to have a healthy collection of poetry on display. In addition, she had a full shelf of magazines. These were an eclectic mix covering topics from cycling to gardening to world travel to DIY to mountaineering to the animals of prehistory. I was still pondering this final category when the front door reopened, admitting Laurel and a man I could not quite make out due to the narrow angle of the door and my inconveniently restricted view of the hallway.

His voice was quiet, but there was something about the quality of it that made me think I might find him rather intriguing.

Laurel pushed wide the door of the sitting room.

In accented tones, I heard the male voice say, 'I'll go in, shall I?'

'Please,' Laurel said. 'I'll be with you in a minute.'

Chapter Three

The man was a disappointment. He was no more than an overgrown boy with a deep voice, a foreign accent and an Adam's apple that protruded more than was normal.

Cédric, as I would learn he was called, looked uncertain as he took a seat in the spot I knew to be Laurel's. Before she entered the room, perhaps sensing his mistake, the young man moved to the opposite chesterfield. He released the large canvas bag that had been slung over his shoulder and let it slide to the floor.

Laurel's head appeared around the door.

'I should have asked,' she said, 'Tea?'

'No,' he said. 'No, thank you.'

'I'll just get my stuff, then.'

This time, when he was left alone, Cédric reached forward and picked me up. His hands were red and there were rough hacks at uneven intervals across the flesh of his fingers and palms. Despite this, it did not seem to cause him pain to touch me.

I have learned that there are two types of people: those who pick up a book with a genuine interest and an intent to read the story contained within and those who pick up a book as an act in and of itself and are, in fact, disinterested in the world that lies within its covers; these, in my opinion, are those who have no interest in commitment. Cédric slotted neatly into the latter category.

I was already back on the coffee table when Laurel appeared with a textbook and a notebook. She was wearing more formal attire than that which I had seen her in before. This took the form of black knee length boots, a green corduroy skirt that skimmed the top of said boots and a black, form-fitting jumper.

'I hope you don't mind working in here,' she said.

'No. I told you. It's okay.'

'The kitchen's a riot, I'm afraid.'

Cédric nodded. A little curtly, I thought.

'Verbs,' he said and asked Laurel to conjugate those he had set her for homework.

At the end of a rather tedious lesson, Laurel thanked her tutor and left the room saying that her purse was in the hall. On her return, she thanked him again and held out a twenty-pound note.

Cédric was on his feet. He returned the canvas bag to his shoulder. I could see now that it had, on its front panel, an image of three books with different coloured spines, stacked on their sides. There was a quote in large letters underneath: "There is no friend as loyal as a book". In the years that have passed since, I have contemplated this phrase often: turning it this way and that.

But back to Cédric.

It was clear as they stood together that he was at least a foot taller than Laurel, who was tall. He took the money and, with an awkward bow, said, 'Merci beaucoup.'

Despite his apparent desire to leave, Laurel offered to make him something to eat. She told him there was a pizza in the freezer that would be ready in no time. Cédric dismissed her kind offer.

During the course of their lesson I had pieced together some facts about this unusual pairing. One fact was that Cédric was a postgraduate student who worked part-time in Laurel's care home. Another was that he was willing to forgo his apparent discomfort around women to earn extra money by helping his boss improve her French. A third was that notwithstanding Laurel's protestations that she remembered nothing from school and felt she must have been crazy to choose French as one of the Highers she was doing at night school, she did, in fact, know rather a lot and was able to accurately answer every question she was asked.

These are the things I thought I knew.

Imagine then my astonishment when, through the open door, I witnessed the gauche young man lean forward and kiss his middle-aged student. To be fair, Laurel appeared to share my shock. Her initial surprise, however, did not seem to prevent her from participating in what turned out to be a rather lengthy and involved encounter. An encounter which led them both to undress, whilst still in the hallway, and resulted in Cédric following Laurel to an unknown location in her flat.

I found the noise that subsequently emanated from what I presumed to be a room, other than the kitchen, on the opposite side of the hallway to be something of a distraction. It seemed Cédric was a rather more loquacious lover than he was a tutor.

An hour or so later, Laurel returned, still naked, to the scene of their original tryst. She righted the coat stand and scooped up the pile of clothes on the floor. Cédric was next to appear, by now fully clad if a little dishevelled.

He crossed the hallway and took his leave.

After a little more time had passed, Laurel returned to the sitting room, now in a pair of comfortable-looking blue pyjamas that were adorned with a multitude of white clouds.

She sat down on her usual chesterfield and was quiet at first.

She reached forward and picked me up.

She was silent as she held me in her hands.

Her grip grew tighter.

'What the fuck was I thinking?' she said, looking directly at me.

Pulling me closer to her face, so that I could feel her breath, softly and even more slowly she said, 'What the fuck was I thinking?'

Her voice grew louder.

'Really, Laurel,' she said, even though she seemed to be addressing me, 'Shagging the hired help. Really? What the fuck, fuck, fuckety, fuck were you fucking thinking, you stupid, stupid, stupid, stupid cow. Stupid cow. Stupid cow. Stupid cow. What if he makes a complaint? Oh fuck. What if he complains?'

It seemed as though she was asking me this question.

I would have liked to have provided her with some comfort, had it been within my gift.

I would have liked to have been able to point out that it was in actual fact Cédric who had pressed his mouth to hers. Cédric who had put his hands on her arms and had manoeuvred her body until it rested unsteadily against the coat stand in the corner to which I had fortuitously – for the purposes of witness and reassurance – had a clear view. It had been Cédric, after the coat stand had toppled over, who had guided her body to the floor and had tugged petulantly at her clothing.

Granted she had participated. She had returned the kiss. She had pulled just as vigorously at his clothing. But it had been Cédric who had initiated the action that had occurred. It was not her fault that they had stumbled into a room across the way, leaving their clothes where they had fallen. Additionally, whilst he may have looked like no more than a child, he must have been at least in his twenties so she need not torture herself with regards to his age.

Despite my best efforts, Laurel still appeared to be trapped in a fury of self-loathing. She cycled through a number of insults: she called herself stupid; desperate; a desperate old bird who should know better and a stupid, desperate old bird with terrible taste who should know better. Eventually, she made the aforementioned pizza and ate it whilst answering quiz questions that seemed altogether too simple for her.

When Laurel went to bed, she left the curtains of the sitting room open. With the bay window unadorned, I had a view of the immediate cityscape and the night sky beyond. I found both to be quite mesmerising. As the bay window stretched upwards from the wooden floor, I had an uninterrupted view of the windows in the block of flats on the other side of the road. Most, but not all, had their curtains closed. Only one of these flats, however, had the lights left on.

This flat appeared to be occupied by a group of alternately thirsty and frisky twentysomethings. From their movements, I also imagined that they were playing music, loudly. It seemed they did not care whether or not their antics were observed as they took no steps to hide them from anyone on this side of the street or from prying eyes that may choose to study them from the street below. This indifference seemed fraught with risk. It also seemed morally irresponsible as there could well be children on this side of the road who, unable to sleep or awoken by a night terror, had gone to their window seeking the solace of the moon and had instead received an education in the ways of the adult world. It was almost daybreak when these young reprobates headed to what I presumed were the bedrooms of their abode.

The next morning Laurel ate toast and jam in the sitting room. The television was on, but she did not appear to be watching it. In between mouthfuls, she assured herself, or perhaps me, that everything would be fine. I saw in her a steely determination and believed she was right.

After the drama of the previous evening, I rested on the coffee table and spent the day in something akin to a dream state. In this condition, I conjured a series of scenarios that Laurel might, at the very minute I invented them, be facing. They were all variations on the same theme.

In the first, I envisioned her in a neat and tidy office at the care home, sitting behind a computer at a large wooden desk. There is a knock on the door. Laurel shouts, 'Come in.' The person on the other side hesitates. She shouts, 'Come in,' a second time. The door opens and Cédric enters the room. Without flinching, and with an air of disinterest, Laurel says, 'Can I help you?' Her impertinent paramour loses his nerve and scuttles from the room.

Next, I imagined her happening upon Cédric in a patient's room, then in the canteen, then in the car park and then in a narrow corridor while she wheeled one of the residents out to the garden.

Each time, the Laurel in my vision was steadfast and serene.

That evening a less than composed Laurel slumped into the flat. Her face was red and it looked as though she had sweated her way through the day in a nervous panic. She did not come immediately into the sitting room. Instead, she changed into more comfortable looking clothing and made herself something to eat. From the aroma, I identified it as fried fish and boiled vegetables, perhaps cabbage.

It seemed she was intent on doing penance.

After I heard noises I identified as clearing up and washing dishes, Laurel entered the room.

I expected her to sit down and turn on the television. She did neither. Instead, she picked me up and took me to the kitchen.

The kitchen was indeed a riot. However, whilst the work surfaces were clean but in no way tidy, most of the mess seemed to be on the large table that filled the recessed area at the back of the room. This was, of course, my destination.

As suspected, Laurel possessed all of the items I associated with the acquisition of knowledge: books, textbooks, notepads, coloured folders, a plethora of pens and pencils, a receptacle in which to keep them, a ruler, a desk diary and a dirty coffee mug.

The books, textbooks, notepads and coloured folders were arranged lengthways on the table into subject areas, with a little leakage around the edges. These subject areas were: History to the left, English in the middle and French on the right. The non-subject specific items crowded in a space between History and English that had been eked out for them.

In all of this hubbub there was a hollow of light oak still visible.

It was on this spot that Laurel set me down.

Chapter Four

Laurel sat down on the kitchen chair nearest to me.

She drew it in towards the table.

She seemed to think better of this and scraped it back out over the floor, filled the kettle and hit the switch that would cause it to boil. She took a clean mug from the oak mug tree and made herself a coffee: strong and black. Exchanging the used mug on the table for the one she now had in her hand, she disposed of the old one into the sink and sat back down.

Laurel nudged me with the outside of her wrist as she reached towards the French section. She was drawing a textbook to herself when she blasphemed and put her forehead on the table. Her dark hair touched my cover as she did. It was even more like silk than I had guessed.

She pushed the textbook back into place. She raised her head and touched me. With the tips of her fingers, she slid me two or three inches over the wood until I was directly in front of her.

'There you are,' she said.

I was confused.

Laurel had addressed me the previous evening, but I had presumed that I was merely a substitute for herself: a surrogate to which she could address her concerns.

This time, however, it felt as though she was actually speaking to me.

'It's been a while.'

These words led me to wonder if she remembered our encounter in Sandra's classroom. What followed would disabuse me of this notion.

'I remember you well,' she told me as she lifted me up. 'You are the crème de la crème. When I brought you home from school, Mum said that – 'Ah, the crème de la crème, Laurel, the crème de la crème'.'

As she spoke, Laurel's fingers held me tightly yet with tenderness. Her mahogany eyes seemed to look straight through my cover to the story within. She raised me to her cheek. It was soft, softer even than her hands. A texture I imagined might be like that of velvet.

Her eyelashes touched me. They were damp.

'I miss you, Mum,' she said.

I was back on the table and she was crying: heaves and sobs. Her eyes were no longer beautiful. Angry veins streaked across them. Puffy lids squeezed open and shut, forcing unwelcome drops of salted water to land on my front cover.

She left me alone in the kitchen.

When she returned, her face was lovely once more.

'Sorry about that,' she said. 'You'd think by now I'd manage to get through a memory of my mother without bawling. Seems not. And Dad wonders why I won't talk about her. When he does. And he does. I just block out whatever he's saying. I look like I'm listening, or at least I think I look like I'm listening, but in my head, I'm repeating la, la, la, la over and over again – la, la, la, la. Until he stops recounting whichever holiday or birthday or picnic or special meal or hill walk he happens to be describing whilst inspecting my face, looking for a reaction, any reaction.'

I was in her hands as she spoke. Her grip was firm but not so tight as to be uncomfortable.

'To be fair, it happens less now,' she said. 'He was always doing it those first couple of years. That, or crying. I used to wonder if he was the same at work. Breaking down in front of patients. I decided he couldn't have been though. I don't think he would have lasted long as a GP if people couldn't get a prescription for penicillin without him weeping over his dead wife.'

Laurel was now in full control.

It seemed as though she had deposited whatever emotion she had felt in a small lead-lined box, which she had then sealed securely and squirrelled away in the far reaches of the deepest recess of her mind.

'And now look at him. Lord God of his Living with Loss group. The Master of Mourning. Offering a helping hand and a shoulder to cry on to every grief-stricken soul he meets. It keeps him out of my hair, I suppose.'

My attention was now, of course, drawn to her hair.

I found myself examining it as she talked. It was really rather pretty. Its smooth waves were a jumble of different shades: black, the precise brown to match her eyes and strands that appeared to be the blackest shade of purple. It was, in my opinion, just the right length. Its cut complemented her face as it drew the observer's eye lengthways in a manner that made the distance from brow to chin seem not too long and the distance from one ear to the other not too short. Had it been a different length or style, her appearance may well have lacked balance.

'It's as if he has a new lease on life. He peddles my mother's death as a topic of conversation. A way to heal others. I could never say that to him though. It would give him something else to analyse. To talk about. He'd tell me, not for the first time, that in terms of Elizabeth Kübler-Ross's model of grief, I'm stuck at stage two. Anger. I'll give him bloody anger. Him and all those women he has fawning over him. Listening to every word that falls from his mouth. It's disgusting. My mum would be appalled. Knowing her memory had been reduced to little more than a pick-up line.'

It seemed to me that this was a less than fair analysis of James Buchanan and might have more to do with the fact that Laurel may indeed be stuck at stage two.

My train of thought was disturbed by the sound of a metallic tap, tap, tap at the door. Laurel put me down and raised herself up, pressing both hands against the table.

I heard the front door open. Her voice was tense as she said, 'Cédric?'

'Can I come in, please?'

'I don't think that's a good idea.'

'Please.'

I heard his feet on the wooden floor of the hallway. The door shut behind him.

'I'm working,' Laurel said. 'I need to study. I've got classes the next two nights and I have homework.'

'Maybe, I could help?' Cédric said.

'I don't think so.'

'I could do it for you, maybe?'

'It's an essay on Britain between the wars.'

They were in the kitchen now. Laurel was resting the small of her back against the sink.

'I want to talk to you,' he said, edging closer to her.

'There's nothing to say. It was stupid and it can't happen again. I mean it, Cédric. I don't know what I was thinking.'

Her voice was firm.

'Can I have a coffee at least?' he said. 'I walked all the way from work.'

'That was stupid,' she said. 'What was wrong with the subway?'

'Just a coffee,' he said.

'Fine.'

Laurel motioned for him to sit at the table.

He chose the seat closest to the English section and pushed it back until it touched the wall behind, creating space between himself and the large mound of books and folders.

It seemed there was a question in his voice when he said, 'We could have worked in here.'

Laurel said nothing.

'Perhaps next week we will work in here.'

'No,' she said, as she poured boiling water into the last two mugs on the mug tree. 'We won't.'

Laurel handed Cédric his coffee and sat back down on the seat nearest to me. She removed a French language textbook from its pile, made a space for it near the edge of the table and sat her hot drink on top of it. Following her example, Cédric did the same with a copy of *King Lear*.

I was horrified. The heat from Laurel's coffee radiated out towards me. I watched the steam rise from her mug and realised that someday this might happen to me.

In the exchange that followed, Laurel told Cédric that she

no longer required his services as a tutor. She explained for a second time that what had occurred between them had been a mistake. She said she hoped that, if they had occasion to cross paths at the care home, he would act with the professionalism his role required.

Cédric was silent in the face of her reasoned argument.

When they had finished their drinks, Laurel motioned for him to leave.

'Can I say something?'

Laurel nodded.

He scuffed his chair around the table towards her. Her face looked stern as he did, but she did not stand up.

'I understand,' he said, reaching one of his red raw hands.

I willed her to stand up.

He rested his hand on her knee. He repeated that he understood how she felt. He pulled his seat even closer to her. He told her she was beautiful. His face was close to her cheek as he told her she was beautiful for a second time. It was then that she relented and dissolved into his arms.

Actually, she did not.

In the heat of the kitchen, and of the steaming coffee mug next to me, it seems I had got ahead of myself.

Laurel's voice broke in.

I realised the drama had changed course.

Laurel was on her feet. She directed Cédric to the door. There would be no repeat of the previous evening's antics she told him. She assured him that whilst those antics had indeed been quite nice, they could not possibly lead to any sort of relationship and would therefore never happen again.

It seemed, to me – now that I was fully aware of what was actually happening – that Cédric was more upset at Laurel's choice of the words "quite nice" than he was at the dawning knowledge of the way in which his evening was now doomed to end.

Once we were alone again, Laurel told me she had in fact been tempted by the young Frenchman's advances.

'But I checked his personnel file,' she said, 'and he's only twenty-four, for pity's sake.'

She then informed me that, having now also googled him, she was grudgingly impressed by the scholarly sounding doctoral thesis he was working on – a detail the recruitment agency had failed to mention, possibly due to the fact that it could well have created the wrong impression with regards to his commitment to the position of porter for which they recommended him. Laurel added that she was not, however, sufficiently dazzled by his apparent academic prowess to embark on any further madness with a temp almost twenty years her junior.

The next revelation of the evening was that Laurel did not have to write an essay on Britain between the wars. Apparently, the topic of Britain between the wars was not even on the curriculum. However, it had, she said, seemed like the sort of subject about which Cédric would have neither the requisite knowledge or interest.

Laurel's final confession of the night was that I, too, was not on the curriculum.

Chapter Five

I had been implicated in a lie.

The falsehood?

That I was a set text on Laurel's Higher English course.

This was simply not true.

The reason for the fabrication, or "our secret" as Laurel liked to call it, was that when her father had told her of Iris's offer, she had not been able to resist the opportunity to get her sticky hands – her phrase – on a book that belonged to his new love interest.

Unfortunately, I was not able to correct her erroneous framing of the relationship that existed between Iris and James Buchanan as our conversations were very much a one-way affair.

Despite not being on the curriculum, I was allowed to stay on the kitchen table with those texts that had, in actuality, been prescribed. These were, in no particular order, the aforementioned copy of *King Lear*, a copy of *To Kill a Mockingbird* and an assortment of short stories and poems that were contained in a blue folder labelled "Short Stories" and in a red one labelled, "Poems". Over the course of the next few months I would come to learn that the poems proffered differing views on war and that the short story folder contained, amongst others, the stories, "The Telegram" by Iain Crichton Smith and, "A Time to Keep" by George Mackay Brown.

Laurel seemed to be most enthralled by the poetry she had

been set and would often recite poems aloud. The one to which she returned most often was "Anthem for Doomed Youth" by Wilfred Owen. I cannot deny that when she read those words I would find myself sad and frightened in equal measure.

Laurel spent many nights in the kitchen and she often spoke to me, referring to me as her talisman. What seemed strange however, was that despite her obvious affection for me, she never actually read me in the conventional way. Instead she would begin her study sessions by opening me up as though I were a magic trick and, by turns, she would take solace, counsel or cheer from whichever words or sentences caught her eye.

Laurel entertained few visitors. Cédric never did return and Christmas was almost upon us before I saw James Buchanan again. He clanged on the door unexpectedly. I listened intently as Laurel showed him into the sitting room and denounced his extravagance, complaining about the number of presents he had brought.

'I've not even got a tree up,' she said.

'Can't a father shower his only daughter with gifts?' he replied, before assuring her that most of them were just little mindings.

'Who helped you? You didn't wrap them,' Laurel said, adding, 'You can't tell me that you're responsible for those ribbons and bows.'

'I might have had some help,' James said, without answering the question.

'Let me guess… Aileen? No? Helen? No? Iris? Yes? Am I right?'

It was hard to tell how engaged James was in the dialogue of disembodied voices as Laurel did most of the talking. I had to insert imaginary smiles, grimaces and the occasional shrug of the shoulders in order to gain a better sense of the tone of their exchange.

Laurel eventually gave up tormenting her father and offered to make him a coffee. I was pleased when I saw him walk into the kitchen behind her. He was dressed as I had expected and was exactly the mix of dignified-yet-cheerful that I remembered.

Laurel's back was turned to him, busy with the preparation of hot drinks, when he began to examine the table. He picked up one of the folders in the history section and began to flick through it. He ran a finger down one of the sheets inside and commented that it looked as though the syllabus had not changed much since his day.

'You mean since the olden days? Or the days of the dark ages?'

'That's enough,' he said, smiling the smile I had imagined had spread across his face whilst I eavesdropped on their earlier conversation.

James put the folder back down. He turned towards the English section. I saw his hand approach and I fully expected to feel his fingers on my cover. However, I was bypassed in favour of the copy of *To Kill a Mockingbird*.

He picked it up.

'So, you're doing both?' he said, raising his voice into a question. 'This and *The Prime of Miss Jean Brodie*?'

'What?' Laurel said as she turned.

I saw her eyes flit from the book in his hand to me.

'We are,' she said. 'The teacher's trying to cover every eventuality. The prose questions were a total bugger last year, apparently.'

'Is that the technical term?'

Despite the levity in his voice, I felt sure that he was, at best confused by his daughter's answer, and, at worst, unconvinced.

'That seems an awful lot to read,' he said, in a way that suggested he may have questioned the veracity of what he was being told.

Laurel took a leaf from her father's book and changed the subject.

'Will it just be the two of us for Christmas dinner or is Aunt Grace coming up?'

'I thought we might go out,' James said, once more successfully evading a direct question.

'Really? How many times have I suggested that in the past and had to listen to you say you wanted nothing to do with plastic turkey and boiled-to-death Brussels sprouts?'

James did not respond. Instead, he feigned interest in the book in his hands.

'Why the change of heart? Dad?'

He looked sterner than I had ever seen him as he put down the copy of *To Kill a Mockingbird* and said, 'I just thought it might be nice. And…'

He did not finish the sentence.

'And?' Laurel asked.

'And Helen invited us to join herself and Iris.'

'That makes more sense.'

Ignoring his daughter's tone, he continued, 'She's taking Iris to a twelve o'clock sitting at Òran Mór. She thought it would be nice if it wasn't just the two of them, so she asked if we'd like to come too. Poor Helen has to go to her parents' house in the evening and do it all over again. And I thought that if she's willing to have two Christmas dinners because she cares about a friend, it was the least we could do. I also thought you might enjoy it.'

'So, Aunt Grace isn't coming up?'

'No.'

I was surprised, and a little disappointed, by Laurel's response to her father's suggestion. I knew of her interest in Iris and could not fathom why she seemed unable to enthusiastically embrace the opportunity to meet a woman about whom she seemed so curious. It appeared that where her father was concerned, she could not be trusted to behave in a rational manner. I remembered overhearing James Buchanan talk about the way in which he had behaved after his wife's death and wondered if this might be at the root of Laurel's difficulties.

What James said then challenged this assumption.

'I know it's your first Christmas on your own and in this place. I thought some company, other than me, might be good.'

Had I ears, they would have pricked up.

I chastised myself for not wondering at a woman of Laurel's age being unencumbered. I suppose I had assumed that, like Sandra, Laurel had merely chosen to focus more on her career.

'I don't want to talk about this.'

'You never do. It's been months and I don't even know why you left him.'

'I told you I don't want to talk about it,' Laurel said, in a tone that seemed intended to shut down the conversation. 'All you need to know is that it wasn't my fault.'

'I've never suggested it was,' James said, continuing to talk about it.

'You didn't have to,' she said, with more than a hint of venom.

He looked truly hurt as he defended himself. 'That's not fair. I liked Christopher. I can't say I didn't.'

An unpleasant noise escaped from Laurel's throat.

'But you're my daughter,' he said, 'and I've supported your decision without question.'

'He was always very good at getting people to like him,' she said.

After this day they only ever referred to Christopher in oblique terms in my presence. I was left to wonder about this man who had caused Laurel so much hurt and distress that his very name was off limits between father and daughter.

When James left, I fully expected Laurel to pour herself a whisky, in the likeness of her father, or a glass of red wine, as Iris may have done.

She did neither.

Instead, she made herself a mug of tea that smelled surprisingly like my memory of the aroma of freshly cut grass.

Laurel was off for almost three weeks over Christmas and the New Year. During this time, she took me with her wherever she went. Mostly I was transported in her backpack, but there were times when she would dress smartly and drop me into a leather handbag – it was tan in colour and had soft lining with vertical stripes in pink and green and brown.

We went mainly to cafés. Once there, Laurel would order a complicated sounding coffee. She would then sit down at a table and use me to create a buffer between herself and the other customers.

This, I confess, is merely my interpretation of the situation. I do not know for certain why she would lay me on the table in front of her and then raise me up in her hands, thereby creating the impression I was being read. I was not. Let me assure you, I can tell the difference.

My most enduring memory of this time is of the afternoon that Laurel took me to the Winter Gardens at the People's Palace. A band played music in one corner. The café was busy, but despite this, she managed to find a table. It was small and had only one chair. The table next to us was just as small but had three people sitting at it.

I found the neighbouring trio quite fascinating. Their hands and faces looked as though they had been fashioned out of pink crepe paper. They wore knitted apparel in cream and various shades of blue. Each one had a head of tight white curls tinged with pastel. I decided, by the way they were quietly bickering, that they must be sisters. One had iridescent powder sprinkled from her forehead to her chin. It seemed that she was the instigator of whatever conflict there was amongst them.

'He did not,' she said.

'Yes. He did,' said the sturdiest of the women.

Agreeing with her hardy sister, the frailest one said something akin to, 'Mm Hm.'

The first one wagged a knotty finger and said, 'I'm telling you, he did not.'

'And I'm telling you, he did,' said the second.

'MM HM,' said the third, nodding her bony head emphatically.

I never did find out who he was and what it was that he was supposed to have done, or not done.

'I'll tell you who did, though,' said the first. 'That bus driver with the lazy eye.'

'Never,' said the second.

'Never,' agreed the third, in something of a whisper.

I felt Laurel's hand tense.

I surveyed the room.

A couple had entered. The man was unremarkable. His companion, however, was striking in that she looked uncannily like a younger version of Laurel.

The couple joined the café queue. This line of men and women of assorted sizes and shapes, stretched back to the door. It blocked our only exit.

Laurel grabbed at her handbag. She stood up – abandoning a hazelnut macchiato and an uneaten scone on which she had spread raspberry jam – and pushed past the old ladies in a way that incited the powdered one to snarl something about manners.

Even though the leather handbag was now over Laurel's shoulder, I was still in her hand as she made her way to the garden part of the Winter Gardens, which, unlike the section with tables, chairs and a band, was virtually deserted. She sat down on a bench in the midst of the desolate rainforest and tried to regulate her breathing.

When she was calmer, she muttered, 'Fucking bastard,' and sat me down next to her on the wood of the bench.

Laurel twisted her body. She strained her neck up and into a corkscrew. She was, I presumed, attempting to spy on the unremarkable man and her young doppelgänger by his side.

Chapter Six

We sat for an age on the bench.

We were screened from prying eyes by pelargonium, fishtail palms, ice plants, birds of paradise and a battalion of subtropical pine trees.

I began to wonder if the unremarkable man had even noticed Laurel's flight into the ferns and, if he had, whether or not his eyes would have had any interest in prying. In the short time I had been able to observe him, it seemed his attention was fixed on his girlish consort and her alone. As I considered this matter, Laurel picked me up.

Her hands were clammy as they held me too close to her face.

I heard the unremarkable man address the girl on his arm.

'You're such a silly thing,' he said.

I would like to be able to report that she did something else, but, in truth, she wrinkled her nose and giggled.

'Am not,' she said, tilting her cherub cheeks downwards.

He reached a hand inside her wool coat and wound it around her waist.

'You are very silly,' he said.

'Fuck sake,' Laurel growled.

I knew from his face that he had heard her.

He hardly moved his head as his eyes swivelled to look round.

'Fuck sake, Chris. Here? Really?' Laurel said without raising her head from my pages.

As he guided the girl away by the arm, I heard her say, 'Who was that, Christopher?'

I imagined he would not answer her question until they were far away under the cold December sky. I also imagined that his answer would not be wholly truthful.

Laurel sat me back down on the bench and exhaled a long, low breath.

When we were on the subway, she slipped me out of her handbag. The air in the carriage was heavy with the scent of sweat and cinnamon. Our fellow commuters were, on the whole, people wearing bulky clothing who gripped multitudinous plastic bags in their hands. I deduced that these red-faced passengers had lately been engaged in the act of last-minute Christmas shopping – a pastime I had heard extolled in jangly television advertisements.

The smooth leather of Laurel's handbag lay beneath me on her lap.

Above us both, Laurel rested the heel of her hands on my front cover. Her fingers stretched up into a blunted peak.

The crush at the mouth of the carriage rose and fell and rose again as the train ate up the stations on its circular route. I watched as the same names went by for a second and a third time: Bridge Street, West Street, Shields Road, Kinning Park, Cessnock. The tide of passengers dipping and surging, dipping and surging.

We were on our fourth sweep of the map when Laurel stood up and dropped me into her bag.

She did not leave the flat for two days.

Finally, she coaxed herself into outdoor clothing and – with me and a gift-wrapped object shaped very like me in her backpack – cycled to her father's house.

After greeting his daughter with the words, 'Merry Christmas,' James Buchanan told her she looked lovely. Despite still being incarcerated, I could tell from the tone of his voice that he was forcing himself not to comment on the fact that the only nod his daughter had made to the season was to pair her khaki trousers, which were neither smart nor new, with a red polo neck jumper.

Laurel's hand brushed my cover as she reached into her backpack in order to liberate my neighbour.

'Let me guess,' her father said. 'Socks?'

'Funny,' Laurel said, her voice deadpan. 'It's a biography of Genghis Khan. I thought it would be right up your street.'

I was not allowed out of my prison all day.

I confess to being a little upset that whilst Laurel, for whom I still feel both great affection and respect, saw fit to bring me with her like some sort of amulet, she did not allow me to see the events of the day unfold. I am therefore, I admit, left disinclined to comment overly much on what transpired, other than to say that once we were in what I presumed to be a restaurant I was able to recognise Helen and Iris's voices and I am happy to disclose that Iris sounded well, if, by the end of the meal, a little intoxicated. I knew this was not the case with Laurel as, unlike Iris, she refused every offer of prosecco and wine that was made to her.

I was on the kitchen table in Laurel's flat when the clock on the wall informed me it was four in the afternoon. Despite the fact I had earlier heard James Buchanan's pleas for his daughter to stay longer and at least have a coffee with him now that they were home, I still did not expect it to be quite so early.

Laurel's face was flushed. I presumed it was due to a combination of her woollen polo neck and the speed at which she had cycled through the city streets. It seemed I was correct because right there in the kitchen in front of me, she peeled her jumper over her head, revealing a tight black top underneath. She tossed the rejected item of clothing over the chair at the bottom of the table and sat down next to me.

'Well she wasn't terrible, I suppose. A bit of a drinker maybe,' she said, into the warm air of the kitchen. 'Then again, it is Christmas day and she is going back to an empty house. Although, I was too and I didn't have three glasses of wine.'

Laurel reached out and touched me. Her fingers pressed into my cover.

'Chris didn't like me drinking. He said I was apt to embarrass myself. But that's not why I stopped. I didn't do it for him. I just stopped enjoying it. Now I can't even stand the smell. Especially beer. The stench of it on someone's breath.'

Laurel made an ugly face.

She pushed herself back from the table and boiled the kettle. As she immersed the tea bag in her mug, I could detect, from across the kitchen, the smell of cloves and liquorice.

The first time Laurel took me to her bedroom was Hogmanay.

The walls of the room looked like they might benefit from a fresh coat of paint. Unlike the sitting room, they appeared to be yellow not by design but due to age. When she put me down next to it, the digital clock on her bedside table declared in green that it was 20:24. Laurel chose a CD from a vertical rack that sat on the floor near her bed. I recognised the voice as Suzanne Vega.

'Mum gave me this. On tape,' she said. 'For my birthday.

The music took me back to the Wilsons' attic. I thought of Heather and of Thomas, which led to inevitable thoughts of Violet and life before. I realised that I had become so preoccupied with Laurel and her willingness to have a relationship with me, that I had become side-tracked. In that moment, I knew with my every fibre that nothing could ever truly replace that which I had lost, or, for any length of time, diminish my thirst for it.

Tom's Diner was playing quietly in the background as Laurel began to speak.

It was then that she first addressed me as Brodie.

'I'm sorry about the early night, Brodie,' she said. 'I hate Hogmanay. Maybe I didn't mind it when I was young. I can't say I remember. But I know I've never been thrilled by the thought that another year is dead and gone. Chris used to say I was a weirdo. He loved all that tramping about in the middle of the night trying to get a view of the fireworks while you're crushed up against a bunch of handsy strangers angling for a quick snog. I just remember being cold. Every year. Cold. Right in my bones.'

As I let the name settle, I lost the train of her speech.

Brodie. A fine moniker. The family name of that most distinguished member of the Edinburgh Town Council and skilled maker of cabinets, Deacon Brodie who, according to the Miss Jean Brodie of my pages, "died cheerfully on a gibbet of his own devising in seventeen-eighty-eight". Indeed, his was a lineage she claimed for herself. Willie Brodie: master of the double life, up until the moment he was not. I accepted the name with gratitude.

Laurel picked me up and put me on the duvet in front of

her. She was sitting crossed-legged.

'This is the first year I've been able to just say fuck it and go to my bed. No doubt he'll be dragging that child about the city. She looked like she'd be happy to hang onto his shirttails. Didn't she? Blech. Oh, Christopher you're so marvellous. What an amazing brain you have. And I'm just a silly little girl. Blech. Fuckwit.'

Laurel took a breath. 'That's not fair,' she said. 'It's not her fault.'

Luka was playing now. Laurel closed her eyes and began to sing. Her voice was quiet as she did: 'You just don't argue anymore. You just don't argue anymore. You just don't argue anymore.' She opened her eyes and sat quietly while Suzanne Vega sang Ironbound.

Laurel lifted me into her lap. 'It's not her fault,' she said, again. 'I'm sure she didn't throw herself at him. Why would she? And I'm quite sure he never told her about me. Or, if he did say something, he wouldn't have told the truth. I bet he got off on all the sneaking about.'

Laurel stared straight ahead. 'She'll see through him soon enough,' she said. 'He'll not manage to pretend to be nice for long. She'll do something that gets right under his skin and that'll be it. Honeymoon period over.'

She started to hum along with Solitude Standing.

'I'm glad it's raining,' she said. 'I hope it's pouring at midnight.'

In the months that followed, Laurel began to take me everywhere with her. I would often be left in the bag in which I had been stowed while she worked at the care home or attended a class or met friends at the pub or visited her dad.

It was during this time that I learned how to focus exclusively on whichever voice I was most interested in and ignore the clatter of extraneous noise that seemed so intent on obscuring it. Often, it would be Laurel's words I would follow, but this was not always so. A case in point is the day Laurel lost me. It was the morning of her first exam: Thursday 1st May 2014; Higher English.

She had taken me to a café. There was no need for her to remove me from her backpack; as has already been established, I was not on the curriculum. Despite this, she lifted me out along with her copy of *King Lear* and the hardback notebook she used for the collection of quotes and the writing of literary essays. I was to the left of her coffee cup; the objects she actually needed to have on the table were to the right.

I presumed we were close to her final destination as, according to her watch, it was almost seven thirty and I had heard her say that the exam was due to commence at nine.

Laurel was jotting down notes when a female customer at the next table caught my attention. She was talking into her phone. There was something about the way she looked and the way in which she spoke that led me to believe she warranted close observation. Her brightly coloured lips dripped syrup into the mouthpiece of her mobile phone. I screened out the voices of the other patrons and listened only to her.

Uh huh. York's lovely, but I'd rather be with you.

(   )

That's just Cheryl. You know what she's like. Up with the lark. She's whining that we're leaving today and she wants to get out and about. At this hour.

(   )

A walk round the wall, I think. You know me, I'll need at least two coffees before I'm fit for it.

( )

No. Not a big night. Just us girls talking.

( )

I was going to pick up something for Rose. What d'you think she'd like?

( )

Really? A book?

( )

I better run, too. Cheryl's tapping her foot.

( )

Love you, more.

We were, even I knew, somewhere in Glasgow and not anywhere in York; I complimented myself on my ability to spot a bad human.

Laurel looked down at her watch. She said, 'Oh shit.'

She stood up.

She tugged at her jacket, pulling it off the back of her seat. In doing so, she knocked her chair into the table, unsettling it and everything on it. She grabbed at the table top. She managed to steady it before her coffee mug could smash onto the floor. She looked relieved as she dropped the notebook and the copy of *King Lear* into her open backpack.

She hurried to the door of the café and ran out of it.

I saw the door close behind her.

In her haste, Laurel had failed to notice that I had fallen to the floor.

The bad human at the next table reached down and picked me up.

The café door was pushed open again.

Laurel rushed in.

She ran over to what had been our table.

A waitress was wiping it with a cloth – a cloth I was sure was not clean.

'Brodie,' Laurel said.

The waitress looked up from what she was doing.

'My book. I left it on the table. I need it. I need my book.'

The waitress shrugged at Laurel.

As she did, the bad human slipped me into her handbag.

Part Five. Rose
2014 - 2018

Chapter One

Once inside the cramped faux-designer handbag, I grieved the loss of Laurel. She had been a fine guardian and, I might almost contend, a friend.

My thoughts, though, had no option but to turn to the stranger to whom I would soon belong. My keen listening skills had left me in no doubt that this person would be called Rose.

I had two points of reference for someone with this name.

The first was contained within my own pages – Rose Stanley, who was, quite erroneously, famous for sex.

The second came from a book in whose presence I had once spent some time. It was a Ladybird classic of the "much loved" – according to the spiel on the front – Brothers Grimm story, *Snow-White and Rose-Red*. As is my want, whilst in the company of this, rather chatty, book, I had questioned it on the story held within its covers.

In doing so, I had learned that unlike her fairest of the fair sister, Snow-White, Rose-Red had lips that were the deepest of red, like that of the flower for which she was named, and her hair was as black as ebony. I wondered if my Rose would be similarly arrayed. I was hopeful that she might be.

I feel it right that I should make a confession at this juncture.

Much as I had experienced a deep connection to Laurel, I was hopeful that Rose might be more akin to Violet or

Heather. I had found the vigour of my first two guardians enlivening and, in the wake of my time with Iris and Laurel, I felt in need of a long draught of the elixir of youth.

One of my neighbours in the handbag began to play an irritating tune. I read the words *Nialls Mob* on the screen of the annoying object. I presumed this was shorthand for Niall's mobile phone and was horrified by the absence of the apostrophe.

A hand with long lacquered nails reached in to remove the phone. I overheard the bad human laugh.

I would, in time, come to know the bad human as the-bad-evil-human-called-Gaynor-who-took-me-captive-and-thus-deprived-Laurel-of-a-dear-and-loyal-companion but for the purposes of clean prose I will shorten this to Gaynor, for now.

I heard Gaynor tell Niall that she, too, was counting down the hours. She said that she missed him so much she had convinced Cheryl to get an earlier train. She would be home by six.

We did indeed get on a train, but, if the clock function on Gaynor's phone was to be believed, we did so within the hour. The destination of this train was Edinburgh. I learned this from the return ticket next to which I had been slotted.

Once we had exited the station, Gaynor pushed her way through what seemed to be busy streets before spending time in a succession of heavily perfumed shops. Her burgundy nails, that had each been carefully shaped into a point, reached in and out of her handbag all afternoon, removing her large leather purse and dropping it back in again, often hitting me on the spine in the process.

I spent much of this time trying to work out the following: why Gaynor was lying to Niall; what she had been doing the previous evening whilst in Glasgow, not York, and with whom she had been doing it.

I am sad to report I was never able to answer these questions.

According to the time displayed on the phone, we arrived at the house closer to seven. After extracting what I had found to be a most convenient of timepieces, Gaynor deposited her handbag in the vicinity of the door through which we had passed.

From the faint sounds that reached me, I had decided that Niall and Gaynor must be engaged in the preparation of dinner and that I was in for an uncomfortable night on the hall floor. I was therefore surprised when, having not heard the tap-tap of her high heels coming towards me, the handbag was opened and Gaynor's fingers lifted me into the light.

In the café, I had presumed her hair was dyed blonde, but I now found myself unsure if it was or if it was just unnaturally fair. Her large blue eyes were heavily made up in shades of gold and brown. Her cheekbones were prominent thanks only to the line of peach blusher that defined them. It looked as though she had recently reapplied dewy paint on her lips.

Without moving from the hall, Gaynor read my back cover and flicked through my pages. The haste with which she did so, however, meant she failed to notice Sandra's inscription, which had faded only slightly with the passing of years. I was sure she had not seen it because she did not stop to read it.

It was at this point my attention was drawn to her left hand. I saw a large diamond. It was mounted on a band of white gold and sat proudly on her ring finger.

'Gaynor,' Niall shouted, in what I felt sure was an Irish accent.

'A minute,' she said in reply.

Before she walked into the kitchen, she turned to the gilt-edged mirror on the wall. She smoothed her long hair and leaned in until she was so close, her breath was on the glass. I presumed she did this in order to satisfy herself that she was still as beautiful as she believed herself to be.

When we arrived in the kitchen, Niall had his back to us. He was chopping what I assumed to be vegetables.

The black leather of his belt and his shoes looked to be of good quality but his grey trousers had a shine to them that I did not find appealing. I could see through the white of his shirt that his waistline was a little thick. He was also not as tall as I presumed he, or indeed Gaynor, might have liked.

'Look,' Gaynor said, holding me out to him.

He did not turn around.

'Niall. Look,' she said.

This time he swung around to face us.

'My hands aren't clean,' he said.

He held them up as if to demonstrate. I noted he was still holding the knife. I also noted that despite how he looked from the back, his countenance was in fact most pleasing. He was short, granted, but his face was strong and his eyes were unlike any others I had seen. They were a weave of dark brown and dark blue and light brown and light blue, all together, and each keen orb was encircled by a fringe of long black eyelashes. I admit I felt a little overcome in his presence.

'I thought you'd be pleased,' Gaynor said. 'It's a classic. It says so on the back.'

She then proceeded to tell Niall a labyrinthine tale about how she had searched high and low and then, whilst exploring the length and breadth of what sounded like an excessively long cobbled lane, she came across a charming bookshop. This was where she had, apparently, found me. She declared that it had taken her ages to choose just the right book.

'I felt sure Rose would like it because it's set in Edinburgh.'

'I'm sure she'll love it,' Niall said.

Unfortunately, his tone suggested that he was in no way convinced that Rose would in fact love me.

'Why don't you put it in her room while I finish here?' he said.

This was an unfortunate suggestion because it meant that I was cast out of their company and would have to wait weeks before I saw another human being.

On the plus side, that next human being I saw was Rose.

I heard her before she came into view.

She stamped up the stairs in a way that alerted me to the presence of someone new in the house. When she pushed open the bedroom door, I saw at once that her appearance was in no way similar to that of Rose Stanley, her hair being neither blond nor short. However, I thought a case could be made for her being not unlike her fairy tale counterpart, Rose-Red, in that her hair was in fact a surging tide of black and her lips were as bright a red as it seemed possible for them to be. Her eyes were a singular colour – the blue of the darkest blue in her father's eyes – and she was small.

It was clear that she was young but at this moment I found myself uncertain as to her actual age. I thought she could be eleven or twelve. But, as I studied her, I also thought she might be nineteen or twenty. The truth, I would find out later, was somewhere in the middle.

She was weighted down by bags that hung over both of her

shoulders. I could hear Niall somewhere behind her, saying he could have helped. The door swung shut on his voice.

Rose dropped one of the bags from either arm onto the floor and then threw the two that were still on her shoulders onto the bed. The smaller of them, which was constructed of a scratchy material I thought might be hemp or jute, landed on me. By the weight of it, it seemed it must contain the unlikely combination of clumpy boots and dictionary-sized hardback books.

I hoped that rather than this being an intentional act of cruelty, Rose had not in fact noticed that I was there.

It was while I was pinned to the bed in this way that I heard music. Despite the circumstances in which I found myself, and whilst I could identify neither the artist nor even the genre, I was pleased to hear it. I focused on its tone. Thankfully, this enabled me to distract myself from the discomfort I was being forced to endure; a burden that might otherwise have been too heavy for me to bear.

Rose began to sing along. Her voice was ethereal.

In addition to this dulcet refrain, I was aware of noises that suggested she was unpacking her bags and depositing their contents into the wardrobe and drawers. I hoped she might soon finish with the two on the floor so that she could tackle those she had hurled onto the bed. In particular, the hefty one by which I was being crushed.

It seemed she somehow became aware of my plight, for as soon as I had this thought, Rose lifted up the bag and set it down on the floor.

It was then that she noticed me.

She bent down.

I knew her hands would be soft as they reached out towards me. She touched me with the tips of her fingers and then eased me up towards her face. I could see the faintest of frown lines pucker her pale brow as she moved me from the bed to the dressing table.

Once she seemed satisfied that all of her belongings had been appropriately stowed, she picked me up and took me downstairs.

She walked through the kitchen into an airy conservatory.

'Did you get me this?' she asked.

Her accent was a Scottish Irish blend that favoured the former over the latter thanks, I would learn, to having been born in Edinburgh and having spent most of her formative years, up until recently, on this side of the Irish Sea.

Her father grinned as he said, 'Is that an accusation, darling?'

'What was it doing on my bed?'

Niall Fitzgerald looked a little hurt as he said, 'Rose, darling, it's just a gift. Gaynor thought you might like it.'

At that, Rose dropped me onto the tiled floor.

'Now then, Rose, come on.'

'I don't want it. I don't want anything from her. I said I'd spend the start of the holidays here, with you, as long as she didn't come anywhere near me and now she's been in my room. I'm phoning Mum.'

Niall picked me up from the floor and placed me on a small glass table. He asked his daughter to sit down. It took him a while, but he eventually convinced her to do so. What was most notable in the exchange that followed was how calm Rose's father stayed in the face of her unkind words. She made it abundantly clear that she despised Gaynor and was distressed that her father, who was so smart in so many other ways had not been able to see through her. When Niall said it would mean a great deal to him if she could begin to think of Gaynor as a member of the family and treat her with the respect that was appropriate, Rose spat back at him that she would never think of that woman as anything other than a conniving witch and that if her father actually went through with the wedding, she would not be there and she would certainly not be wearing some hideous dress designed to make her look like she was twelve years old.

Whilst I was saddened by the way in which Rose had chosen to speak to her father, I had thought she was on solid ground up until this point in her argument. It seemed to me that any dress could well make her look as though she were still a child, immaterial of its design.

Rose began to cry.

Chapter Two

I had observed Niall's face keenly as his daughter shouted and waved her arms, it neither reddened nor creased. His voice was even and his eyes remained kind.

'It's just an adjustment,' I heard him say. 'It's not about Gaynor. I know that. It's about us: you and me. And you'll always be my wee girl. You know nothing can ever change that.'

He drew her tiny, resisting form to himself and held her. His arms, like his face, were resolute. I saw the tension release from Rose's body, at least for a moment, as Niall assured her that everything was going to be alright. He said she must know that he loved her more than anything else in the world, more than anyone else. It was at these words that the stiffness re-entered first her spine and then her shoulders.

Rose followed her father into the kitchen.

As good fortune would have it, my position on the glass table was not terrible; I was able to watch Niall, his back to me, preparing their meal and I could still hear their conversation. He told Rose he was going to cook her favourite dinner. It seemed this lifted her mood. Her voice regained the delicate quality I had detected earlier when she sang in the bedroom; it was almost musical as she told him about her flight from Dublin.

A delicious aroma reached me in the conservatory as I listened to the satisfactory sound of what I believed was steak being prepared.

'It's lovely, Dad,' she said as they sat just out of sight at what I presumed was the kitchen island.

'Listen, darling,' he said. 'You're only here for three weeks. Could we try to have a nice time? Please? I haven't seen you since Easter.'

Rose did not reply.

Niall changed tack. He asked her about her exams. Rose was non-committal on this topic, also. She told her father that he knew all there was to know, having phoned her every night during them. She said her feelings towards them had not altered in the two weeks since they had ended. She was pleased, however, that school was finally over and she was relieved she only had to endure one more year of it.

'I don't think you'd have felt like that if you'd stayed in Edinburgh,' Niall said, a little cautiously. 'You used to love school.'

Rose did not respond.

Niall said, 'You know you can always come back here to do sixth year.' His voice rose, suggesting there might be a question, or even a request, implied in this statement.

'Don't start, Dad.'

'I'm sorry, darling,' he said. 'I won't mention it again. Cross my heart.'

It took Niall less than a day to break this promise, by which time I had been moved into a small, informal sitting room. Niall had carried me there that morning.

I have to admit, I was a little disgruntled at his decision to relocate me as I had spent a pleasant night under the stars: the conservatory having been constructed almost entirely out of glass.

Rose and her father were watching highlights from the first week of Wimbledon on television and were discussing their hopes that Andy Murray might win his second in a row, when Niall raised the contentious subject again. I was glad he had broken his vow because the dialogue that followed was most illuminating.

If you will be generous enough to allow me a moment of flagrant exposition, I will share the pieces of biographical gold that I was able to mine as a result of this most productive piece of eavesdropping. In the spirit of full disclosure, I should explain that in order to provide the most useful account, I have ordered this explanatory treatise chronologically and have, in addition, inserted salient facts gathered at other times:

i.   Rose was born in Scotland;

ii. Rose's parents are both Irish (they met as students in Edinburgh);

iii. Rose's parents never married but she was given her father's surname, Fitzgerald, as they agreed a child named Rose Fitzgerald may fare better in life than one named Rose Hogg;

iv. Rose's parents lived together until she was three (or thereabouts);

v.   Rose's parents remained on good terms and for many years lived only one street away from one another in order to share parental duties;

vi. when Rose was fourteen (or thereabouts) her mother married a lawyer named Fergal (with whom she had also been at university);

vii. when Rose was fifteen (or thereabouts) Fergal accepted a job offer in Dublin;

viii. Rose and her mother moved with Fergal to the Irish capital, after a great deal of soul searching all around;

ix. Niall visited his daughter regularly;

x. when Rose was sixteen (or thereabouts) her mother, Niamh, produced two children (the test tube twins, as Gaynor was in the habit of referring to them);

xi. Niamh, being almost forty, greatly appreciated any and all assistance Rose could provide with her boisterous baby boys, Dermott and Declan;

xii. Rose, a most dutiful daughter and half-sister, did not feel able to return to Scotland to finish her schooling, despite a deep desire to do so (she had not fitted in at her school in Dublin; she, in fact, hated it with each and every fibre of her being and missed her Scottish school and her Scottish schoolfriends).

Their exchange – which at times veered towards heated debate on the part of the younger Fitzgerald – left Rose, for the second time in as many days, both in tears and threatening to call her mother.

Niall had remained even-tempered, even amiable, throughout. When Rose began to cry, he apologised for having brought the subject up and assured her that it was truly the last time he would do so.

It was not.

Whilst this was all very interesting, I found myself preoccupied with thoughts of Gaynor and what had become of her.

I felt quite sure that ordinarily she shared the house with Niall – although it seemed unlikely that Rose had been informed of this controversial living arrangement. I could not fathom where she might be. I hoped she was not back in

"York" doing whatever it was she had done on her last visit to this fictive version of what I knew to be a very real town in the north of England, one, which if the opportunity were ever to arise, I would be keen to visit.

Due to the cursedly robust nature of the soundproofing in the solid example of Scottish house construction that now served as my abode, I had not gleaned any information in the weeks since Gaynor had allowed me to fall from her cold fingers onto Rose's bed. I therefore knew nothing of whatever plan had been hatched to conceal her from Rose. Indeed, I knew precious little of her relationship with Niall other than the troubling details I discovered on that first day in May. Except, of course, that she appeared to be considerably younger than him.

As luck would have it, once Rose had retired for the evening, Niall, still in my presence, phoned her evil-stepmother-to-be. Gaynor did not answer the phone. This prompted Niall to leave a nauseating message, which did little to elucidate the situation.

'It's me again, darling. I miss you. I promise I'll speak to Rose tomorrow. She's just a bit fragile at the moment. I'll call you later. Love you, darling. Did I mention I miss you?'

As far as I could tell, Niall had left for work before Rose emerged the following morning. She slouched into the television room, as I had now begun to think of it, with a bowl of cereal in one hand and a spoon in the other. She threw herself down onto one of the comfortable-looking chairs. Somehow no milk was spilled on either the cream fabric of the seat or on Rose's outfit of black leggings and a short-sleeved red floral dress. She watched breakfast television whilst crunching her way through the brown flakes in her bowl. By reason of our close proximity,

I was able to scrutinise her young face, for that is what it appeared to be; too young for the age I now knew she must be – seventeen, give or take a birthday.

There were dark shadows underneath the blue oceans that served as her eyes, but, inexplicably, even these did not make her look like she could be much beyond her first decade. I wondered when a change would occur; I tried to imagine how she might look once her face had undergone the transition that was already evident in her body. As I watched her jaw move hypnotically, I imagined that this question was at times a concern for Rose also. I felt quite sure that she would likely be anxious for it to happen. I felt equally as confident that in years to come she would lament all that she had lost by virtue of the transformation.

In the week that followed, I was entirely untouched. I did not mind, too much, however, as I was reasonably well entertained: the room in which I was resident appeared to function, at least in the evening, as the heart of the home.

It seemed peace had been brokered between father and daughter for Rose and Niall came and went harmoniously. During this time, accompanied by the quiet din of murder mysteries and some rather dull programmes on home improvement, they would reminisce about years gone by. I came to understand something of the texture of Rose's childhood from these conversations. It seemed that, up until the move to Dublin, she had been happy, as had both of her parents. To his credit, I detected that Niall did not harbour feelings of bitterness towards either Niamh or Fergal. It sounded, at least from what he said to his daughter, that he was pleased his erstwhile love had found happiness with a man he seemed to deem worthy of her and of Rose; a man he felt could be trusted to participate in the parenting of his daughter.

Their truce lasted only until the Sunday afternoon of the Wimbledon final.

Despite their disappointment that Andy Murray would not be playing, father and daughter gathered in the television room to watch the battle ensue on centre court.

I did not hear a key turn in the front door.

I did not notice a figure enter the room; I, too, was engrossed in the televisual spectacle.

The first instant I was aware of Gaynor's presence was when her voice broke into the commentary.

'There's my favourite girl,' she said, quite inexplicably.

I cannot say whether it was Rose or Niall who looked most shocked. I would say that an expression akin to horror passed across both their faces. Gaynor, however, appeared wholly unaware of the distress her appearance had quite evidently caused.

She swept across the room and leant down to, I presume, embrace Rose.

As she did, Rose leapt to her feet.

This resulted in something of a collision. Sadly, Gaynor's body blocked a significant portion of my view. However, it was evident to me that the top of Rose's ascending head had glanced Gaynor's descending face.

Reeling backwards, Gaynor turned around.

Blood issued forth from her nose.

The scene that followed, was, as you can imagine, quite dramatic. In short, Gaynor insisted that she had been attacked by Rose. Horrified, Rose maintained that it had been an accident. Niall chose to side with his daughter.

After Rose fled into the hallway, Gaynor and Niall were

left standing either side of the table on which I lay. By this point in the proceedings, Gaynor had staunched the flow of blood using a white cotton handkerchief Niall had produced from somewhere about his person. She was using this now unsightly cloth to dab at the tears that refused to cease and desist.

Without moving towards her shaking form, Niall asked Gaynor to calm down. He told her it had just been a terrible accident and that she was fine. He kept repeating: you're fine; there's no harm done; you're fine.

This, however, did nothing to appease his unhappy fiancée.

'Come away with me into the kitchen, darling,' he said. 'I'll fix you a drink and we can get you properly cleaned up.'

Niall reached out and took Gaynor's hand.

Chapter Three

My disappointment at having been left alone was tempered only by the fact that they had not turned off the television. In fact, this did not happen until the early evening, by which point I was heartily sick of armchair experts.

Niall came in and put an end to the voices in the corner.

As he left the room, he tipped up his head and shouted, 'Rose, darling, we're off out for a bite to eat. Won't be long.'

I heard no reply.

Now that the din had been silenced, I was able to consider what might have transpired in the aftermath of Gaynor's bloodied nose.

I decided that the most likely course of events was that once Niall had settled her with a drink and a fresh handkerchief, he had joined his daughter in her room and sought to do likewise, minus the alcohol. I hoped he had been able to both calm and appease Rose and that he had perhaps even convinced her to stay. As I mulled this thought over, I came to realise that much as Rose did not care for me, I had begun to care quite deeply for her. There was a vulnerability about her that I found compelling and I had developed something of a fellow feeling for her based on the fact that she too had had her life-course altered through no fault, or choice, of her own.

I was therefore greatly heartened that whatever had in fact occurred, Rose was still there the next morning. She even returned to the scene of the crime and chomped her way through a bowl of cereal. I presumed that Niall and Gaynor were at work because the nine o'clock news was just beginning as Rose turned on the television.

I was wrong.

A programme about buying houses in need of renovation was partway through when Niall joined his daughter. He, too, looked to be wearing pyjamas. Thankfully, when Gaynor joined them moments later, she had changed out of her nightwear, which I was quite sure would be inappropriate attire outwith the bedroom.

Niall was the first to speak.

He told his female companions that he was grateful to both of them for their understanding and their willingness to put the events of the previous day behind them.

He turned his head from one side to the other as he explained how important they each were to him and how he dearly hoped that Rose would discover what a special person Gaynor was, if she would only give herself the chance to do so. He said he was incredibly thankful to Rose as she had promised him that she would try. Despite the smile that appeared to have been carved into Gaynor's face, I was sure I noticed her wince at the word "try".

Niall then seemed to recap part of a speech he had given to Rose the previous evening. From what he said, I was able to deduce that it had always been the plan that he and Gaynor would take two weeks off to coincide with Rose's visit and that those two weeks began that morning. It seemed that Niall and Gaynor had felt, despite not consulting Rose about it in advance, that this would be a perfect opportunity for Rose to get to know Gaynor properly. The wedding was in September, after all, and Gaynor would dearly love if

Rose would agree to be a bridesmaid. At this, Rose's face, which had seemed unhealthily pale, flushed red. I did not seem to be alone in noticing the change in her appearance, for Niall ended his speech at this point with the words, 'but let's not get ahead of ourselves.'

Gaynor, her carefully made-up face a study in forced composure, said, 'I really hope we can have a nice time together, Rose.'

Rose did not speak, but the muscles around her jaw appeared to clench more tightly. It seemed she had decided that saying nothing was the safer path.

'So, why don't you take yourself upstairs and get ready, darling, and I'll do the same,' Niall said. 'We're going to whisk you away on a magical mystery tour.'

Rose was rising to her feet when Gaynor stretched forward and touched me with her icy fingers. With a supercilious smile she looked directly at Rose and said, 'Your book.'

Gaynor held me out towards her young rival as she said, 'I hope you like it.'

Rose became a statue in the room.

It seemed clear to me, that, in this action, Gaynor was rather recklessly attempting to seize the upper hand. Rose, I gathered, had made promises to her father, but in this moment these assurances were being sorely tested. I can only assume that it was in deference to such vows that Rose reached out and took me from Gaynor's hand. Her short fingernails were sharp as she accepted me from her evil-stepmother-to-be.

Rose's nails dug further into my cover as she climbed the stairs. I could well have felt aggrieved at this, but I chose to accept the discomfort; I knew Rose was not to blame.

She dropped me onto the dressing table. As I reoriented myself, I noticed that the bedroom looked different. The plain cream bedding was now covered by a woollen blanket in deep red. Cushions in various lighter shades of this colour had been stacked in front of the cream pillows and there was a deep pile rug on the floor. It, too, was red.

In addition, there was now a large picture on the wall. It was a print of a painting by Raoul Dufy and appeared to be his impression of a room, perhaps a room he himself had known. The entire scene seemed, to my untrained eye, as though it had been pink-washed. Before I try to describe it further, I feel the need to apologise for what I know will be my inability to convey the beauty I beheld within it.

In the foreground, there was a small round wooden table; only its top was visible. On this, there was a vase of flowers. Behind the vase of flowers, a painting hung on the wall. In this painting, the one that was hanging on the wall of the imagined room, there was a vase of flowers.

Raoul Dufy's name and two dates, 1901 and 1931 were written at the bottom of the print in what I took to be the painter's hand. In between these two dates, the following phrase had been inscribed: *30 ans ou la vie en rose.*

In the days that followed I found myself unable to divert my attention from the pink room and the picture of a vase of flowers within a picture of a vase of flowers. I would torment myself with the thought that if I were to concentrate with every atom of my being, I might find myself able to move from this room to that room.

You may be unsurprised to learn that, no matter the intensity of my focus, I never managed this feat of transcendental teleportation.

In the moments when I was not attempting to thwart the physical order, I directed my thoughts towards Rose.

I was pleased she had attempted to make the bedroom her own. I did wonder however how much encouragement and, or, help she had received from her father. I hoped he had done no more than merely drive her to whichever repository of décor and soft furnishings it had been necessary for her to visit in order to infuse the room with at least some sense of her personality.

I, however, digress. I should, for the purpose of the proper telling of Rose's story, return to that first morning I spent on the dressing table.

I observed Rose prepare for the day ahead, both physically and mentally. First, she removed her pyjamas and replaced them with a pair of black leggings – a form of uniform it seemed. She added a number of layers in the form of a long black t-shirt and an equally long red blouse. She pulled on knee length black socks which she ruched down and a pair of black midcalf boots that were stout in their construction.

I thought her style was a little reminiscent of Violet's and found myself heartened by this notion, if a little surprised as almost three decades had passed since I had observed Violet don equally stalwart footwear. This train of thought began to cause me pain, so I dismissed it and focused once more on the here and now.

In terms of what I presumed to be mental preparation, Rose sat down on the edge of the bed and folded her head and then her arms out over her knees. She stayed in this position until I heard Niall shout, 'Rose. Rose. Are you ready, darling?'

She unfurled, applied red to her lips, courtesy of the lipstick to my left, and extracted a small black handbag from the wardrobe.

When Rose returned that evening, she looked even paler than when she had left. She pulled out the stool from the dressing table and took a seat in front of me. Despite her proximity to the mirror, she did not appear interested in her appearance. Instead, she unzipped her handbag and eased out a mobile phone that looked to be almost as long and wide as the bag in which it had been contained.

I watched as she used the keypad to write the following message: Back now. Horrible. Hope boys behaving. Almost immediately after sending, the phone in her hands sprung to life.

(   )

I can't even tell you, Mum.

(   )

I know but I just don't like her.

(   )

I am trying.

(   )

I am.

(   )

I need you to be on my side about this. Tell Dad it's not on. I can't stay in the same house as that woman.

(   )

It's not the same, Mum.

(   )

It's not. Fergal's nothing like her.

(   )

I do want Dad to be happy.

(   )

I'll try. I promise.

(   )

So how are the boys?

(   )

No!

(   )

Completely naked?

(   )

He did not!

(   )

That Dermott will be the death of us. You'd never catch little Prince Declan doing that. Not in a public park.

(   )

I suppose they're asleep?

(   )

I'll try and catch them tomorrow. Maybe we could Skype?

(   )

Bye. Love you. Bye.

It was another couple of hours before Rose put out the light. In the meantime, she sent myriad texts and ate two mallow type biscuits that she had dug out of one of the large bags that was ordinarily stowed under her bed – when not being raided for foodstuff. I assumed she had brought it with her from Ireland. I thought these delicacies, which, according to their packet were Original Kimberley Biscuits, looked as though they would taste very good: the inner spongy, sugary filling was surrounded by an outer sandwich that radiated the faint aroma of ginger. Their downside, however, was the fact that they seemed to be impossible to eat without the shedding of crumbs. These tiny particles fell from Rose's mouth into the creases of the bedclothes that surrounded her. I felt quite sure this would diminish the quality of her sleep, as in the case of the princess in *The Princess and the Pea*; a book I had encountered during my time in Violet's bedroom.

Over the nights that followed, I would have occasion to watch Rose eat a variety of biscuits from the bag I had come to think of as her treasure trove of treats. These were, in order: original Kimberley's; chocolate-covered Kimberley's; Mint Clubs; Fruit Clubs; Custard Creams and Orange Creams.

Rose never overindulged, having no more than two in any one sitting.

In this time, I also listened to one half of a number of whispered conversations Rose had with a boy called Ryan, which led me to believe that she was in the first flush of a romance. It seemed likely that many of her written communications were either to, or from, him. Unfortunately, she did not often use her mobile phone at the dressing table, preferring, I presumed for reasons of comfort, to sit on her bed with pillows and cushions piled up at her back. I was therefore unable to read their text messages and was forced to imagine what they might contain based on the one-sided phone conversations I had overheard.

Chapter Four

Whilst I was frustrated by my lack of access to the many epistles on Rose's phone, I was happy that, even so, I had less fettered access to her life than say her parents.

I knew about Ryan, which I was sure neither of them did, and I knew he was a major factor in Rose's decision not to return to Dublin early, as she had threatened to do.

Thanks to her penchant for reminiscence, I was aware that Rose and Ryan had rekindled an old friendship as a result of an accidental meeting six months earlier during the Christmas holidays, some of which Rose had spent with her father. This was evidence enough for me to be quite sure that Ryan was, in fact, from Edinburgh.

As the hushed phone calls increased, and became more intimate, I discovered that Rose's daily runs were merely a cover, allowing her to meet up with her young beau. I also learned that Rose was now considering not only extending her holiday, at the home her father shared with Gaynor, but she had even begun to contemplate returning to Scotland to undertake her last year of schooling. This became known to me not only as a result of her steamy phone exchanges with Ryan, but also from the way in which she had begun to frame her calls with her mother.

Seeds were sprinkled night after night as follows: a brief mention of how nice it was to be back in Edinburgh; an acknowledgement of just how much she had missed the city; an anecdote about meeting up with old school friends; an acknowledgment of how much she had missed their company; a story about bumping into a former teacher; an acknowledgement of how much she had enjoyed school up until she moved to Dublin; an acknowledgement that she had missed out on spending the last two years with her father; a confession that she had had a deep desire to make the most of the time she might have with her father before he got married to the wicked witch of the east.

Rose's strategy culminated in a tearful Skype call with her mother two nights before she was due to board the plane for her return journey to Dublin.

Minutes later, there was a knock on the bedroom door.

Niall entered the room for the first time since I had been placed on the dressing table. Rose was cross-legged on the bed, sniffling. He motioned a request to sit down next to her. She nodded in assent.

'I just had your mum on the phone, darling,' he said.

Rose's fingers felt their way under one of the pillows behind her. She removed a tissue and blew her nose.

'She says that maybe you would like to stay on for a bit.'

Rose blew her nose for a second time.

'You know I'd love that but before I go changing any flights, I wanted to check it's what you really want,' He extended his hand towards her. 'Is it? Is that what you want to do, darling?'

Snuffling, Rose nodded her head.

Niall's face contorted a little in a manner that I could only surmise meant that he was thrilled by this unexpected change of heart but was trying not to influence his daughter by alerting her to his delight.

'I'm worried about Mum though. How will she cope with the boys?' Rose said, sounding genuinely remorseful.

Niall reached out and took his daughter's hand in his.

'Your mum would never want you to think that way, Rose, darling. You know that.'

He went on to assure Rose that both he and her mother had only ever wanted what was best for her. He reminded her that that was the very reason he had agreed to her move to Dublin; back then it had seemed like the right thing for Rose, being that there were two sets of grandparents in the city as well as Niamh and Fergal to care for her. Niall pulled his daughter's hand close to him and said that now she was seventeen, and with the situation at school, maybe it was time for a rethink.

Rose looked wretched as she nodded.

I, however, found this development to be most welcome. I had not relished the thought of being abandoned in an empty room for all eternity, or until Gaynor had decided to dispose of me by means of pulp machine or flame, and I had been quite certain that Rose had no intention of packing me into one of the bags under the bed and taking me with her to Dublin – a city I would dearly have loved to have visited, temporarily, and then be brought back to Scotland in order that I might somehow find my way home.

This change in circumstance meant that I now had more time to try to encourage a bond with my young custodian, a task to which I had earnestly applied myself for over a week (in the moments when she was in the bedroom and I was not engaged in the pursuit of cosmic transfer to allow me to journey into the pink room in the painting).

I did, I can assure you, realise the enormity of a project whose sole objective was to cause Rose to feel anything towards me other than hostility – due to my association, in her mind, with Gaynor.

I should also say that I was in no way sure I had in fact any powers of telepathy. However, the relationship I had experienced with Laurel had cultivated within me a sense that such a possibility may exist.

When Niall was safely downstairs, Rose phoned Ryan in order to convey the exciting news that she would not be leaving in two days. She assured him she would tell him all about it when she saw him on her morning run. She ended the call with a promise to meet at eleven o'clock in their usual place.

I found myself wondering where this spot might be: a park; a café; a street corner; a bus shelter. I tried to picture Rose and Ryan, in the form in which I had chosen to forge him, sharing an embrace in each place. As a result of this less than scientific survey, I decided that their secret spot was most likely to be under an oak tree in the nearest park.

The next thing I saw Rose do was push herself off the bed and make her way towards the dressing table. She sat down on the stool and placed her mobile phone not an inch away from me. As she began to type a message to her mother, I speculated that I might indeed have the facility to bend human actions to my will.

The missive she composed was brief and more than a little dismal. She opened with an apology, stating that she was sorry she would not be home to help look after the boys. She then asked her mother to please understand the difficult situation in which she found herself. Rose wrote that she felt terrible, torn as she was between two parents whom she loved equally. She ended with a further expression of remorse regarding the fact that her mother would be bereft of her assistance for the remainder of the summer.

Whilst she was writing this, I admit, I began to worry that Ryan was not a good enough reason for Rose to decide to abandon her mother and choose to live with her father, and Gaynor. My limited experience of matters of the heart suggested that it may not be altogether sensible to trust, unconditionally, the object of one's affection.

Rose, however, appeared smitten and determined to do whatever it might take and, indeed, forgo all that she would have to forgo, in order to further explore her nascent relationship with this young boy. If he was a young boy.

This, I realised, was no more than an assumption. It was, whilst highly unlikely, possible that Ryan was not a teenager at all. What if he was actually a twenty-something-year-old man who taught art or music at her former school or the father of one of her old Edinburgh friends? Once I had had this thought, I found it difficult not to worry about such an eventuality.

The following morning, Rose pulled on black Lycra leggings and a rather tight orange t-shirt. After lacing up her running shoes, she disappeared out of the bedroom door – intent, I presumed, on her assignation with the irresistible Ryan.

When Rose returned to the room that afternoon, she appeared flushed. After a noise I presumed indicated she was in a nearby shower, she re-entered the bedroom in a large fluffy blue towel. She removed her phone from under her pillow, where she had stowed it before leaving the room, and phoned someone I would come to learn was a friend from her former school in Edinburgh called Kate.

(   )

Hey. It's Rose.

(   )

Fitzgerald. How many Roses do you know?

(   )

Don't worry. It's fine. Anyway, you'll never guess.

(   )

I wish! No. I'm going to be staying at my dad's house for the rest of the holidays.

(   )

I'm not sure yet. I might. We're still talking about it.

(   )

It would be great. I hate that school in Dublin. It's full of total bitches.

(   )

I've missed you, too. It was lovely to see everyone at Philippa's. It was so nice of her to invite me, considering how long I've been away.

(   )

What? Ryan Donnelly? No. What do you mean?

(   )

I might have seen him a couple of times. Just bumping into him.

(   )

Olivia? I didn't know that. He said he wasn't going out with anyone.

(   )

I would never. You know that.

(   )

Are you sure they're going out?

(   )

That's my dad shouting me. I better go.

(   )

Bye. Bye.

Rose immediately phoned another number.

(   )

Are you going out with Olivia?

(   )

Kate. I was just on the phone with her. She seemed pretty certain.

(   )

I didn't think it could be right. Sorry.

(   )

I am. Really sorry. And you're right. I shouldn't have accused you without hearing your side.

(   )

Really? I didn't think she was like that. She sounds like a total stalker.

(   )

Same time, same place?

(   )

Bye. Bye.

As you can imagine, I found all of this rather disturbing. However, I was at least able to console myself with the knowledge that the undoubted cad was at least a youthful cad.

I confess I also found myself relieved that Ryan's seemingly convincing denial had ensured Rose was still keen to stay in Edinburgh. However, I now knew the situation to be precarious and recognised that events could take a terrible turn at any moment thanks to the unreliable nature of a hormone-driven youth. If this were in fact to come to pass, I might well once more find myself alone, or perhaps more troubling, at the mercy of Gaynor.

I will also admit to a small moment of self-congratulation, as, without even having met this individual, my instinct had told me that I (and indeed Rose) should be wary of him.

Chapter Five

By early August, I had come to suspect that it had been agreed by all interested parties that Rose should finish her schooling in Edinburgh. I presumed this had been deemed the most sensible course of action in order to ensure she had, academically at least, a productive present and a bright future.

It was, by my calculation, a Sunday morning when I learned my intuition, and my listening skills, had proven flawless once more.

It began with a sharp rap on the bedroom door.

Without waiting for permission, Gaynor entered.

Rose was still in bed.

Despite the fact that the strong sun had long before forced its way through her insubstantial curtains and had bathed the room in light, Rose pretended to be asleep.

'I know you're awake.'

Rose did not stir.

Gaynor picked up the dressing table stool and put it down next to the bed, close to Rose's head. She sat down on the stool, her long legs crossed at the knee. The high-heeled shoe on her left foot rested on the metal frame of the bed. She tapped the patent leather toe against it, impatiently.

'I know you're awake,' she said, again. Her voice sounded more determined, despite the fact it was quieter than before.

Rose pushed herself up into a sitting position. She stretched an arm over the opposite edge of the mattress and grabbed at one of the red cushions she had pushed to the floor the previous night. She placed it behind her back.

'What?'

'Ground rules,' Gaynor said. 'I think we should agree on a few things before you move into my house on a more permanent basis.'

'Dad's house,' Rose said in a manner that suggested she was ready for an argument.

'That attitude is exactly why I'm here. I want it stopped. Now.'

Rose rolled her pretty eyes in a way that made them look anything but pretty.

'When you're under *my* roof,' Gaynor continued, tapping her toe menacingly against the metal, 'you'll show me respect.' She leaned closer towards Rose as she said, 'If not, I'll make sure your beloved daddy knows exactly how much of a nasty little bitch you really are. Understood?'

Rose stared straight ahead. Her arms were folded in front of her in what looked like a pose of teenage defiance.

'It won't take much for me to convince him that his little princess needs her mother, no matter the sacrifice that might mean on our part.'

She placed the long fingers of her right hand on Rose's nearest forearm.

Rose looked as though she was about to speak, but no sound escaped her mouth.

'Good,' Gaynor said, her plastic smile in place. 'I think you understand.'

Gaynor shut the door soundlessly as she left.

In the wake of this incident, Rose did not respond as I

imagined. She did not run to her father; she did not phone her mother in tears; she did not pull her phone from under her pillow and vent her spleen to Ryan.

Rose sat where she was and ran her left hand in a gentle motion, back and forth, over the area of her forearm where Gaynor's nails had bitten into the skin. She soothed herself in this way for what felt like hours.

I found my attention begin to wander to the pink room in the painting.

The next thing I was aware of was Gaynor. She had re-entered the bedroom and the door behind her was closed. I wondered, not for the first time, if she possessed powers of a demonic nature.

'One more thing,' she said. 'I expect you to be at our wedding in the beautiful dress I bought for you with a smile on your face.'

'It doesn't fit,' Rose said, quietly.

'Don't worry, darling,' Gaynor said, drawing out the word "darling" with an exaggerated mock Irish accent. 'I've made an appointment for you with my seamstress. She'll fix it in a jiffy.' As she turned back towards the door, she said, 'It must be so awful for you, still having the body of a twelve-year-old.'

With that, the wicked witch of the east was gone.

The following Saturday, when Rose was out for her morning run, two men appeared in the bedroom. Niall was at their back. As he entered the room, he began to give them instructions. They were to remove the dressing table, on which I sat, and the stool. These had to be carried downstairs, out of the front door and into the garage. It might be a bit of a squeeze on that half landing, one of the men suggested. Niall's entire face became a smile as he said, 'What comes up, must go down.'

He told them that once the dressing table and stool had been safely stowed, they would be able to bring the desk and chair up the stairs.

'I'm afraid I'd be more worried about how you'll get that desk up the stairs,' he said. 'My fiancée chose it and her taste can run to the extravagant.'

Niall used his foot to manoeuvre one of Rose's clumpy boots under the bed as he told the men that he had asked his daughter to get the room ready for them.

'But that's teenagers for you,' he said, still smiling.

Whilst keenly watching this action unfold, I also found myself thinking that I was surprised Rose had allowed anyone into her room when she was not present. I reasoned, however, that it was likely the only incriminating item was her phone and she had, as was her habit, taken it with her on her "run".

I also remembered that I had witnessed her reach under the bed and rearrange the bags that resided there – she had pushed back the one I thought of as her treat treasure trove and had then positioned a different one in front of it. The thought occurred too, a little tangentially, that her stockpile of snacks must be getting rather low.

Niall cleared a path for the men and then turned his attention to the dressing table. The drawers were, upon his inspection, empty, and there was not much for him to remove from the top. Rose did not seem to wear makeup, except for her obligatory red lipstick. An example of which was, in fact, my only companion. She did have more of them, all red, but this particular specimen was the only one she had ever left beside me. I had already surmised that the others, and any additional items she used on her face, hair and body, were kept in the family bathroom next door (an expansive cream coloured room I had glimpsed on both of my journeys to the bedroom). It seemed likely that this was a facility of which Rose had sole use. I supposed Gaynor had her own equally large bathroom: one that adjoined the master bedroom and was bedecked in black and gold.

You may wonder why I appear to have been unperturbed by these goings on and, indeed, the question of what might happen to me when these removal men removed the dressing table, thus rendering me homeless.

In truth, I found myself to be wholly composed for two reasons.

The first of these was that I had confidence I was destined to be relocated to the desk, being as I was the perfect object for such a piece of furniture (I was thrilled by the thought that, to begin with at least, I might have the desktop all to myself; it seemed to me that it was the red lipstick who had cause for concern).

The second reason for my sense of calm was that my experience of Niall up until this point caused me to believe he would take good care of me.

The men muttered their assent.

For reasons I could not quite fathom, Niall popped the red lipstick into his pocket. He lifted me up and placed me onto the bed.

The dressing table was then removed. I felt sorry for it as it left. I imagined that its new lodgings would be markedly inferior, and frigid in winter.

The sounds I was able to hear the two men emit thanks to the open door suggested that they did indeed have problems negotiating the staircase with the dressing table and then significantly more difficulty when it came to doing the reverse journey with the desk. A desk that I would come to agree was, in fact, as extravagant as advertised.

Rose's bedroom was not small. However, it appeared to be tiny when, red faced, the men dragged the desk into it.

The dressing table had been stationed against the back wall, facing the foot of the bed. However, once the desk – a thick rectangle of carved wood on equally thick legs – had been tugged across the carpet into this same spot, it seemed that the gulf that had previously existed between the two original items of furniture had now been entirely overwhelmed by the interloper.

I found myself wondering where the chair Niall had mentioned might go, as there appeared to be no room for it between desk and bed. The balder of the two men seemed unhappy (his heavier companion, who I would later come to presume was named Frank, merely seemed exhausted).

'I knew it,' the balder man wheezed. 'I said to Frank, there's no way that'll fit.'

'It'll be fine,' Niall said, even though it clearly would not be fine.

'If she sits on the end of her bed, maybe?' the balder man said.

'That's not a terrible idea,' Niall said, as though he genuinely believed it might not be a terrible idea.

The balder of the two men made a face that suggested it was indeed a terrible idea and said, 'What do you want us to do about the chair?'

'Bring it up. We'll put it in that corner. It'll be a great place for her to hang her clothes,' Niall said, in what I presumed was an attempt to lighten the mood.

Both men left the room. Frank returned with the chair.

I watched from the comfort of the bed as Niall sat down on the chair and sank into, what appeared to be, deep concentration.

I realised that I felt rather melancholy.

The incident had reminded me of the attic and of Alan Mackintosh. It seemed I could not think of him without a certain sadness. I wondered if it would be possible to ever experience a memory of him and it not be accompanied by this same ache.

Whilst I was thinking my thoughts, it seemed in concert Niall was thinking his own. After a while, he shouted through the still open door, 'Gaynor, can you come here a minute?'

Gaynor appeared in layered grey leisure wear.

'Will you look at the size of this thing,' Niall said.

'Why did you get them to put it there?' she asked, as though confused.

'That's where it was to go.' Niall said, sounding as though he was the one who was actually confused.

'I didn't realise. I thought it was for under the window,' she said, sweetly.

I was quite certain that she had known full well that it was intended for the spot the dressing table would vacate. Had I not found her so reprehensible, I might have been impressed at how quickly, and decisively, she was able think on her feet.

'But we'd have to rearrange the whole place,' Niall said.

I thought he too must be aware that this pretence was merely a way for her not to have to admit any error of judgement on her part.

'It'll only take us a moment,' she said. 'I have it all in my head.'

She explained that it would be very simple to merely move the wardrobe to the other side of the bed, move the bed over to that side of the room a bit, move the chest of drawers to the foot of the bed and then move the perfectly-sized desk under the window. She also mentioned she was quite sure she had shared this vision with him when they had been in the antique shop on Dundas Street. It was just a shame he had not asked her to supervise the men, she said.

'If you'd been wearing something other than a negligee when they rang the doorbell, I might just,' he said, his face once more a smile.

Gaynor wagged a pointed finger at him as she said, 'That black satin nighty is very respectable, Mr Fitzgerald.'

Chapter Six

By the time Rose returned, the bedroom was the room of Gaynor's vision.

For the sake of an accurate account, I find myself compelled to admit that Gaynor had proven herself to be surprisingly strong and fit that morning. She had certainly held her own in the lifting and shifting of heavy objects. I might even say that she and Niall made it look like it was an altogether easier task than the two men actually employed to lift and shift had made it look.

I should also confess that the bedroom looked fine – and by "fine" I mean adequate, tolerable, middling, acceptable. This was true with the exception of a bothersome lack of balance that had been created by the rejigging of the place. The pink-washed picture was no longer centred above the metal headboard of the bed. This lack of symmetry would annoy me for the rest of my tenure. Unfortunately, no one else seemed to be disturbed by it. Rose did question it that first day but when Niall had pointed out that either the print would be in the centre of the wall or the centre of the bed, she chose to have him leave it where it was. She did however point out that none of this had been in the least bit necessary as she would have been happy to do her homework at the dressing table – a comment that, it seemed to me, caused Niall to look a little disappointed in her.

But I race ahead.

Thanks to Niall, when Rose pushed open the door, I was alone on the desk as predicted.

She leant the weight of her body against the door to close it.

She stayed there, supported by the heavy wood, while she surveyed the scene. She did not move until Niall attempted to open the door behind her.

'Do you love it?' was his first question.

Rose answered with a question of her own.

'Did you have to rearrange the whole room?'

'Doesn't it look a lot better?' he said. 'I'm not sure why we didn't have it this way around from the start.'

'Maybe because the bed's not in the middle of the wall?' Rose suggested.

It was then she commented upon the off-kilter picture and disappointed her father with her apparent lack of gratitude for the large antique desk beneath the window – on which he had clearly spent a small fortune – and, indeed, for the fact he was, it could be argued, attempting to make whatever adjustments were necessary in order to accommodate a teenage addition to his home. Even if these adjustments did not seem to have involved the teenager to any meaningful degree in the decision-making process.

To her credit, Rose may have thought precisely this, but she did not say it.

Niall's smile returned as he reached into his pocket and said, 'I believe this belongs to you, my little Rose-Red.'

Rose took the lipstick from him.

'You know I hate when you call me that,' she said.

It appeared from my prime position under the window that she, in fact, very much liked him calling her that.

I was not alone on the desk for long. Over the course of the following week, in addition to the stubbornly present red lipstick, I was joined, in dribs and drabs, by the standard scholastic instruments. Of these, the only notable item was Rose's pencil case. It was metal and red. For reasons that escape me, I found its curved edges really rather lovely.

I would not be joined by books, jotters and folders for yet another week, when Rose started school.

Before I saw Rose in her uniform, I saw her in her bridesmaid's dress.

On this noteworthy evening Gaynor had rapped on the bedroom door. As usual she did not wait for an answer before she entered.

She teetered in wearing high heeled shoes that appeared to be impossibly high for the purpose of walking, or indeed staying upright.

The dress was in the long garment bag she held aloft.

Gaynor announced she had picked up both dresses on her way home from work and she wanted Rose to try hers on. Rose complained that she had already attended a final fitting and that there was therefore no need.

'Humour me,' Gaynor said through her wicked witch smile.

'I'm in the middle of texting my mum.' Rose replied.

Gaynor stayed where she was, holding the garment bag out in Rose's direction.

'Fine,' Rose said, without looking up from her phone.

For a minute or two, they both stayed exactly where they were.

'I'm going downstairs to speak to your father. I'll be back in ten minutes to see what it looks like.'

Gaynor turned around. She used her free hand to lift Rose's dressing gown from the brass hook on the back of the open door. She let the dressing gown fall to the floor. She hung the garment bag where it had been and tottered out of the room, closing the door behind her.

I could see Rose's eyes fill with tears as she put her phone down and uncrossed her legs.

She removed her outer layers. She placed her red polka dot dress and then the black leggings on the bed near her phone. Not for the first time, I studied the muscular tone of her small frame and noted, also not for the first time, that it offered proof, if any was necessary, that no matter what else went on during her morning runs, there was actual running involved.

Rose picked up her dressing gown and laid it over the end of the bed. She then reached her small hands up to the garment bag.

As the bag was unzipped, I expected to see swathes of pink satin material or some equally shiny fabric in pale blue or lemon. I did not anticipate raw silk in a dark shade of red.

The style of the dress was a little elaborate in that it was off the shoulder; had a stiff bodice and a full skirt, but otherwise it looked as though it was designed wholly with Rose in mind. I wondered if both Rose, and I, had judged Gaynor too harshly.

I replayed every occasion I had had to observe her. Based on this evidence, I judged that there must be a motive for the seeming olive branch that aligned with Gaynor's interests and Gaynor's interests alone.

Rose stepped into the dress.

With a great deal of difficulty, due not to the fit but to the trickiness of its tiny buttons, she fastened herself in. The only mirror in the room was mounted on the wall above the chest of drawers. Rose therefore had to stand on the bed in order to see what she looked like. This is where Gaynor found her when she entered the room, without knocking.

'Beautiful,' Gaynor said, in a way that suggested she might actually mean it. 'Your dad will be so happy. And you almost look your age.'

Rose glared at her.

For once, she was taller than her step-mother-to-be. Perhaps that is what gave her the confidence to say, 'I'm doing this for my dad. Not you. You'll never be a mum to me. Or anything close to it.'

'I wouldn't want to be, darling.' Gaynor said, and left the room.

Rose slumped onto the bed.

She was still lying in the same heap when her phone started to play a now familiar tune. She reached out to it.

I heard Niamh's cheerful voice change as she saw her daughter's face on the small screen.

'What the matter, darling?' she said.

Through her tears Rose told her mother how miserable she was that her father was actually going through with the wedding. Niamh attempted to lift her daughter's spirits, but she failed. It was only when she said that she wanted Rose to know that it was not too late for her to change her mind and come home, that Rose stopped complaining and declaring herself to be miserable. Everything was fine, she assured her mother. She explained her outburst away by saying she was just having a bad day.

'Let me have a proper look at that lovely dress,' her mother said.

Rose pushed herself off the bed, stood in front of the door and held out her phone to allow her mother to examine the dress through the sorcery of modern technology.

'Don't you look beautiful,' Niamh said. 'It suits you perfectly.'

And it did.

****

Rose had been at school for almost a week when, one evening, her fingers reached across the desk in my direction. Her hand was warm. 'I know it's not your fault,' I felt her say to me, 'I just don't want to have to look at you.' She pulled out a drawer I had not even known was in the desk. Her eyes turned away as she slid me inside.

****

I drifted through undifferentiated days and nights. I played and replayed each era through which I had passed. I moved in and out of the chapters of my life. I grew to understand that I was wholly bound up in the lives of my guardians. A tenderness for each one blossomed at the very depth of my being. Despite long years of imprisonment in the dark, I even learned to love Rose.

Part Five. Daisy
2018

Chapter One

During the years I spent in the drawer, I was deprived of a most cherished faculty: my sense of time. My world was devoid of clocks, calendars and the light by which I might track the passing of days.

I should mention, however, that I did not spend the entire three years, three months and three weeks (or so) in absolute darkness: the drawer was opened, and quickly closed again, on three separate occasions. Each time this happened, Rose incarcerated another object.

I would come to believe that my fellow inmates must also have been given to Rose as gifts by the wicked witch of the east. The first of these was a slim, black bottle of perfume. Initially, I found the smell that emanated from it overpowering, but as time went on the fragrance, or my ability to perceive it, diminished. The next outcast was a leather-bound diary – one I imagined Gaynor hoped Rose would use to incriminate herself. The final object to be sequestered was a small, round mirror with material on its reverse that depicted intertwined roses and thorns.

My ability to listen keenly was undiminished and provided me with some diverting, if limited, intelligence. This was particularly true early on.

Of most interest during this dark period were the occasions on which I heard a male voice, that did not belong to Niall, in the bedroom. It seemed clear to me that this caller must be Ryan and I assumed these assignations must be happening when the house was empty and both he and Rose should have been at school. It did not take much imagination for me to picture what was taking place outside of my prison.

The noise in the room eventually dwindled to silence. I had a growing awareness that, like me, the bedroom had been abandoned. I fell into a state I have come to think of as something akin to hibernation.

I was roused at some point by the thump of a door.

I heard Rose's voice.

I heard bashing and banging and words I choose not to repeat.

I heard Niall enter the room. His voice was soothing, at first.

After what developed into an unholy argument, I heard the door slam.

Rose opened the drawer.

As I adjusted to the daylight, I could see that she was crying. Her dark hair was pulled back from her face in a thick black band. The dark shadows beneath her eyes were more pronounced; her cheekbones higher; her lips thinner and paler. She no longer resembled the Rose-Red of a book cover.

There was a large open black bag on the floor. She dropped me, and the perfume bottle, the diary and the mirror, into it. I landed on something soft: the raw silk of her bridesmaid's dress. I saw Rose's, still small, hands descend and grasp the top of the bag. She tied it in a knot.

I was in darkness once more.

Niall's voice returned. It was gentle.

'I'm sorry, Rose, darling,' he said.

He tried to reason with her. It seemed he had not expected

this kind of reaction when he had phoned the previous night. He really did not think she would mind if they were to redecorate her room and give it to Sophie. It was not as if Rose lived with them anymore, or had even spent very much time at the house since she had left for university. In fact, in the eighteen months since Sophie had been born, Rose had not stayed overnight even once. Now that the new baby was on its way, Sophie would need to move out of the nursery. Granted it was Gaynor's New Year's resolution to get on with the project as the baby was due at the end of March but Rose had not needed to rush across from Glasgow, especially on such a horrible morning. They would have moved her stuff into the garage for her. The roads must have been terrible, he said again, with concern. In what I am sure he thought was a gesture of genuine goodwill, he told her Gaynor planned to put bunk beds in Sophie's new room, so that Rose could stay whenever she liked.

Rose did not respond with anything more than a loud sniffle during this entire monologue. I wondered if she was sitting on the bed as he spoke or if perhaps she was standing facing him.

'Wouldn't it be lovely,' Niall said, 'if the baby was born on your birthday.'

I imagined this possibility did not, in any way, thrill Rose.

'I have to go, Dad,' she said. 'I've got everything I need.'

'At least let me help you carry it all out to the car.'

'I can manage,' Rose said, in a tone I was quite sure would have convinced him to allow her to do just that.

Despite my surroundings, I felt a distinct chill when the front door was opened. Rose pitched the bag in which I was stowed into what I presumed was the boot of her car. It was even colder in there than the wintry blast of the outside world had been. I could feel and hear other items being thrown in around me. After what I presumed was another trip to and from the bedroom, I felt a heavy weight rest on top of the black bag. I believed it to be the framed Raoul Dufy print.

During this uncomfortable, but short, journey, I had only enough time to wonder about two things: where Gaynor and the oft mentioned Sophie had been during the melee and what was about to happen to me.

The car stopped.

I felt Rose slide the picture off the black bag. She then lifted the bag up and out of the assorted jumble.

The boot thudded shut.

Rose carried the bag a few steps and then opened a door which closed behind her with the tinkle of a bell.

She wanted to donate a few things, Rose told an unseen woman. She enumerated the contents of the bag. The woman thanked her.

'Could you sit it just over there?' the woman said and explained that Daisy would unpack it when she had a chance. They had been run off their feet all morning, apparently. She said it was the same every year and ventured that it must be all those New Year resolutions.

I heard the bell jingle a second time.

The woman shouted, 'Daisy. Another load.'

'Coming,' a voice replied.

A moment later, the first voice clarified the situation.

'To be fair, it's not exactly a load. Just the one bag. A bridesmaid's dress and some other bits and bobs.'

'Just as well. There's hardly room to swing a cat back there,' the new voice said. 'What we could do with is people coming in and buying stuff, rather than just dropping it off. I've got a big pile that's no use for anything but recycling. When I'm finished, I'll bag it all up and leave it at the back for Ed. That should free up a bit more room at least.'

'Did anyone ever tell you you're a star?' the first voice said.

The black bag that contained the bridesmaid's dress, and me, was carried into the back room.

A while later, Daisy opened it.

Her face was glorious.

I cannot say that her face was in actuality glorious, but it certainly seemed that way to me. Thick, red spirals of hair spilled over her shoulders. Her eyes were large ovals, dark hazel in colour. Her smile was broad and revealed a gap between her two front teeth. There were freckles on her lips and a light dusting over her nose.

I knew immediately she was a Munro.

Chapter Two

You may be sceptical of my claim that the instant I saw Daisy, without her even having touched me, I recognised that she was somehow related, by blood, to Violet. You may even assume that it is only because of what I was to learn later that I have reinvented the encounter and have allowed myself to believe that I experienced this revelation. If that is your belief, it is unlikely there is much I can do to convince you of the truth of my epiphany, other than to offer you a sincere and solemn oath that it did indeed happen.

I also admit, which may add weight to my account, that at that moment I still had no inkling as to the second heritage coursing through the veins of the young woman who peered in at me.

Had I taken note of her sharply elfin chin and the luminescence of her cheeks, I may have come to the discovery sooner, but I was distracted by the width of her smile, the gap in her teeth and the speckles of brown on her lips so, somehow, I overlooked it.

I was not the first item that Daisy removed from the bag.

Her long Sandra-like fingers reached first for the leather-bound diary. Only when she had flicked through its empty pages and set it aside, did she lift me up from the folds of the red dress.

Her touch was gentle. I also noted that her nails were clean and had been cut short. She was kneeling next to the bag.

Holding me in one hand, she got to her feet a little awkwardly.

I sensed by the way in which she looked at me that she considered me something of a find. In my new, rather lofty, position, I was able to see that the back room was indeed an overcrowded mess. I immediately became concerned that if she set me down without taking a careful note of my location, I might be lost to her.

I would soon come to realise that I should have had no such fear.

Daisy carried me out into the main part of the shop.

'For under the counter?' Joyce, the woman whose voice I had already heard, asked.

She looked different than I had imagined.

Her frame was tall and broad. This robust body did not seem to be in keeping with the soft sing-song of her voice. In addition, she had sections of purple and pink through her shoulder length grey hair.

'Busted,' Daisy said, with a grin. 'Could you price it? I don't like to do it when I'm going to be the one buying it.'

'I swear you spend all your wages in here. I thought you were saving up?'

'One more book. That's all,' Daisy said. 'I promise.'

'Doesn't your mum run a book shop?' Joyce asked in a tone that suggested she already knew the answer.

'I like old things; what can I say?' Daisy said.

'I hope you're not referring to me, Daisy Hunter,' the older woman said.

'No.' Daisy pursed her freckled lips and stretched the word out as far as it would go.

'Cheeky mare. Are you sure it's wise to upset the person who's about to decide on a price for that?' Joyce said, nodding her colourful head in my direction.

Daisy handed me over.

'It's in pretty good condition,' Joyce said. 'How about we say fifty pence?'

'Are you sure?' Daisy asked.

Joyce picked up a pencil with her free hand and clicked a button at one end to extend the lead at the other. It looked very sharp.

I was relieved when Daisy said, 'Is it okay not to write it on? I'll give you the money at the end of my shift.'

With that, Joyce placed me on a shelf under the counter.

Once there I wondered about Daisy's age. I settled on somewhere in her mid-twenties. This then led me to wonder as to the path Daisy had taken that had brought her to this current moment and to the charity shop and Joyce. My ruminations, however, lacked both depth and potency. A most distracting sense of excitement had taken hold of me as I felt quite certain that I would soon be taken home by a member of the Munro family.

The doorbell tinkled on and off for what I presumed to be hours.

Each time, as Daisy had feared, those who brought in donations left again without buying anything, adding, I was sure, to the quite literal stock pile in the back room. Most of the donors were women and many were on first name terms with Joyce. They each had a variation of a story on the New Year's resolution theme.

A number mentioned that their significant other, and, or,

children would be horrified when they noticed the precious things they never used, wore, played with, watched or listened to, had disappeared.

Joyce laughed each time, as though it were the first.

Every time the bell tinkled to indicate Joyce was once more alone, she would yell, 'Another load,' and I would hear Daisy shout back, 'Seriously?' or, in what I presumed to be irony, 'Marvellous!' or 'Do they think this place is the charity shop equivalent of the TARDIS?'

I was able to see Joyce's face throughout and it seemed clear to me that she enjoyed the repartee and, more than that, that she liked the younger woman very much. I felt this would bode well for my future: a future I believed I was destined to spend with Daisy.

As I contemplated this further, it occurred to me that for the first time in my history I had been chosen by the person to whom I would belong. I was not a gift to be accepted or rejected. It seemed, if I could allow myself such a thought, that this should be a more secure position than those in which I had found myself in the past.

'Four o'clock,' Joyce shouted.

Daisy's freckled face and red hair appeared over the counter. 'That was the quickest day ever,' she said, setting a pound coin down next to me.

'That's the benefit of being busy,' Joyce said, handing over the change.

Daisy's long fingers picked me up. A canvas bag hung across her body from one shoulder to the opposite hip. She opened its flap and placed me inside.

The next time I saw light was in the hallway of Daisy's flat.

She removed me from the bag and carried me into her front room.

On the wall by the door there was a floor to ceiling bookcase. Admittedly, it looked to have been made out of reclaimed wood by a carpenter who was only moderately skilled, but it was full of books and not so full that its occupants looked to have been squeezed into place. In addition, the room contained a wooden desk upon which there were small book towers, three or four high. A low wooden coffee table was similarly arrayed.

Thankfully, there were no molehills of books on the floor.

I surveyed two small sofas. Both looked to be a little lumpy and bumpy. They had been covered with the same type of material. The only difference was that one was green and the other had a floral pattern – in the same green, but also with pinks and yellows. The sofas were in the centre of the room facing one another across the coffee table.

The room had a bay window in the far corner, in front of which was a round table. I was not sure of the material of the table as it was draped in a yellow cloth that extended to the wooden floor boards. On it, there was a small vase in green glass. I thought it would benefit from an arrangement of flowers – daisies would have been both pretty and appropriate, but I supposed they may be difficult to come by in early January.

I wondered where I might be headed.

I thought, if I had my choice, I would be apt to select the tallest of the low book towers on the coffee table.

Once more, I had occasion to speculate as to whether it was in any way possible that I had the ability to invoke a psychic connection, for this is exactly where Daisy laid me down.

The book beneath me was a rather crochety copy of Mary

Shelley's *Frankenstein*. It did not seem best pleased to no longer occupy the prime position in the sitting room. It was quite clear that I was an unwanted intruder and an even more unwelcome weight – despite my slender frame.

As I settled into my new surroundings, I became aware that there was no television anywhere in sight. Only Sandra's sitting room had been similarly bereft. Indeed, I had come to think of a television as a prerequisite of any such space. There was, however, a laptop on the desk and I would come to learn that this was the medium via which Daisy would receive audio and audio-visual entertainment. Indeed, it proved to be a most versatile object; Daisy also used it as a repository for her other amusement – writing.

This, it seemed, was a major preoccupation.

That first evening, Daisy carried a dinner plate in from the kitchen and nudged the laptop further back on the desk in order to set it down. Simultaneously, she ate her meal with a fork and set something, which seemed to me to be a film that had been paused partway through, in motion. It was at this point that I regretted my choice of location. The coffee table, it seemed, was not in fact the prime piece of real estate in the room, that title went instead to the desk, on which there were, as mentioned, a number of low book towers I could have been placed atop.

I wished for a transfer.

The *Frankenstein* book, I was quite sure, had a similar longing.

It seemed Daisy was deaf to our desires.

From my less than ideal position, I was still able to see Daisy's plate. Her meal looked to be decidedly unappetising. It appeared to consist of potatoes, carrots and minced meat all of which had been mixed and mashed together in a most unattractive fashion. I suspected it had been cooked in the microwave – an object with which I had become familiar whilst resident in Laurel's kitchen.

My clues to this were the speed at which it had appeared and the distinctive binging noise I heard moments before its arrival. I did hope, with perhaps a little too much fervour, that this meal was not something that had been produced in a vast vat in a factory prior to being packaged in plastic, but rather that Daisy herself had prepared it from scratch at some point earlier. Her pallor caused me to worry that it had in fact been the former and that she often skimped on nutrition in this manner.

Due to the way in which the laptop was now positioned, I could no longer see two-thirds of a framed photograph to which my attention had previously been drawn. The picture was one of Daisy flanked by the people I presumed to be her parents. One thing I had noted before the laptop obstructed my view of her was that Daisy, smiling her wide gap-toothed smile, appeared even more freckled. I had therefore presumed it had been taken on a family holiday somewhere warm, although, my evidence for this was clearly rather scant.

The portion of the photograph I could still see was of the man's tanned face. He was bald, so I could not tell if he had once had red hair. His eyes looked to be dark brown. They were small, so it was difficult to be sure. He, too, was smiling, but his mouth in no way resembled Daisy's.

Thankfully, once she had finished eating Daisy carried the laptop over to the floral couch and sat down. At first, she balanced it on her knees, but after only a few minutes, she set it down near to me on the coffee table. Having decided upon what type of film she was watching – a period drama – I returned my focus to the photograph as it was visible once more.

The woman's hair was short and dark. Her face, whilst long, ended abruptly in a small, pointed chin. Her skin looked smooth and peach-pale with not a freckle in sight. Her eyes were her most notable feature. I thought they must have caught the light of the camera flash, for they appeared to be shards of sapphire.

I found myself in a maelstrom of thought.

Daisy was Heather's baby.

Chapter Three

Daisy continued to watch her film.

Two women, who had once enjoyed esteem and a certain stature as a result of secretive work they had undertaken during the war, were able to overcome the fall in their social standing and the prejudices of the day in order to solve not one, but three murders, all of which had been perpetrated by a middle-aged mortician.

During this time, I tried to fit together the unwieldy pieces of the jigsaw with which I had been presented.

In doing so, I was struck by the revelation that Daisy's connection to Violet had not come through her mother. It therefore followed that the unknown man in the photograph could not be Daisy's father, because that honour, I realised, must go to Thomas Munro.

Daisy stretched forward and closed her laptop.

As she retired to bed, she turned down the thermostat by the door and put out the light.

Initially the room was just dark, but before long it was both dark and cold. I remembered Joyce's suggestion that Daisy may lack self-discipline in her approach to financial management. It seemed to me that an improvement in this area may have resulted in the necessary funds to allow her to more adequately heat her home. I was also reminded that it was early January and whilst I was pleased to possess the knowledge of which month of the year I found myself in, I knew that it was unlikely these overnight lodgings would be anything other than unpleasantly chilly for weeks to come.

As the night dragged, I had occasion, when not thinking about Heather and Thomas and Violet, to think about the way my relationship to the passing of time had changed. Here I was comfortably settled on a small stack of books that was situated on a perfectly nice coffee table that was in turn surrounded by all manner of interesting items and I was allowing myself to be tortured by the fact that each second of each minute of each hour seemed to linger in the most dilatory fashion. It was especially galling that I should feel this way seeing as, until very recently, I had been trapped in the dullest of dull drawers.

I chastised myself.

I refocused and became lost in the mental gymnastics required to try to unpick the puzzle of Daisy Hunter. Time accelerated. Whilst I was contemplating the unpleasantness of Heather performing the sort of act required to conceive a child with Thomas Munro, the fruit of his loins appeared.

She wore a long pinstriped nightshirt in white and blue, thick black socks and a green woollen cardigan that stretched beyond the hem of the garment beneath it. When combined with the red of her hair, this ensemble risked contravening regulations regarding the number of disparate colours that should be displayed at any one time on any one body. I was unsure such a rule existed, but, based on this evidence, I felt that if it did not, one should be enacted forthwith.

Due to the aroma which escaped from it, Daisy carried a mug of what I felt sure was strong black coffee. She settled down on the floral couch, tucked her feet underneath her and held the mug in both hands as she drank. Her eyes were shut as though she was deep in thought. As I observed her at such close quarters, I saw that even her eyelids had not been spared their share of freckles. I also noticed the thickness of her eyebrows and noted that they, and her eyelashes, were an auburn brown, not the red of her hair. Both reminded me of Violet. From my memory of Thomas, all of his hair, even the fine down on his arms, was a robust red. He, too, had had many freckles, although, I was sure, they were lighter in colour than hers. It was only when Daisy put her mug on the coffee table that I saw her chin, which marked her as a Wilson.

Interesting as this survey of her features might have been, it answered few questions. It certainly did not explain why Joyce had called her by the name of Hunter.

Daisy opened her laptop and caused it to broadcast a radio station. She left with her mug and returned with it replenished. In her other hand she carried a mobile phone. She wrote a message and then set the phone on the coffee table.

I could see that her text – Great. I'll be home by 6 – was in reply to one from a contact she had designated as Mum. I was pleased to note that the previous message had been an enquiry seeking to know whether it would be convenient for the sender to drop by that evening.

I did not see Daisy consume anything other than coffee, but I did hear clattering noises from the room I presumed to be the kitchen that sounded like she first toasted bread and then used a knife to spread it with something – I presumed butter – before the knife was discarded into a metal sink. The fact I could smell toast, may well have helped me to identify these associated noises.

Daisy did not return to the sitting room.

I heard the front door thud shut.

Time slowed to a crawl.

I attempted various distraction techniques but it seemed that the knowledge that in a matter of hours I would see Heather again, rendered my normally useful strategies useless.

Fortunately for you, you do not need to endure such agonies. I will proceed directly to the moment Heather entered the sitting room. Actually, perhaps I should begin a little earlier.

A key turned in the lock of the front door.

I listened to the sound of it yawn open.

I heard it close.

The clock on the wall above the desk said it was five twenty-five.

Footsteps padded to the kitchen. I knew this was where they had gone because, moments later, I heard the noise of an electric kettle being filled and then coming to the boil. When the sitting room door began to swing in towards me, I fully expected to see a disarray of red curls.

Instead, I saw Heather.

I have often declared myself to be pleased about this or that without really feeling anything. However, in this moment, I did experience what I can only imagine to be happiness.

Despite the fantastical schemes I had spun in my daydreams, in truth, I had not expected to recover that which I had lost.

To preserve what sanity I have, I choose not to dwell on my lack of self-agency, as it is a reality about which I can do nothing. However, in that moment, as I beheld Heather, it occurred to me that it was possible for something that might be called fate or good fortune to break into one's life and turn it aright. Had the circumstances been otherwise, I might have dwelt longer on this thought.

I drank in Heather. Her body still neat and muscular. The blue in her eyes sharp and clear. Her hair no longer short nor black, but chocolate in colour and cut in layers that moved as she walked.

I found myself back in the attic. I recalled that she had so often been consumed by sadness. I remembered her distress. The version before me, coffee in hand, looked like an adult form of the one I had known, and yet she was very different: her spirit having somehow been allowed to flourish.

I saw in her a contentment I could not have predicted. I also saw Daisy.

There was something in Heather's movements that suggested her daughter had more in common with her than merely the pretty elfin chin they shared.

In the hand not holding coffee, Heather carried a small plastic bag containing an unknown object. I admit I was intrigued.

She sat the bag down on the table, close to me. With the benefit of being able to survey it from the top of the small book tower, I could see that it was book-shaped, dark in colour and had white writing on its cover. The writing appeared to relate to a disease. I was perplexed that she should think to bring this as a gift.

I became distracted from the strange book by an unexpected aroma. I was sure I could detect more than a hint of liquorice somewhere beneath the more dominant fragrance of well roasted coffee beans.

Heather held the mug containing the odd-smelling coffee in

both hands. Her eyes were closed as she drank. I noticed that there were soft creases on the once taught skin of her eyelids and that her forehead was now criss-crossed with the finest of fine lines. As I traced the landscape of her face, I could see that it held both Dorothy and John Wilson, yet she in no way resembled either one.

The noise of the front door slamming shut interrupted my reverie.

Heather opened her eyes.

'I'm in here, love,' she shouted.

'I'm just going to get changed. I'll be there in a minute.'

'We're not going anywhere fancy,' Heather shouted back.

As we waited for Daisy, I scanned the bookshelves near the door to see if there was any other reading material relating to the illness in question. Halfway down I was discouraged to see, lined up one next to the other, four books on this particular disease. I turned my attention to the book towers on Daisy's desk. One of these vertical collections – that was otherwise comprised of non-fiction titles relating to nutrition and meditation – contained two more.

Heather sat her empty mug on the coffee table. This act seemed to summon Daisy, for it was at this moment that she appeared.

Daisy reached down to give her mother a hug and then, as Heather was sitting in her preferred spot, she sat down on the green sofa opposite.

She sank into it, tucking her unshod feet between two lumpy cushions.

'Are you cold?' Heather asked, a note of concern evident in her voice.

'No. Are you? I can turn the thermostat up.'

'I'm okay, but you look frozen. Are you feeling okay?'

It was true. Despite thick tights and a cosy-looking jumper, it did appear as if Daisy might be cold.

'Mum, what have I told you? I'm fine. Stop looking for something to be worried about.'

'I'm not. You just look cold. And very pale.'

'Well, I'm absolutely fine,' Daisy said. 'Where's Dad?'

Heather explained that she had received a text to say he was still caught up in a meeting so would meet them at the restaurant.

'I could have got the bus,' Daisy said in a way that suggested she was a little annoyed.

'It's just as easy for me to pick you up when I'm driving this way anyway,' Heather said. 'And it's very slippery underfoot.'

'Mum, I'm twenty-five. I'm perfectly capable of making my way into the city centre without falling over and breaking my neck.'

'Do you see the nurse this week?' Heather asked.

'She's still on holiday and I don't want to talk about it. How many times? If there's anything you need to know, I'll tell. This is exactly why I moved out.'

'I'm sorry. I know. New subject,' Heather said and then paused as if to think of one.

'Your dad and I are talking about going to London at Easter time. Do you fancy coming down with us?'

Daisy asked if she could think about it. She said she would like to see the family but she did not know how she felt about taking time off before the summer. She reminded Heather that she was only just back at work and did not want to be seen to be taking advantage.

'You were off sick, for goodness sake,' her mother said in reply.

The muscles around Daisy's jaw seemed to tighten as she said, 'Can I just think about it, please?'

'Of course.'

Diligently ignoring the book-shaped plastic bag on the coffee table, Daisy asked her mother if she would like another coffee. Heather said she would and then stood up to follow her daughter into the kitchen.

On her way out of the door, Daisy turned up the thermostat.

I had to presume there was room enough in the kitchen for them to drink their coffees, for they did not return with them. I imagined a slim breakfast bar and two high stools. It did not seem to me to be a very comfortable option.

Unfortunately, their voices, whilst audible, flowed too quickly and too quietly to easily make out individual words.

I heard the front door close behind them.

According to the cuckoo clock on the far wall, that had seen better days, it was a little after seven.

Chapter Four

Despite the fact that neither Heather nor Daisy had drawn the curtains against the chill of that January night, the room grew warm.

I decided I would attempt to engage the mysterious book.

After I had assured it of Daisy's benevolent nature and her evident love of reading, the book, a copy of *Multiple Sclerosis: Life After Diagnosis, Fifth Edition*, began to open up.

From the depths of its plastic prison (a state of affairs from which, I promised, it would soon gain liberty), it began to reveal something of itself and a great deal of its contents.

It was, if I am honest, more than a little self-important.

Assuming that I might be interested, it took great pains to explain that, in a person with multiple sclerosis, the immune system labours under the erroneous assumption that an imaginary enemy has declared war and, deciding attack is the best form of defence, it launches an offensive that breaches the blood-brain barrier. Rogue immune cells then wreak havoc and, it claimed, in the resulting fray, a protective shield known as the myelin sheath is destroyed, leaving nerves injured and exposed.

These acts of sedition and the resulting damage are, apparently, what cause the symptoms associated with multiple sclerosis.

I feel it important to point out at this juncture that I found its use of military metaphors when describing human illness, to be both inappropriate and disturbing. I therefore felt disinclined to continue our inchoate friendship.

The book, appearing irritatingly unaware that I had cooled towards it, began to gratuitously rattle off a seemingly endless list of symptoms.

Numbness, tingling, burning, tightness, pins and needles, severe itchiness, hypersensitivity to touch, pain, loss of the sense of the body's position in space, impaired sense of smell, impaired sense of taste, stabbing pain in the face, a sensation like an electric shock running down the spine when the head is tilted down, muscle weakness, loss of muscle tone, increased muscle tone, muscle spasms, tremor, foot drop, impaired gait, problems walking, paralysis.

On and on, it went.

Loss of balance, loss of coordination, jittery eye movements, changes in voice quality, including hoarseness, breathiness, nasal tone and poor pitch control, trouble swallowing, loss of vision, eye pain, diminished colour vision, double vision, blurred vision, bladder problems, bowel problems, impotence, reduced libido.

And on.

Insomnia, breathing problems, problems regulating heat and cold, seizures, short and long-term memory problems, attention difficulties, slower information processing speed, difficulty finding the right words, confusion, sensory overload, depression, mood swings.

I admit I could take no more. I switched my attention to the swirling pattern of the rug and awaited Daisy's return.

As I did, I tried not to think about why Heather might have bought this dreadful book and why Daisy possessed others on the same topic. Likely, I thought, there were previous "gifts" from her mother. I was, however, unsuccessful in my endeavour and by the time I heard the front door being pushed open, I was in a state of fear – or as close to this condition as it was possible for me to manage.

A man's voice said, 'I think you need some WD40 for that lock.'

'There's just a knack to it. It's a lot easier when you're not wearing gloves,' Daisy said.

'A few drops wouldn't hurt' he said. 'I'll pop by with some through the week.'

'Stop fussing, Dad. You're getting as bad as Mum.'

As they entered the room, the man was gasping in mock horror.

'And after me agreeing to share your sticky toffee pudding,' he said.

Heather did not follow them in.

I heard the kettle begin to boil and her voice shout, 'Decaf all round?'

Daisy and the man she referred to as Dad both raised their eyebrows.

'I'm okay with leaded,' the man shouted in reply. 'It's early yet.'

'Me too,' Daisy shouted.

There was no reply from the kitchen.

The man and Daisy were sitting on the floral couch.

He leaned in towards her and said, 'I don't know what your mum was on about; it's lovely and warm in here.'

Daisy smiled her wide, gap-toothed smile.

'I told you,' she said, a little conspiratorially.

Heather appeared with three mugs on a tray.

'Can you move some of those books?' she said.

Daisy cleared a space for the tray. In doing so, she sat a small stack of books on top of the book-shaped plastic bag and swept the entire pile to the far end of the coffee table.

'There you go.'

Heather made no comment as she set the tray down.

'Daniel,' she said, pointedly, 'fully leaded as requested.'

'Likewise,' she said, handing the second mug to Daisy.

'Thanks, Mum,' Daisy said. 'I have cut down. Honest. This is only my second today.'

'It's your choice,' Heather said, now on the green couch opposite. 'But you know caffeine makes it difficult for the body to absorb vitamins. And you also know the importance of sleep.'

As I watched the exchange, I wondered if Heather was aware how much like Dorothy Wilson she had become. I presumed she did not possess the requisite self-awareness, as, otherwise, she may have been able to resist the temptation to offer advice that sounded more akin to judgement.

Whilst I was sure Daisy was bristling inside, she indulged her mother and told her she was aware of each fact and that, for the most part, she was eating well and sleeping well.

'I just wouldn't want you to have another relapse.'

It was Daniel's turn to speak.

'Heather,' he said. 'That's enough. Daisy's quite capable of looking after herself.'

Thanks to Daniel, the focus moved away from Daisy's health, or lack of it, and onto his assertion that the weather was due to get even worse. He said he had heard they were in for a monster snowstorm. To which Daisy and her mother both told him he must be wrong. Daisy said she could not remember the last time a really decent amount of snow had fallen in Edinburgh.

'I wouldn't mind if it did, though,' she said, grinning. 'Do you remember that year you took me up Calton Hill to go sledging?'

'On a tray,' Daniel said. 'You were fearless. And you couldn't have been much more than seven or eight.'

He looked across at Heather and said, 'Remember how tiny she was?'

As though she had not heard this aside to her mother, Daisy said, 'It was the year you got married.'

Heather smiled.

The tension in the room was gone.

Daniel looked very much like the framed-photograph version of himself. His accent was firmly Edinburgh. I would even go as far as to venture the Edinburgh of Granton or Trinity. His step-daughter had similar tones, but if you were to pay close attention you might also detect something of Glasgow and, hidden in the depths of certain vowels, possibly even a smidge of London.

Heather's voice was virtually unchanged.

'*The Prime of Miss Jean Brodie*?' she said, leaning towards me.

'I found it in a bag of donations,' Daisy said as Heather lifted me up.

Had I not already been certain she was indeed Heather Wilson, I would have known it from her touch.

'I had a copy once,' she said, as she opened me.

I felt the pulse in her fingers accelerate as she said, 'Where did you say you got it?'

'Joyce said a young girl handed it in,' Daisy said. 'I didn't see her. Why?'

Heather was staring at Sandra's handwriting.

'Mum?'

Heather's blue eyes filled with tears.

'It's mine.'

'What?' Daisy said. 'What are you talking about, Mum?'

Heather said nothing. She stood up and carried me over to the other couch. Daniel moved to let her sit next to her daughter.

I was still open at the inscription page.

'I never thought I'd see it again,' she said.

Heather explained that a friend had given me to her to read. She had not seen me since she was at school.

'The inscription. See,' she said, as she turned the page to face Daisy.

Daisy took me in her hands.

'That's amazing,' she said.

'What are the odds?' Daniel said, a little chirpily.

I was suspicious he did not fully grasp the significance of what had just unfolded. He did, however, seem pleased that the conversation had taken a turn in a new and less controversial direction.

'So, Violet?' Daisy said, still holding me. 'That Violet?'

She was now looking straight at her mother.

'I'm sorry, love,' Heather said. 'I'm really tired and I have to be up at the crack of dawn tomorrow. We'll talk later. Okay?'

She gave Daisy a look that silenced any further questions.

Heather stood up. She lifted Daniel's mug and then her own.

'That'll be me finished then,' he said, although not unkindly.

From the hallway, I heard Heather invite herself back over. Daniel would be away that weekend at a conveniently timed management development course and Heather could think of no better way to spend a Sunday afternoon than with her daughter.

When they had gone, Daisy picked me up.

She sat down on the floral sofa.

She found the page with Sandra's inscription and followed the words with one finger. I felt her skin touch the blue ink that had long ago become a part of me and I let myself believe that I was almost home.

The next day when Daisy returned from work, she called her mother in order to interrogate her. It seemed, despite Daisy's persistence, that Heather was able to convince her daughter that this discussion should wait until they were together.

Despite Heather's effective evasion, the call was still somewhat illuminating. I did at least learn that Daisy had lain awake the previous night thinking about me and about Violet and Sandra.

On each of the following days when she would return from work, after she had eaten what I was now sure were microwave meals at her desk, Daisy would sit on the floral sofa and alternately pay attention to her laptop and to me. The benefit of this movement between us both was that she kept us at close-quarters – the laptop on her legs and me on the lumpy cushion by her side. Not only did this mean that I had regular and precise information regarding the time, day and date, I was also able to watch Daisy search the internet for information on individuals named Sandra Galbraith and Violet Munro.

On the second night, I observed her perform a search on Thomas Munro. She did this only once and did not seem able to bring herself to click on any of the links that were offered to her.

It became evident to me that Daisy knew certain key facts about the absent branches of her family tree. Otherwise, she could not have known which surnames to add to the Violet and Sandra of my inscription and would not have chosen to initiate an inquiry into the name Thomas Munro.

It was also apparent that Daisy had sufficient patience not to demand her mother immediately come and explain herself. I found myself wishing she possessed a little less of this quality.

I am sad to report that it was on one of these nights that I read an obituary notice for Sandra. It said that she had been a much-loved sister to Mark and Jane, aunt to Violet and Thomas, great aunt to Jack and Chloe and a beloved teacher to many. It also said that she had died at the age of seventy-five after a short illness. The notice was dated 16th February 2017.

I admit I grieved not only for her death, but also for the fact that she had been alive eleven months earlier. Somehow this knowledge made me feel her loss all the more keenly.

Sunday eventually arrived. Thankfully, before coffee was even made, they settled down on the couches to talk.

The discussion Daisy and Heather had that afternoon was only the first of many. These, sometimes strained,

Chapter Five

There were certain things I noticed about Daisy during those early weeks in her sitting room.

The first was that she was apt to drop things. This was linked – sometimes, but not always – to the second: her tendency towards miscalculation. For instance, she would misjudge exactly where the desk was when trying to put something on it, or the top of the coffee table. Both of these shortcomings were less of a problem when she was holding something unbreakable, like keys or a box of tissues. Mugs containing hot liquids were, however, more of an issue. Thankfully, the flat's original floorboards seemed able to take a lot of abuse.

These foibles could be explained away as little more than clumsiness, as could the frequency with which she tripped over invisible hazards. This could not however be said of her habit of launching items across the room. She did not do this in anger, but rather it seemed to be a reflex to some unseen stimulus.

The first time I witnessed this odd phenomenon I was on the coffee table as she wrote a birthday card to a friend named Naomi; inexplicably the pen in Daisy's hand flew into the air, arched and landed near the bookcase. Daisy appeared to be as surprised as I was by this unexpected occurrence. She swore quietly and retrieved the pen.

Before she finished writing the card, she used the rounded end of it to erase a score she had inadvertently made. This was my first introduction to the wonder of erasable pens.

With this as my evidence, in addition to what I had learned during my encounter with the dreadful book and Heather's reference to the possibility of a relapse, I reluctantly deduced that Daisy had the relapsing remitting form of multiple sclerosis. It would, however, be many months before I would have this diagnosis confirmed.

An interesting fact, or at least one that I found to be interesting, was that the aforementioned hideous book languished in its bag for days before Daisy removed it – as though in its pages it held droplets of the very plague itself. Without opening it, she squeezed it between two books of a similar ilk, causing the only instance of overcrowding in the entire bookcase. This led me to conclude that she had a horror of being exposed to the sort of information she knew it must contain.

Daisy did not take time off that Easter to visit London with Heather and Daniel. I had, in fact, forgotten they were going as it had not been mentioned for months, at least in my presence. I was therefore surprised one Saturday after Daisy had returned home from work when her laptop began to sing a tune to signal they wanted her to join them on a videocall. Daisy clicked on the green button to indicate she accepted the request and I saw their faces appear in the rather grand front room of the house belonging to Daisy's Uncle Jonathan and Aunt Natalie, both of whom were present.

It was very satisfying to see Jonathan and Natalie.

I had long imagined what they might look like. Jonathan did indeed resemble his father, down even to the steel rimmed glasses and the matching silver-grey of his hair. Natalie appeared as though she was in the habit of seeking professional assistance to allow her to look twenty years younger than the age she must actually be.

Heather did most of the talking, interrupted occasionally by Natalie who seemed most upset that her favourite niece had not been able to visit.

It seemed Jonathan had spoiled them – that afternoon they had been to see a matinee performance of the musical, *Wicked*. According to Natalie, she had seen it three times before and it was simply wonderful.

Heather then explained they had a booking the following lunchtime at a restaurant Daisy seemed to have heard of and they would be joined by Kirsty, Elspeth, their partners and children. When she heard the news that she would be missing out on the opportunity to spend time with her older cousins, Daisy seemed genuinely bereft.

'Next time, Daisy-blossom,' Natalie said, just a mite too breezily for my taste.

'I'll give the girls your love,' Heather assured her, also seeming a little irritated by her sister-in-law.

After the call, Daisy stayed on her laptop and wrote a message to Kirsty explaining how sad she was that she would not be at the lunch. I thought it was interesting that Daisy did not copy Kirsty's sister on the missive and surmised that this most likely suggested Elspeth's personality had not improved with age. She then left me alone with her laptop while she went to the kitchen to microwave a meal.

I was thus able to enjoy rereading her email in the two minutes before my most recent nemesis – the vexatious screensaver – activated. When Daisy returned, having rather unusually eaten her meal in the kitchen, she was dressed to go out.

I hoped this might mean she would bring someone home with her and I would have the opportunity to eavesdrop on a conversation between her and someone other than her mother. However, when the front door was pushed open in the wee small hours, I could only hear the sound of one set of footsteps.

Often, when I was alone in the sitting room, I had occasion to wonder why Daisy was not in the custom of bringing people home – friends or lovers. I had witnessed her interaction with Joyce and knew her to be socially competent. She was also, in my opinion, a quirkily beautiful young woman. I was aware that she sent and received a seemingly appropriate number of emails and texts and that she went out at least two evenings each week. The fact that she always returned alone was of concern to me.

Daisy had not performed a search on Violet's name in weeks when she did so one Thursday night. She looked up her address via an online telephone directory. There was only one Violet Munro in Glasgow.

I knew from the calendar icon on the laptop that the date was the seventeenth of May.

Daisy used her phone to take a picture of the address.

The next day, she did not leave for work at her normal time. She entered the sitting room, still in her nightshirt, at ten in the morning. She drank coffee, ate toast and then left to get dressed.

She looked really rather chic when she returned.

She had made efforts to tame her spectacular mane of red hair, tying it back in a ribbon of black velvet. She was wearing expensive-looking black trousers I had not seen before, a cream jumper in wool I presumed to be cashmere, a trench coat in a similar shade that had something of a swing to it and short black leather boots. Over her shoulder was a leather satchel. She had tied a silk scarf around her neck; it was cream with a black border and was decorated with tiny flowers I presumed to be daisies.

She walked steadily towards the coffee table, bent down, picked me up and put me into her bag. I am pleased to report that it was roomy inside; the only other items it contained were her keys, phone, purse, a tiny notepad, pen, vanilla lip balm and a packet of tissues.

For this reason, and because I felt quite sure that we were about to embark on an adventure that would ultimately involve Violet, I found myself experiencing something I believe I can quite confidently describe as joy.

We were on a train when Daisy removed me from the satchel.

The seating was in a configuration of four, with a small plastic table in the middle. There was a young woman to Daisy's right and an elderly lady in the seat diagonally opposite. The elderly lady was wearing a sea-green raincoat. The large button at the top was undone and I could see that she was also wearing a pale pink jumper and a string of grey pearls. She had placed her triangle of a handbag on the empty seat next to her, along with a cloth shopping bag.

The train was busy, but not so busy that anyone attempted to sit down on the vacant seat across from us that the elderly lady had claimed with the overspill of her belongings.

Daisy sat me on the plastic table. Despite being white, I was quite sure it was not clean. I was therefore pleased when she took me in her hands and began to read.

'Did you not do it at school?' the elderly lady asked in an Edinburgh accent – Marchmont or Bruntsfield was my guess.

It seemed almost to have been an accusation.

Daisy smiled her wide gap-toothed smile and shook her head to indicate she had not.

'I thought they always did it.'

Daisy lifted her head from my pages to look over at the elderly lady.

'I think the other half of our year did,' she said. 'We read *To Kill a Mockingbird*.'

The elderly lady's face crinkled in mild distaste.

'But that's American,' she said.

She dug into her cloth shopping bag and removed a copy of a magazine called *The People's Friend*. It seemed Daisy's literary revelation had extinguished her interest in conversation.

The girl to our right gave a slight nod and a wry smile in our direction that seemed to indicate she was amused by the exchange and was standing in full solidarity with both Daisy and Harper Lee. I was surprised as I had imagined she was impervious to her surroundings, due to the music that was being piped into her ears.

Daisy returned to the business of reading.

Despite the rumbling movement – of both train and people – and the attendant thrum of noise, she was a most attentive reader.

She closed me over at the end of chapter two and placed me back in the satchel. Before long she was on her feet. I pictured the scene beyond my confines as we moved our way through an imagined throng in the station and out into the streets of Glasgow. It was not long before we were in what I took to be a shop. Daisy bought a card and a gift bag. These she slotted into the satchel next to me.

We were on the subway when she freed me once more.

I was pleased to be out in the light but less than pleased that I was only out to be used as a means of holding flat the card she had bought so that she could write on it. I could feel the movement of the pen as it stroked my cover. Despite the jolting movement of the carriage, her penmanship felt fluid and would look, I was sure, quite attractive.

Once the card was written, she put first it and then me into the gift bag. We rested there, on her knee, until the train reached her desired station.

The air was warm as she walked through the streets to her destination.

From inside the bag, I glimpsed blossom trees in pink and white.

Daisy stopped outside a Victorian tenement.

She pressed a buzzer mounted on the stone wall near the door. A voice I identified as belonging to an older and rather polite gentleman said, 'Yes?'

'Delivery for flat six,' Daisy said.

'I'm sure she's in herself,' the voice said, sounding a little put out.

Nonetheless, I heard the low grumble that signalled the door mechanism had been released.

Daisy pushed at the heavy door with her shoulder.

She climbed the stone stairs to the landing on the third floor.

She sat the gift bag down.

I felt myself tilt backwards.

I saw the underside of a yucca plant and extrapolated that the bag was leaning against the plant pot to which it belonged.

I heard Daisy's steps move further from me.

A door opened.

'Hello,' said a voice I knew belonged to Violet.

I heard Daisy's boots on the concrete flagstones. She continued walking.

'Hello,' Violet said again, more loudly this time. 'Did you leave this?'

The footsteps stopped.

It seemed Daisy now had no option but to respond.

Chapter Six

'It's for your birthday,' Daisy said.

Violet stepped out of her flat.

She bent down and picked up the gift bag.

'Will you come in?' she asked.

Her question was met with silence.

'Please?' she said.

Still there was silence.

Eventually, Daisy said, 'Just for a minute then.'

They were in the hallway when something in Violet's behaviour or in her demeanour led Daisy to say, 'You know who I am.'

'Of course,' Violet said. 'Please, come on through and have a seat,'

Even with the narrow view I had of the sitting room, I recognised the high ceiling with its centre rose and the exquisitely intricate cornicing.

'Do you want me to open it?' Violet asked.

Thanks to the inscription, I knew her birthday was still two days away. Despite this fact, I presumed Daisy must have given her consent, for Violet's hand removed me from the bag.

We were in Sandra's sitting room.

As if on instinct, Violet opened me at the inscription page. Her face was as I remembered although perhaps a little thinner.

Her thick auburn curls were cut to her chin and streaked with grey. Her eyes were as large and as bright as I recalled.

'I never thought I'd see it again. How do you come to have it?' she said. 'I did always suspect Thomas had taken it.'

'He did. He gave it to my mum. But that's not how I got it,' Daisy said. 'I work in a charity shop. Someone handed it in.'

'Really? That's incredible,' Violet said, somewhat stating the obvious.

'My mum couldn't believe it when she saw it.'

Daisy shifted a little uncomfortably in her seat and said, 'I didn't think you'd be in. My mum said you're a teacher.' She added, almost apologetically, 'It's why I came today.'

Violet explained that she was in fact a teacher, but said she was off sick because she had been a bit under the weather recently.

Daisy told her aunt that she was sorry to hear this.

'I hope it's not anything serious,' she said.

'I'm fine,' Violet said. 'I just needed a bit of a rest.'

'Why?' Daisy asked, her question more curious than impolite.

'I'm fine,' Violet said. 'Honestly. It's just I've got multiple sclerosis and I had a relapse a few weeks ago.'

The way in which Violet told Daisy she had multiple sclerosis made it sound as though it were no more serious than the common cold. However, when Daisy told her aunt that she too had it, Violet began to cry.

Both women apologised – Daisy for blurting it out and Violet for her tears.

'I had heard it could run in families,' Daisy said. 'And we didn't know of anyone on my mum's side.'

Violet apologised for a second time. It was as though she

felt responsible for her niece's neurological ill-health. She said that after she was diagnosed she had started to wonder if it had come from her grandfather Galbraith's side. He had moved to Glasgow from Aberdeenshire in the 1930s, she explained, and no one knew anything about his family.

'They don't even really know if it is genetic,' Daisy said, as if to make her aunt feel better. 'It's just what some people say.'

Violet now apologised to Daisy for having forgotten her manners and asked if she could make her a cup of tea, or perhaps a coffee. She had cake, too, she said.

I hoped that Daisy would not leave me for the kitchen as I did not want to miss out on any of their conversation. Thankfully, when she rose to do so, Violet insisted she sit back down.

With Violet out of the room, Daisy walked over to the bookshelves. She lightly ran her fingers over some of the books. As she did, I noticed that the Larkin book was still in his place and had lost none of his haughtiness.

Violet returned with a tray. On it were two mugs, two small plates each with a slice of cake and a matching milk jug and sugar bowl.

'I forgot to ask if you take milk or sugar.'

'Just black,' Daisy said and for the first time since the train journey, she smiled her wide gap-toothed smile.

'Very wise,' Violet said. 'I have a weakness for sugar, I'm afraid.'

They were quietly eating cake when Violet said, 'Do you mind if I ask you a question?'

Daisy shook her head.

'Can I tell your dad you were here?'

Daisy said she would rather if Violet did not, for now. She motioned towards me and said that she agreed with her mum that finding me must be some sort of sign. Perhaps the universe was trying to tell her something she said, but she was not ready to see her father.

Daisy told her aunt that was not why she had come.

She told Violet that ever since she read the inscription, she had been thinking about her. She remembered the visit Violet had made to London. Daisy had only been little, but she remembered Violet taking her to a park and she remembered that they had picked flowers. She remembered Violet's kindness, her beauty. She remembered her love.

Daisy told her aunt how for weeks now she would wake up in the middle of the night with one thought in her head: the book wanted to go home.

Violet dabbed at her eyes with a tissue.

I thought of her sixteenth birthday and the girl I could still recognise in the face I now beheld.

Violet picked me up.

'Thank you,' she said. 'I'm so glad you found it and that it brought you here.'

I learned many things that afternoon.

I learned that Thomas now lived in Manchester with his wife and children and that Violet truly believed that he would dearly love to have contact with Daisy if ever that was what she wanted. I learned that Violet had inherited Sandra's flat and had moved into it a few months earlier when her own house had sold. She said she had been married once; her diagnosis had put an end to something that had been dying anyway.

Daisy asked Violet about her illness.

It started when she had just turned thirty-four, she said. She had had a terrible headache for a few days and then lost the sight in her right eye. There had been other things too, numbness, mainly, so tests had been run.

'Uch, a lumbar puncture.' Daisy said.

'I thought the MRI was worse. I didn't know I didn't like small spaces until I was in that machine.'

'You mean the noisy coffin,' Daisy said.

Violet laughed.

It seemed that Daisy found the conversation cathartic. This was interesting to me as I thought she had no interest in speaking about, or even thinking about, her illness.

'Did people do that thing?' she asked. 'Tell you they know someone who has it?'

'Or they know someone who knows someone who has it,' Violet said.

They both laughed now.

'No one had ever spoken about it before, but as soon as I was diagnosed,' Daisy said, 'every person I met wanted to tell me about someone they'd never mentioned before who had it.'

'It is a strange phenomenon,' Violet said. 'Even worse when they finish it off with *and they're not even in a wheelchair.*'

'No, no, what's worse,' said Daisy, sounding almost excited, 'is when they tell you the person's only been in a wheelchair for a year or two.'

They spoke about being confined to bed and the sense of isolation it brings; they spoke about being put places they did not want to be – slid into an MRI scanner, for the fourth time, or folded into the foetal position for a lumbar puncture; Daisy spoke about the way time becomes elastic when you have a relapse – that brushing your teeth can take close to an hour and yet it seems as though no time has passed at all; Violet spoke about the way in which you can be present and invisible all at once; they spoke about the frustration of being trapped indoors when you want to be outside; they spoke about the feeling of being left behind; they spoke of being talked over, not to, of being moved this way and that, of being poked and prodded, of feeling like an object.

They also spoke about how wonderful the smell of toast can be when you notice it for the first time in days.

They delighted in the ease with which you can eavesdrop on the conversations of others because they have forgotten, or did not even notice, you are there.

They spoke about the importance of distracting yourself from the thoughts that come unbidden and are unhelpful – anxiety about the future and the impossible desire to return to *life before.*

'I started writing poetry,' Daisy said. 'I didn't mean to. Words kept rattling around in my head so I began to write them down. It's how I learned to manage the neuropathic pain. I would get so lost trying to arrange and rearrange the words that I'd somehow forget about the sensation of broken glass in my hands.'

Violet told her she would like to read some of it.

'I'm not saying it's good,' Daisy said. 'But writing it seemed to help.'

She told Violet about a time when she had bumped into someone in the street. She knew this woman, she said, but would not describe her as a close friend. The woman asked, as people do when they bump into you, 'How are you?' Daisy said that she did not know what got into her, but she found herself answering the question honestly.

'She couldn't get away quick enough. I felt stupid and embarrassed and angry with myself.'

Daisy said she had gone home and written a poem and had felt better as a result. She said the words just tumbled out. She closed her eyes and began to recite the poem as though she were reading it from a page in her mind.

You are huge
granite grey
yet unspoken
as you sit
sipping
peppermint tea
on the Laura
Ashley chaise
longue opposite.

I see brows knit
faces turn flint
if I even hint
at you –
how rude
to allude
to the recumbent
gargantua
in the room.

Others dance
around you
romance you –
infer
if you were there
how benign
you would be
how mannerly.

You wink
as you sit
unsaid
patiently
sipping
herbal tea
on that chic
pink chaise
by Laura Ashley.

Violet clapped her hands.

'Exactly,' she said. 'That's it. Exactly.'

I cannot say that I understood why it captured the incident described in just such an exact fashion, but I realised that my own experiences had at least given me something of a point of reference.

'If ever there's anything,' Violet said, her voice beginning to trail. 'Anything I can do.'

'I don't usually like talking about any of this,' Daisy said. 'So maybe if we could just have the odd conversation. Even if it's only over the phone.'

'Of course.'

'And I'll warn you now, I'm a bit of a lunatic,' Daisy said, through her gap-toothed smile. 'Because mostly I want to live like I don't have it. I don't even want its name mentioned. But then, very occasionally, I want people to acknowledge what a great job I'm doing. It's a bit screwed up, isn't it?'

'That's your Munro/Galbraith DNA coming through,' Violet said, smiling the same wide smile. 'I apologise. You're probably a bit stubborn too. Am I right?'

'I get that from both sides,' Daisy said.

Daisy stayed and talked into the evening. When she left, she promised to return soon.

Alone in Sandra's sitting room, Violet held me in her hands.

She turned to my inscription page and traced the words as Daisy had done.

I heard her silently thank her aunt for the best birthday present, ever.

Gillian Shirreffs is a Glasgow-based writer and researcher who has a Doctor of Fine Arts degree in Creative Writing. In her thesis she explored the relationship between object and illness, with specific reference to multiple sclerosis. The creative element of her doctorate is *Brodie*, a novel narrated by an object. The idea for this method of interrogation came during months of bed rest. Gillian's work has appeared in *thi wurd* magazine, The Interpreter's House, The Polyphony, The Common Breath, and in the anthologies *Tales from a Cancelled Country* and *Alternating Current*, amongst others. In a former life she was an HR director, living and working on both sides of the Atlantic. In another former life, she was an English teacher.